Annie Payne spent most of her life as an NHS nurse, midwife and clinical network manager but now concentrates on writing full time. She has written extensively for television programmes such as *The Bill*, *Doctors* and *Heartbeat* under the name Candy Denman and has published a medical mystery series and novella under that name too.

Now she happily writes novels in a posh shed in the garden in between playing with her six grandchildren and walking her dog, Dennis the Cockapoo.

THE DOCTOR

ANNIE PAYNE

avon.

Published by AVON
A division of HarperCollins*Publishers*
1 London Bridge Street
London SE1 9GF

www.harpercollins.co.uk

HarperCollins*Publishers*
Macken House
39/40 Mayor Street Upper
Dublin 1
D01 C9W8
Ireland

A Paperback Original 2023

1

First published in Great Britain by HarperCollins*Publishers* 2023

Copyright © Candy Denman 2023

Candy Denman asserts the moral right to be identified as the author of this work.

A catalogue copy of this book is available from the British Library.

ISBN: 978-0-00-856200-7

This novel is entirely a work of fiction. The names, characters and incidents portrayed in it are the work of the author's imagination. Any resemblance to actual persons, living or dead, events or localities is entirely coincidental.

Typeset in Minion Pro by Palimpsest Book Production Limited,
Falkirk, Stirlingshire

Printed and bound in the UK using
100% Renewable Electricity by CPI Group (UK) Ltd

All rights reserved. No part of this text may be reproduced, transmitted, downloaded, decompiled, reverse engineered, or stored in or introduced into any information storage and retrieval system, in any form or by any means, whether electronic or mechanical, without the express written permission of the publishers.

This book is produced from independently certified FSC™ paper to ensure responsible forest management.

For more information visit: www.harpercollins.co.uk/green

For all the health and social care workers around the world who died during the pandemic. Lest we forget.

PROLOGUE

'I just need to flush your cannula,' I explained as I drew the curtains around the bed. I can't deny that there was a flutter of anticipation and excitement in my belly.

'I've told him,' she said. 'I told him about what I heard, about what's been going on in the hospital.'

'That's fine. I hope he reassured you,' I said, although it wasn't fine and I couldn't take the chance on what she might have said to him. What if he believed her? What if he hadn't written off her bizarre accusations as a sign of dementia?

I took the syringe I had brought with me, pre-drawn up and on a little tray. I had placed an open ampoule of normal saline next to it, although it certainly wasn't saline in the syringe. As I pushed the plunger down and the liquid entered her vein, she went rigid and tried to pull her arm away, but I was ready for it; after all, she wasn't the first patient I'd killed this way.

I have heard it said that being injected with potassium chloride feels like liquid fire running through your veins until it reaches your heart and, well, then it's all over. Not having been through it myself, I couldn't say, but it certainly seemed painful in my experience of watching people die from it. Sad really, but what can you do?

Once it was over, I straightened her bed and closed her eyes.

Interfering old bitch, I thought to myself as I drew back the curtains and left her looking as if she was peacefully asleep. I didn't hear the emergency buzzer sound until later, and by then, it was much too late to save her.

CHAPTER ONE

The sun was shining as Alison got into her car. It was one of those beautiful autumn days that make you glad to be alive. She took a deep breath of the fresh, cool air and smiled. It smelled different here, slightly salty. There was something about being so close to the sea that reminded her of holidays. She wondered if that would change, when she had been living here longer. She hoped not.

Before starting the car engine, she paused for a moment, looking once again at the house she called home, for the time being at least. Situated on the outskirts of town, it was a real chocolate-box cottage with its thatched roof and the promise of roses around the door in the summer. It had a log burner in the sitting room; she had felt cosy and warm the night before as she sat with Paws, her rescue cat, curled up asleep on her lap. Even though she'd been surrounded by cases and boxes that she had yet to unpack, it felt good to be away from London and the turmoil of the past few months.

And now there was just excitement about what the future might hold. A new day, a new beginning.

She drove along the shore road on her way to work. It probably wasn't the shortest route, particularly in the summer, but she had plenty of time before she was due at the hospital and she wanted to see the town at its best, take in the view that the tourists came for and that featured on a million postcards. She pulled over by the beach, got out of the car and stood by the sea wall looking across the bay to the town that was to be her new home. She could understand why it was so popular, with its sandy beaches and lively marina area surrounded by restaurants and bars. There were plenty of green spaces spread throughout the town, breaking up the rows of houses. It really was lovely. The sunlight was glittering on the water but there was a light, chilly wind. She shivered slightly and wrapped her coat tighter around her and trying to still the butterflies in her stomach, she took deep, calming, breaths of the salty air.

It was unlike her to feel nervous, but she told herself it was only natural to be anxious about her first day as medical director at the local hospital. There was no doubt in her mind that it was going to be the biggest challenge of her life to turn things around and improve its CQC rating. She had come to help, but she knew she would be resented by some, the ones who didn't want to change, didn't think they were part of the problem – though they usually were. She wondered about the chief executive, who she had only met when she was interviewed by the board. Was he a strong enough leader to drive the sort of change that the hospital needed? She knew he had been there only two years, but in that time had not managed to improve the ratings. It was only natural that he was in a hurry to put things right now, before he was ousted by the board, like Alison's predecessor already had been. No one had told her exactly why he had resigned suddenly, but there had been hints dropped during her interview about a clash of values, a disagreement over what needed to be done to improve the hospital. It had made sense and she had thought it a good sign that the chief executive had stood his ground and the board had backed him. They could work together, she thought, and do a good job. At least she hoped they could.

With a final look at the town and the whitewashed villas – mostly B&Bs and small hotels rather than family homes that lined the sea front – she got back into her small car.

Inside, away from the wind, she adjusted the rear-view mirror so that she could see herself and ran her fingers through her straight, shoulder-length blonde hair, checking it was tidy and that she was looking business-like and neat. She needed to make a good impression, not turn up looking like she had been in a force-ten gale. Satisfied, she started the car and drove the short distance on to the hospital. Her hope was that it would be possible to see the sea from her office, but she was pretty sure, located as it was at the back of town, the hospital would be too far inland. From the roof perhaps?

She parked her car in the staff car park and left a handwritten note on the windscreen – giving her name and letting the parking staff know who she was should suffice. She didn't want to get a parking ticket on her first day, that wouldn't be a good omen at all! Grabbing her bag and locking the car, she made her way towards the hospital, a mish-mash of the original building, which was a decidedly ugly tower block from the 1960s, and some more modern additions connected by a number of covered walkways.

It would take time before she would be able to confidently navigate her way around the place, but she had taken a look at the map on their website the night before, and she had a pretty good idea of where to find the main administrative offices where she was to report to the chief executive, Brian Hargreaves. At her interview she'd thought that he seemed nice enough, but nice wasn't what she needed if she was going to turn the hospital around in a short space of time, so she hoped he could be tough as well. She was looking forward to when she could get actually stuck in, because she knew that the morning was bound to be spent doing mundane things like getting her

ID badge sorted, meeting people and being shown her office. It would be a while before she could get on with her real job.

As she went towards the main entrance, she noticed how tired and lacklustre the exterior of the hospital seemed. There were weeds growing in the flower beds either side of the path up to the door and the whole building could do with a lick of paint. She had read the CQC report saying that the hospital was 'in need of improvement', but she hadn't thought they meant the structure. Perhaps that's what happened when morale was low, no one could even be bothered to keep the place neat and tidy. There would be time to address that over the next few months; it might not be important to have a neat and tidy garden, but it gave a bad impression before the public had even got through the front doors. It was then that she noticed the cigarette ends scattered on the ground on either side of the entrance, right next to the No Smoking signs. That would have to be cleared up straight away, she couldn't possibly let it wait. She would have a word with the staff on reception to make sure this practice was nipped in the bud.

She put a smile on her face, not wanting to come across too grumpy so early on, and walked across the reception area to an empty desk with a sign saying 'We're here to help you' – but clearly only when they could be bothered to be there. Smile slipping, she waited a moment or two, but when there was still no sign of anyone coming to help, she continued walking, trying to recall the layout of the building. She made her way to the lifts, head held high and a look of steely determination on her face.

She was left regretting this decision when, having finally managed to rouse someone to let her into the section of the hospital where all the administration staff worked, she found she was not even expected and Brian Hargreaves was away at a conference. Treating it as further evidence that she was needed, that she could really do something to help this hospital improve, she had merely smiled and asked to meet his deputy and the chief nurse.

'And can you let HR know I'm here? It makes sense to get ID badges and such like underway, er, Ms. . .?' Alison looked pointedly at the elderly administrator's name badge which was hanging from a lanyard round her neck but had twisted so that her name and title were not visible.

'Oh. . . Doyle, Mary Doyle,' the woman answered, straightening the badge which lay on her ample, twinset-covered bosom. 'I'm Mr Hargreaves' PA.'

'Good morning, Mary, I'm very pleased to meet you,' Alison said with a friendly smile, trying not to look at the thick pink lipstick that had seeped into the wrinkles around the woman's mouth.

'Yes, of course. I'm so sorry, Dr Wilson. If I'd known you were arriving today. . .' She sat there, looking flustered, touching her tightly curled grey hair as Alison waited expectantly. She wondered why the woman hadn't retired, she was certainly old enough to have done so.

'Could you show me where my office is, Mary?' she finally said when it became clear the woman wasn't going to do anything without being given clear instructions. 'Is it all right if I call you Mary, or would you prefer Mrs Doyle?' Alison tried to see if she was wearing a ring, but couldn't see one.

'Oh, Mary's fine, just fine. I'm not married.' She finally stood up and, grabbing a key card from the top drawer of her desk, led the way out of reception and into the corridor. 'Follow me,' she instructed Alison and led the way along to a door labelled: *Dr Richard Atkinson, Medical Director.*

'I'm sorry, we haven't. . .' Mary once again didn't finish her sentence before opening the door and showing Alison into an office which was little more than a store cupboard. It looked as though her predecessor had merely grabbed his personal belongings when he left, there were files and papers everywhere she looked.

There was no way she was going to hit the ground running. Perhaps it was good that she had arrived a week earlier than they were expecting her, it would take her that long to straighten out her office!

Once Mary had left, Alison made a start on the pile of papers balanced precariously in the tray marked urgent. She moved a waste bin next to the desk so that anything out of date could be filed there and she could ask Mary to shred it later. The other papers she put into two piles, those that needed to be dealt with now and those that could wait until later. She was still only about halfway down the pile when there was a knock at the door.

'Come in!' she called out. The door opened and a woman poked her head around the door.

'Hi, I'm Eliza, Chief Nurse. Mary gave me a call, may I come in?'

'Of course,' Alison replied. 'Sorry about the mess.' She indicated the piles of paper surrounding her.

There was a pause as Eliza picked something up from the chair just outside the office door and then backed into the room.

'I come bearing gifts,' she said as she looked around for somewhere to put down the tray she was holding. Alison quickly cleared a space on the desk by simply dumping a pile of files on the floor. The tray had two cups, a cafetière of steaming coffee, a milk jug and biscuits. None of the crockery matched, but it was a welcome sight all the same.

'I'll leave if you want some time to get yourself sorted,' Eliza said as she eyed the disorganisation around her.

'No, no, it looks worse than it is, I'm sure.' Alison didn't sound all that sure, but the coffee and a chance to speak to someone from senior management was an opportunity not to be missed. 'Have a seat, please. Thank you for coming up and for bringing much-needed coffee.'

As Eliza moved a chair over to the desk and then busied herself pouring coffee, Alison took the opportunity to take a good long look at the chief nurse, her right-hand woman in the job of improving clinical practices at the establishment. Like Alison, Eliza must have been in her mid-to-late forties, but with her short hair in a pixie cut and a small, lithe body, she could pass for much younger, even though her dark hair was streaked with grey. She had an attractive face, despite wearing no make-up, and an infectious smile. In fact, it was more of a cheeky grin, and Alison felt immediately that this was a woman she could work with, could even be friends with. She began to relax.

'I'm sorry there was a mix-up with your start date,' Eliza said once they were settled with coffee in front of them. 'To be honest, Mary could do with a hand, she sometimes struggles a bit. Do you mind if I. . .?' Eliza indicated the biscuit plate.

'No, of course not.' Alison declined to have one herself, and watched as Eliza helped herself to two. 'I did wonder as she seemed a little confused about, well, everything. She's Brian Hargreaves' PA?'

'That's what she likes to be called, but really she's shared across the senior team. Been here since the year dot, way before I came along,' Eliza explained between mouthfuls. 'I think retirement would kill her.'

As a warning shot, this was a very gentle one. Letting Alison know that she would meet resistance if she tried to oust Mary, even if she proved to be completely senile.

'I rather think that's up to the chief executive as she's his PA and I see no reason to interfere.' Alison was letting her colleague know that she was not going to do anything, for now anyway. 'To be honest, I was rather hoping to have an office on the stroke ward rather than here, as that will be my clinical working area. Do you think that will be possible?'

Eliza hesitated before replying. 'Dr Carrick has his office there. He is. . . was head of the Stroke Unit and much as you are senior to him in the hospital hierarchy, I'm not sure he's quite ready to hand over his kingdom just yet.'

Alison knew that it was going to be hard on him, having a stroke consultant from London parachuted in above him, but the poor results from his service was part of the reason she had been appointed. She was going to have to tread very carefully.

'Of course, I won't rush in,' she said reassuringly, but inwardly wondered if that was exactly what she should do. Dr Carrick might leave if she did, but better that than have him hanging around organising resistance to any changes she might need to make. 'I will be doing some clinical sessions in stroke, and I may want to change some things.' There was no may about it, if she was honest. 'But I'll try and be as gentle as I can.' She hoped that Eliza would believe her.

'What made you come to St Margaret's?' Eliza asked. 'I mean, there's such a shortage of stroke consultants, you could have gone anywhere. Stayed in London, even.'

It was a good question and one she had been asked by friends, colleagues, not to mention the board when she was interviewed for the post.

'The challenge,' she gave her stock answer. 'The feeling that I could do some real good here, not just coast along, having an easy life.' She didn't mention the word escape, or that she was desperate for a way out from her life in the city, not even to herself. 'That, and I have always loved the seaside. Good enough reasons?' She smiled, hoping to take any unintended sting out of her words.

'Absolutely.' Eliza stood and picked up the coffee tray. 'Right, are you ready to face the world? I've alerted HR so they are poised and ready to take your photo and get your pass organised. IT will be here at eleven o'clock to get your laptop set up, they have a morning meeting until then and heaven forbid we should interrupt that, so we have time for the full guided tour beforehand, if you're up for it?'

For the first time that morning, Alison felt a sense of relief. She could do this; with this energetic, efficient woman beside her, she could turn this hospital round, no matter how bad things seemed at the moment. She could make a difference, and find herself and a measure of peace while she did so.

'Yes,' she replied with a smile. 'I am definitely up for it.'

CHAPTER TWO

Her tour of the hospital with the chief nurse had given her several ideas of where she should start and the stroke ward was undoubtedly one, along with the emergency department. She felt sure that a certain amount of re-organisation in those two areas would bring the ratings up. Dr Carrick, the stroke consultant had not been on the unit when Eliza took her there. The ward sister, Joyce Fletcher, a plain, no-nonsense sort of woman in her fifties, explained that he was busy in outpatients when she was introduced. Alison knew she would have to work hard to get Joyce's support because she was one of Dr Carrick's greatest fans, according to Eliza. Alison was glad that the nurse had warned her as they walked onto the ward, because she knew that getting the sister onside was vital if she was going to successfully make any changes to their current practices, and she was pretty sure she was going to need to do that. Alison did her best to be friendly, listening carefully as the sister and Eliza exchanged greetings.

'Perhaps you could show me around the ward, Joyce?' Alison smiled at her, hoping the sister hadn't noticed her wrinkle her nose at the smell of cigarettes that wafted around her. 'Introduce me to people? Talk me through your patient pathways? If you have time.'

'Of course, Dr Wilson,' Joyce replied. 'I'm sure I can make the time.' Her quick look around the ward suggested otherwise.

'I'll leave you in Joyce's capable hands then,' Eliza said, before she left.

As they walked around the ward, with Joyce pointing things and people out, Alison got to know more about her. Joyce was single. Not ready for retirement, or 'to be put out to grass' as she put it just yet. There was no doubting her enthusiasm or her dedication to caring for her patients, but Alison was getting a feel for where she would need to make changes.

'And this is Mrs Rossi.' Joyce stopped at the bedside of a woman in her sixties, who Alison would describe as 'ample', if she were being kind, sitting in a chair next to her bed. She was dressed in a hospital gown, with a pink towelling robe over the top, and a pair of sturdy pink slippers on her feet.

'Good morning,' Alison said to the patient, trying to ignore the Tupperware containers stacked on her locker.

There were some Italian pastries visible in the open foil container on the table in front of Mrs Rossi, and a lot of crumbs suggesting she had eaten some already.

'Good morning, darling,' Mrs Rossi said to Alison and Joyce. 'Here, would you like one?' She held out the container. Alison recognised cannoli but there were other pastries in the box that she couldn't name.

'That's kind of you, but not for me, thank you,' Alison said.

'They are homemade, by my daughter, she is a very good cook.' Mrs Rossi was not going to make it easy for her to refuse.

'I'm sure she's a wonderful cook but I've already had breakfast,' Alison explained, 'and I need to finish my tour.'

'She's the best. Here, sister, you take them for the nurses' coffee break,' the woman insisted and after putting the lid on the container, handed it to Joyce.

'The Rossi family run the ice cream shop on the front,' Joyce said as an aside as they continued the tour of the ward. 'And a few of the vans you see around the town, as well. Lovely ice cream,' she added.

'I can believe it,' Alison answered, the pastries had certainly looked delicious.

Alison felt exhausted as she pulled up outside her cottage after what had been a very strange day. Suddenly, she wondered if it wouldn't be better to live closer to the hospital, so that she didn't have to drive at all after a long day, but she knew the importance of creating a bit of space between work and home life. After all, that was one of the reasons she had moved here.

As she opened the door to the cottage, Paws, her sleek grey cat, appeared and wound himself around her legs – a trip hazard if ever there was one, but it was nice to be welcomed home, even if she knew it was just cupboard love.

Once Paws had been fed, Alison opened the refrigerator, hoping something in there would strike her as appetising enough to be worth the effort of cooking. She hadn't yet unpacked all her cooking utensils – that was a job for the weekend – so she couldn't tackle anything that required too much preparation. There was a ready-made salad and some microwave meals none of which tempted her, if she was honest, but she settled on a pasta dish, knowing that she needed to eat something. She had only found time to grab a quick sandwich at lunchtime, and she thought longingly about the pastries that Mrs Rossi had offered her. Perhaps she should have sneaked some to eat at home. With a shake of her head, she looked at the bottle of chilled Cabernet Sauvignon, ready and waiting. She hesitated before taking it out, but if she didn't deserve a glass of wine today, then she never would.

She put her meal in the microwave and took her wine through to the sitting room. Although it was late September, it wasn't yet cold enough to need the heating on, let alone light the log burner, but it was still a room that made her feel warm and cosy. She put her wine down on a side table next to the sofa and switched on the lamp before sitting down and pulling her laptop case towards her. She had downloaded the most recent metrics and wanted to look over them again.

She smiled as she thought about the chief nurse, Eliza. She was so glad that at least one person at the hospital seemed to be on her side and up for the challenge of improving the hospital. Alison had no illusions, her stay at St Margaret's would be short-lived if she didn't manage to do the job she had been expressly brought in to achieve.

She stretched out on the sofa, and having finished his dinner Paws jumped up on her lap, purring. She was asleep before the microwave pinged.

CHAPTER THREE

'Dr Wilson, I'm so sorry I wasn't here to greet you when you arrived.'

Alison had no difficulty recognising the man who strode across the room with his hand outstretched as the chief executive of the hospital trust, Brian Hargreaves, even though it had been several months since she had been interviewed. In his fifties, slim and silver-haired, he came across as competent and friendly, but Alison was reassured that he also looked as if he could be ruthless when needed.

'And this is my deputy, Jonathan Selby, I'm not sure. . .' He turned to his deputy, who also came forward with a smile and his hand outstretched. He was young, handsome and well turned out, without a hair out of place, every inch the ambitious young executive.

'No, we just managed to miss each other last week,' he said.

Alison decided to play nice; she was well aware that Selby had deliberately ignored her repeated efforts to talk to him over the previous week.

'How are you settling in?' Selby asked her.

'Just fine, thank you. I've sorted out the office, got myself up and running with IT and HR.' *No thanks to you*; the subtle subtext was there. 'Mary is trying to organise meetings with all the heads of department and Eliza has been a great help, taking me round and getting me orientated.'

'Great, great.' Selby's smile never wavered; it seemed implied criticism was like water off a duck's back to him. 'And how about at home? House sorted? Is your husband moving down here to join you?'

'Everything's fine, thank you.' She was quite sure he was aware that she was recently divorced and chose to ignore that part of his question. She turned to Hargreaves. 'I'm working on an action plan that I'd like to go through with you at some point.'

He nodded his approval.

'You've hit the ground running, I see. That's good. Let's get Mary to put a meeting in the diary, sometime later this week, is that all right?'

She agreed and allowed herself to be ushered towards the door, smiling to herself at the look of discomfort on Selby's face. *He* certainly didn't like the fact that she had hit the ground running, that was for sure.

As she returned to her office, Alison walked past Mary

and stopped to ask her to schedule the meeting that Hargreaves had suggested.

'Good morning, Mary,' she said, aware that Mary seemed flustered, but equally aware that this wasn't unusual. There was the clunk of a door closing behind her and Alison turned to look down the corridor, surprised to see that there was no one there.

'It's just the wind,' Mary told her quickly.

Alison didn't think that was the case. She couldn't help notice that the chair next to Mary's desk was slightly askew and that there were two cups of tea, both half-empty, on her desk, but only one had traces of her bright pink lipstick on the rim. Still, if Mary chose to lie about her visitors, it wasn't really anything to do with Alison.

'Brian asked if you would set up a meeting between us for later in the week, Mary,' she said.

'I'll set it up and put it in your diary, Dr Wilson,' Mary said, more calmly. 'And I arranged some meetings with the department heads, but you seem to have cancelled them.'

'Well, if you could rearrange them?' Alison asked patiently; she certainly hadn't cancelled any meetings, but she was beginning to learn that Mary wasn't the most reliable secretary and made a mental note to check that they were indeed arranged.

Back in the tiny room that served as her office, Alison was irritated to see that she still didn't have a label for the door. She had removed Dr Atkinson's name plate the first day she was there but had hoped it would not take long for her own name to be up there, certainly not as long as this. She would mention it to Mary, again. Meanwhile, she wrote *Dr Alison Wilson, Medical Director* on a piece of paper and taped it to the door. It would have to do for the time being.

The office was unrecognisable from the room she had walked into on her first day at the hospital. The paperwork that had covered every surface was now mainly gone. What little she couldn't store on the hospital's secure electronic system was all filed away, organised so that she knew exactly where to find it. She had moved the desk round so that it was sideways on to the door and her back was to the filing cabinets rather than the window. Being able to see outside was important to her, even if it wasn't much of a view, across the car park and out to the main road – but she could see the sky and sometimes she needed that more than being able to see anyone walking along the corridor, as Dr Atkinson had clearly wanted. She could imagine him sitting behind his desk, with the office door open, keeping track of the comings and goings of all the other senior staff. She was building up a picture in her mind of the man she had replaced but had no idea if it was a true one or not.

As she looked around her tiny office, she thought back to what had been, what she had lost when she moved to this small provincial hospital by the sea. At the time, the losses had seemed so big that they were insurmountable, but maybe, just maybe, she could resurrect her old life, or build a new one here, by the sea.

The new bitch is interfering in the running of the hospital, interfering way too much for my liking. She is asking questions, wanting to know about every department, actually listening to what she is told. Some people are being far too quick to tell her what they think is wrong with the place and she is even asking for ideas on how to change things. I can't let that happen, can I? She is a nuisance and one way or another she has to go. I have an idea about how to do it. There is a tension, an uncertainty, a brittleness about her that tells me that there's something not quite so perfect about her past. Something that has gone wrong. Personal or professional? I don't know. Does it matter? Not at all, I just need to find it, find her weak spot, that place where I can undermine her, apply pressure and watch her implode. She won't stay here long, I will see to that and I will enjoy doing it.

CHAPTER FOUR

The stroke unit, her ward, was the place where Alison always felt she belonged. When work was hard, or her home life was falling apart, the stroke unit was where Alison would go to think things through as she worked, reassuring and helping her patients. She was sitting in Dr Carrick's office on the ward, having what she had referred to as a strategy meeting and he had called a coffee morning; he certainly seemed to have allocated the same amount of importance to it as one. A small, neat and precise man in his fifties, Alison had taken an instant dislike to him, but was doing her best not to show it.

'If you look at the metrics,' Alison started, holding out the chart she had prepared for him, but he waved the paper away.

'For me, it's about the patient experience and their long-term prospects, not about numbers on a page.'

'Yes, but these numbers reflect the patient's long-term—'

'Now what we need is more therapists,' he interrupted, talking over her as if her thoughts were not relevant, 'and that would undoubtedly help your metrics.'

'I absolutely agree,' she replied and got a startled look from him. 'I have put forward a business plan to increase therapists and I'm hopeful that it will be approved at the next board meeting.'

'That's good.' He nodded and took a biscuit from the plate in front of him, nibbling at it thoughtfully. 'A good start, anyway.'

Alison began to think that she was winning him round, by conceding that he was right about this area. She knew he had been complaining about lack of therapy time since before she arrived.

'But we do also need to look at the other measures – the time it takes to get through the emergency department and have a CT scan, for instance.'

He went to interrupt but she held up her hand to stop him.

'I'm working with the consultant and the ambulance service to get them to pre-alert so that a member of the stroke team can be there, at the door, waiting for any potential stroke patients to make sure they go on the fast pathway and get their clot-busting drugs as quickly as possible.'

'Impossible!' he almost shouted and banged his coffee cup down so hard, Alison worried it might break. 'I can't have senior members of the team leaving the ward to hang around A&E. Not unless you increase the number of staff we have on duty. We need them here, not swanning round the hospital checking out every patient the ambulance service think might possibly have had a stroke. They'd end up having to sort out all sorts of things that have nothing to do with this unit. Migraines, confusion, dementia and we'd lose them from the ward all day.' He jabbed a finger at her to emphasise his words.

'Perhaps if—' but he never let her finish her suggestion that an extra member of staff should be recruited for each shift so that it wouldn't bring their numbers down.

Instead, he stormed out of the room, muttering, 'Absolutely ridiculous!'

Alison took a deep breath and rubbed gently at a spot on her temple that might well be a migraine developing, she thought.

It wasn't just on the stroke ward that Alison was facing opposition to her plans. The A&E consultant was scathing about trying her plan to meet the stroke pathway needs. To be fair, he had much more pressing worries about his own four-hour wait target, which he was failing. He told her he was happy to listen to her plans to use someone from the stroke team to help speed patients through the department to scanning, just so long as she didn't expect him to free up any of his staff, because, just as Dr Carrick had told her, he didn't have anyone spare.

And, as she had suspected, she wouldn't get the support she needed from Jonathan Selby, who was much more interested in making sure he was the chief executive's blue-eyed boy. To top it all, every time she went back to her office, the name plate on her door, albeit only the hand-written one she had taped there, had always fallen off. It didn't seem to matter how securely she fixed it, somehow it was always on the floor when she came back. She suspected someone was doing it deliberately, but complaining about it would just make her look paranoid. So, she contented herself with asking Mary Doyle, once more, to see what had happened to the permanent one that had been ordered.

Her working day seemed to be one long round of battles, or skirmishes, she supposed they would be better described as. She didn't even feel as if home was the haven she that had hoped for. Yes, it was a lovely cottage, and yes, there was always Paws to keep her company, but she hadn't exchanged more than a handful of words with her neighbours or the people who ran the local shop/post office. She really needed to make more of an effort to make friends or at least acquaintances locally if she was going to stay. A big if. She had seen this post merely as a way back to her upwardly mobile career. Sort out St Margaret's and maybe, just maybe, one of the big London hospital trusts would be interested in offering her a post, but if she left having failed, that would be it. No one would touch her, not after what had happened before.

She had to make it work, she had to succeed. Failure was just not acceptable to her.

Closing her laptop, she decided to go home. She might have more success there.

Deciding that she really needed to make an effort to get to know the local area, she thought it would be a good idea to stop at the local convenience store before she went home and maybe pick up some cat treats for Paws to placate him for being out so late.

'Hi,' Alison said as she entered the shop, giving the lady behind the counter a smile.

'Good evening,' she replied, busily rearranging the display of sweets.

Alison picked up a basket and wandered round the shop. She didn't really need anything but she wandered round the shelves, picking up a couple of things, some cat treats for Paws, a tin of salmon and a packet of biscuits she could take to the stroke ward for the nurses' tea breaks, bribery being one of the more effective tools to get them onside. The shelves were packed solid with a vast array of different stock lines, and where shelf space had been insufficient, crates of bottled water and stacks of cereal packets reduced the aisle space still further. She took her basket to the checkout.

'Are you new round here?' the lady asked as she rang the items through the till.

'Yes, very new.'

'Well, welcome to Wayleigh. My name's Jenny.'

'Thank you, my name's Alison.'

'What brings you down here?' Jenny looked at the total on the till. 'That will be five pounds ninety. Cash or card?'

'Card.' Alison held out her card and paid for her shopping. 'I'm working at the hospital.'

'Lovely.' Jenny smiled. 'If you need anything ordered in, or delivered, just let me know, so long as you're local, that is.'

'Thank you, yes. Very local. Just around the corner in fact, Glebe Cottage, such a lovely home.' Alison smiled at the woman and turned to leave. Was it her imagination or did Jenny's smile disappear when she said she was renting Glebe Cottage? Deciding that she must have imagined it, she carried her shopping bag outside to her car.

A man was standing on the pavement, watching the door as if he had been waiting for her to leave, but he turned away from her when she came out. There was something furtive about the way he did so, which made Alison look harder at the man. He was spare and stooped, in his sixties, she guessed, and dressed in what were clearly once smart clothes but now looked unwashed and uncared for, trousers sagging and grubby, his dress shirt frayed at the collar. Alison wondered if he was a local down-and-out, or just a lonely old man, but he hurried away as soon as he realised she was looking at him.

* * *

'Going to the shop was a good thing to do,' she told Paws later, as he licked salmon from his paws and purred deeply. He clearly agreed. He would be happy living on tinned salmon every day. 'It's good to try and get to know the people round here if I'm going to stay.'

She was still a little unsettled by the look on Jenny's face when she told her she lived in Glebe Cottage, and also by the man who had been hanging around outside the shop and, for a moment, a thought crossed her mind that perhaps she might be better off not getting to know the locals.

'But that's just me being silly and letting my imagination run away with me,' she told Paws, wondering if she really ought to be talking to a cat. She looked around the room. It looked much more like home now, even though it wasn't her furniture and some of it, she might not have bought if it had been her choice, but the house itself was perfect.

'I'll get a couple of rugs, and some throws,' she told Paws, having decided that it was probably quite normal even though he didn't seem to be very interested in her plans. 'They would cover up the stained carpet and the worst of the chintz chair covers.' She looked around the sitting room, thinking that an extra lamp in a dark corner would brighten the place as well. 'And maybe, if I decide to stay at St Margaret's, I could see if the landlord was willing to sell me this house, and then we could really make it our home.' She looked at Paws, but he just carried on trying to get the last remnants of salmon off his whiskers.

'Now, I'm going to take a good look at the garden. Coming?'

Dusk was just beginning to fall as she went out through the back door to the small lawn which was surrounded by flower beds. Everything looked a bit straggly, and there were lots of dead flowers on the rose bushes. Autumn was here and the summer long gone. In London, she and Ed had lived in a townhouse with nothing but a small patio garden furnished with a few pots containing evergreen plants that needed little or no care, but still seemed to die and need replacing on a regular basis. There was little change from one season to the next and gardening was not something she was used to having to do, and anyway, Alison hadn't brought any gardening equipment with her. She went in search of any her landlord might have left and found a few bits and pieces in the shed, using the torch on her phone as what little light was left was effectively stopped by the grime on the windows. Armed with a pair of rusty secateurs, she set about deadheading some of the roses near the house where the light spilling out from the kitchen windows helped her see what needed to be done. It would be good to get some garden lights and she might need to find out about a local gardener who could help her keep things tidy. Maybe she could put a notice up in the shop? She would ask Jenny if that was okay next time she went in.

She found it incredibly peaceful, soothing even, as she pottered about the garden as the last of the evening light disappeared. Paws even ventured out to join her, finding a warm spot on the patio to curl up and snooze. She stood and listened. There was so little noise, just an occasional car passing or a child crying to break the silence. London was never this quiet. She wondered if things would have been different if she and Ed had had children. Would they still be together? She doubted it. Children didn't stop men having affairs, they just made divorces more complex. She only had to look at the papers, or listen to her friends to know that.

Friends. She didn't have many, but the few she did have, she treasured. She made sure she was there for them when they needed her, made sure she didn't hurt them. It was a shame the same couldn't be said about them. Her best friend had always been Ed, her husband.

'Ouch!' Paws looked up as she pulled the thorn from her finger and sucked the drop of blood that appeared. At her feet lay several perfectly good blooms that she had dead-headed while her mind was elsewhere. Perhaps gardening wasn't such a good idea after all. It was too dark anyway, and there was a chill in the air. She wondered what her predecessor had done to relax when he wasn't working. Was he a gardener? Did he have a wife? A family? As she gathered the blooms and carried them into the kitchen in the hope of finding a vase, and settled on a jug instead, she thought that he was probably considerably better at relaxing than she was. Everyone was.

CHAPTER FIVE

'Dr Atkinson liked me to give him a written note of any appointments so that he could put it in his desk diary,' Mary told her. 'Belt and braces, Mary, he liked to say, belt and braces. That way he could be sure he never missed anything important.'

'I know, but I don't use a desk diary, Mary, I use the online calendar. So, if you could just flag up any new meetings like this.' Alison showed Mary again how she wanted it done.

'Are you sure you don't want me to write you a little note, just to be absolutely sure, Dr Wilson?'

'It's really not necessary, Mary, and I don't want to put you to any trouble.'

'It's no trouble at all. Dr Atkinson was always saying I was a life saver. He was always thanking me, but then, Dr Atkinson was a really, really, lovely man.'

'I'm sure Dr Atkinson was very nice, but I have to get to the ward now, Mary, because there's a ward round. Could you possibly chase up the name plate for my door? The paper one I put up seems to have disappeared again.'

'Well now, Dr Wilson, you could check on it yourself, as you'll be going past there anyway,' Mary pointed out.

'I really don't have time, just now, Mary, so if you could do that little thing for me?' Alison said as sweetly as she could manage, but one look at Mary's face told her that she was unlikely to do anything that helpful.

Once she arrived, a little breathless and a little late, Alison looked around the ward and the staff who had collected there, ready and waiting for her. As medical director she didn't have to cover the daily ward rounds except when she was on call at weekends, but tried to do them once or twice a week so that she kept in touch with the ward and her patients, and eased the strain on her colleagues. At last, she felt she could relax and be herself, especially as she knew that Dr Carrick was doing an outpatient clinic, so she wouldn't have to deal with any snide remarks or criticism.

As Alison led her team around the ward, she became aware of a bit of a ruckus occurring at the end of the ward.

'Do you want to just go and see what the problem is?' Alison asked Joyce.

'It will just be Mrs Rossi's relatives again. Trying to come and see her even though it's not visiting hours yet,'

Joyce said with a sigh. 'The sooner she goes home, the better.' She looked pointedly at Alison.

'I'll see how she's doing when we get to her,' Alison told the sister, but she was pretty sure Mrs Rossi wasn't ready to be sent home just yet, a decision that was reinforced when she reached the patient.

'How are you feeling today, Mrs Rossi?' Alison asked her as she looked at the charts.

'Oh, I'm much better thank you, doctor,' she said with a big smile. 'My granddaughter just brought me some figs, because I was a bit, you know, bunged up. Figs are so good for the bowels, so much better than all this medicine the nurses keep giving me. Would you like one?' Mrs Rossi held out a bowl of fresh figs.

'No thank you, Mrs Rossi, but it's very kind of you.' Alison tried not to laugh. 'But I'm very pleased that your family are bringing you in something healthy instead of all the pastries.'

'Oh, I can't lie, they brought some of those in as well,' Mrs Rossi answered with a twinkle in her eye, 'but only for the nurses, keep them sweet.' She winked at Alison who didn't need to look at Joyce to know that she was rolling her eyes.

'That's fine, Mrs Rossi,' Alison said seriously, 'if they are for the nurses.'

'I've always been big,' Mrs Rossi told her, 'I live to eat. It's the way I am.'

'Yes, but your blood pressure is not stabilising as much

as I would like.' Alison sighed. She knew that even if she did get Mrs Rossi to lose weight in hospital, she would just put it on again as soon as she got home. Sometimes, a doctor had to just accept the situation and do what they could. 'We really need to be sure we have the right balance with your medication before we send you home, after all, we don't want you coming back in again with another stroke.' Alison turned to Simon Bayliss, her SpR, the unit's specialty registrar who was junior to the consultants on the team but who would be looking for his own consultant post in the near future. 'Can we increase the ramipril to ten milligrams and see how it settles on that?'

'Sure,' Simon replied as Joyce made a note.

As they walked away, out of Mrs Rossi's hearing, Alison continued: 'She needs to mobilise more and let's get the dietician up here again. There's no point in her being on a reducing diet if she's scoffing pastries between meals, but I doubt it will make any difference.'

'It's not just pastries,' Joyce said, 'the family bring her in cheese, bread, pasta dishes and all sorts of other stuff. Sometimes the ward smells like an Italian restaurant.'

'Better than the usual ward smells,' Bayliss said and then quickly shut up when Alison gave him a stern look.

'Is there a husband or one of her children who might listen if I were to talk to them, persuade them that it's important that their mother loses weight?'

Joyce shrugged. 'I can try and find out for you.'

Alison knew the chances of getting someone like Mrs Rossi to lose weight were never going to be easy. She loved her food, she loved her family and she loved her life too much to change, but Alison had to try, for Mrs Rossi's sake.

Alison had been hoping to spend some time catching up on paperwork after the ward round, but Mary had left a message that Brian Hargreaves wanted to see her right away. She hurried to the administration block and up to his office, hoping it wasn't about anything too serious.

'Go straight in, Dr Wilson,' Mary said and Alison did, with only a perfunctory knock to warn Hargreaves that she was doing so.

'Come in,' Hargreaves called, although she already had. 'Why have you told Dr Carrick he can recruit more staff?' he said before she had even had a chance to sit down.

Alison sighed and rubbed the space between her eyebrows. It was going to be one of those days, she could tell already.

'I didn't,' she said calmly.

'Well, he cited your name, and said you had approved it when he went to HR. You might well have promised Dr Carrick more therapy staff but it really isn't your place to do that. It's a decision for myself and the board.'

'I didn't promise him anything, I told him I was putting forward a business case, which I am taking to the next board meeting.' Really, she could strangle Dr Carrick. He knew he didn't have permission, he was just trying to force the issue, and make her look bad at the same time. And he had succeeded!

'That's not what he says,' Hargreaves was saying, 'he said that you clearly told him he was free to go ahead and recruit.'

'Well, he's mistaken.' Alison was trying to keep her temper, and didn't want to say Dr Carrick had lied but she was furious with him. Did he really think she was so green that she wouldn't know the correct procedures for goodness' sake? 'I'm sure I can delay the recruitment process and smooth things over with him, but he is right in one way, we won't be able to improve the stroke metrics or our patient outcomes if we don't have more therapy time available.'

'Is there no way you can reduce therapy time elsewhere to give the stroke ward more?'

'You mean rob Peter to pay Paul?'

'Yes, I mean exactly that. There is a limited amount of money in the pot and it's your job to decide which areas need it most. Just make sure the business plan you present on Thursday tells me exactly where the money for these therapists is to come from, Dr Wilson. Understood?' He looked back at his computer screen, letting her know that their meeting was over.

There was no point arguing further, because she knew he was right, but it didn't make her feel better. Bloody Dr Carrick. She could scream, she really could.

'Oh, Dr Wilson,' Mary said as she marched past her desk.

'What?' Alison said rudely, before seeing Mary's shocked face and taking a deep breath, 'I'm sorry Mary, what can I do for you?'

'I don't want to be a bother.'

'You're not, Mary, honestly, I just got out of bed on the wrong side this morning. What is it?' She indicated the envelope Mary had been holding out to her.

'Your name plate, Dr Wilson, for your office door.'

Of course it was.

'Thank you, Mary, and I'm so sorry to have snapped at you.' Alison took the proffered envelope and went back to her office. She opened it and tipped the name plate out onto her desk. It read *Dr Alsion Wilson, Medical Director*.

She sat down and rested her head on her arms. This hospital! They couldn't even spell Alison right.

'Hello?' There was a knock on the door and Alison sat up.

'Come in!' she called.

'I thought you might be in need of some sustenance.'

Eliza opened the door and came in with a tray of coffee and biscuits. It was like Alison's first day, and she was as glad to see the chief nurse now as she was then.

'You heard?'

'I was in outpatients when Dr Carrick was told you

hadn't approved the extra staff and his voice carries. I'm surprised you didn't hear his reaction from here.'

'I did not tell him he could recruit more staff.'

'We all know that, but. . .'

Alison drank some of her coffee and shook her head. 'He must have known it would scupper any chance he had of getting the staff.'

'Has it?'

'Well, it's certainly delayed it. And made it more complicated.'

Eliza looked at the name plate on the desk.

'Oh, dear,' she said.

'I know. It would be funny if it wasn't so. . .' Alison stopped, as she could see that Eliza was trying hard not to laugh. 'Strike that, it is funny,' she admitted and laughed too, because it was. Funny, trivial and irritating, all at the same time. She sighed. 'Maybe I'll just give up and change my name to Alsion.'

'You have to admit, it has a certain ring to it.' Eliza picked up another biscuit. 'So how are you going to find the money for more therapists?' she asked.

'Good question,' Alison replied. 'I've been over and over the staffing in the hospital and we are already under the recommended levels in every department. If I take any staff from anywhere, I'm just shifting the problem from one department to the next.'

'Dr Atkinson used to say exactly the same. "Re-arranging deck chairs on the *Titanic*," was a favourite phrase of his.'

'That describes it perfectly.' Alison paused for a moment before changing tack. 'He seems to have been well-liked.'

'Very much so, and a good medical director.'

'So why did he leave so suddenly?'

Eliza shifted uncomfortably in her chair before shrugging.

'He had a falling out with the chief exec, I think. I mean, maybe Mr Hargreaves felt he couldn't work with Richard, that he was in some way part of the problem.'

'So, he was pushed out?' It made sense, but in Alison's experience, it wasn't that easy to get rid of senior staff; even if Hargreaves did remove Richard Atkinson as Medical Director, he could have stayed on as head of cardiology, his specialty. As it was, that was another department that Alison was having difficulties with as they were a cardiologist down, albeit a part-time one.

'I'm sure he didn't leave of his own accord,' Eliza said as she stood up. 'I'll leave you to get on with your staffing problems, I have some reports to get out and I can't put them off any longer.'

Once she had left, Alison sat for a while thinking. There had to be something more behind Dr Atkinson's departure from the hospital entirely. It would definitely have been uncomfortable if her predecessor had remained to snipe at her efforts and try and undermine her from his position in cardiology, so she was grateful that he had left, but why would he? She might never know, but that wasn't going to stop her from trying to find out. She went to the door, took down the handwritten sign she had stuck back on her door, as she had every morning since she arrived, and slotted her new name plate into the space: Dr Alsion Wilson, Medical Director. It would have to do.

CHAPTER SIX

It was getting late and everyone in the senior corridor had gone home a long time ago, back to their families, but not Alison. She was still struggling with all the figures on staffing. There was no doubt that St Margaret's was under-staffed across the board, and it certainly wasn't the case that they were being overpaid. There seemed to be no grade inflation going on, in fact the opposite seemed to be true: the vast majority of staff were junior. That was part of the hospital's problem with quality of care, there were not enough senior and experienced clinicians. It was a very different scenario to the one she had left at a major London teaching hospital. The staff numbers there had been much higher, but she had expected that, had known that St Margaret's would inevitably mean a smaller staff budget. She just hadn't expected it to be quite so bad. She clicked into the other hospital finance spreadsheets and tried to make sense of it all. The hospital was busy, and they were being paid what she would have expected, but where was all the money going?

Her other concern was the mortality rate which was higher than expected. She wanted to find out more about it. Her problem was that it didn't seem to be in any one particular specialty. Whenever she had heard of high rates occurring before, it could always be explained by poor standards in one area, an inexperienced surgeon or a high-risk population, but this seemed to be across the board.

As she worked her way through the different files, highlighting any deaths that seemed unexpected, Alison became aware of a strange scraping sound. It seemed to be coming from the room next to hers and, at times, it sounded almost as if it was in the room with her. She looked up from her work and listened, but the noise stopped. She knew that everyone else who had offices on this floor had gone home. It was one of the reasons she would have preferred to have her office on the ward; there was always someone else there, although it would also mean that she was more likely to be interrupted. She listened again, but there was still no sound.

Must be the cleaners, she thought to herself and tried to concentrate on the spreadsheets in front of her, but the noise disturbed her again. It was a scratchy sound, like fingernails on the blackboard. Alison had never been nervy, even as a child she had always been rational and unflappable, but this made the hairs on the back of her neck stand on end.

She stood up and looked around her office. There was certainly nothing that could account for the noise in the room. She listened carefully but, once again, it had stopped. She went to the corners of the room, checking for signs that perhaps the hospital had a rodent problem – unlikely as that seemed on the second floor of a comparatively new building. She moved the waste bin and the filing cabinet by the window, but there was no sign of droppings. Then her silent inspection was shattered by a noise like something falling in the room next door, which she had been told was a storeroom, and then the bang of a door closing. Hurrying to her office door, she threw it open, sure that she would see someone in the brightly lit corridor, but there was no one to be seen in either direction. She tried the storeroom door but it was locked. It had an automatic latch on it, so whoever had been in there would not have had to stop and use a key when they left. Alison stood still. She was sure someone had been in the cupboard, but had then left suddenly when they heard her moving furniture in her office.

She looked up suddenly as there was the click of a door closing that seemed to come from the reception area. Alison hurried along the corridor and turned into reception. Everything seemed to be in order, and the whole place was deserted, as she expected. She looked at the door to the stairs and the rest of the hospital. It looked closed. She went over and gave it a push. It was firmly shut. She opened it and let it go. It closed with a click that was identical to the noise she had heard. Someone had been there, in the storeroom and then in reception. But who?

'Cleaners,' she muttered to herself again and gave herself a mental telling off. It had to be the cleaners. There was no sign of any cleaning equipment and a quick check of the waste bin by Mary's desk showed that it hadn't been emptied. Perhaps it was the supervisor just checking what needed to be done. She had to be less jumpy. Who else would be up on the senior corridor at this time of night? This was a hospital, for goodness' sake, not a haunted house, and she wasn't a hysterical teenager.

All the same, she decided to stop working and head home. She was too tired to be working effectively and if she was over-reacting like this, she would be better off with a glass of wine and a nice long soak in a hot bath. She packed up her papers, closed down her laptop and headed for the way out.

As she went down the stairs and along the corridor to the main hospital, she could see that it was a busy night. On a whim she decided to visit the emergency department and see how the staff were managing with her new protocols to help reduce waits.

To her dismay she found several trolleys in the corridor to the side of the unit, all containing sick, frail, elderly and confused patients. There was only one nurse trying to look after them all, as well as other patients in the main unit.

'No beds?' Alison queried.

'They're just trying to free some up on elderly care,' the nurse told her. 'There's been a bit of a rush.'

'How long have these patients been waiting?'

'Between three and. . . five hours,' the nurse told her guiltily. Not that she had anything to feel guilty about, it wasn't her fault the hospital was full. But she had told Alison that the patients were either already breaching the maximum four-hour wait or soon would be. She moved into the main emergency area. It was made up of curtained bays in a U-shape around a nurses' desk in the centre. There was an abandoned dressing trolley next to the desk, covered with blood-stained swabs. Grim-faced, Alison took it and moved it into the sluice area which already contained a similarly used trolley, an overflowing laundry hopper and a pile of used bedpans. This wouldn't do. The room was a clear health hazard.

Alison went back into the main room, where there was some shouting. She headed straight towards the bay where it was coming from.

'Get your bloody hands off me!'

'What's going on?' She pulled the curtain aside as she said this and was met by a stunned silence. A young, male doctor, dressed in scrubs, was attempting to suture a nasty cut on his patient's head, but the patient didn't seem to be cooperating.

'I'm trying to treat this man.' The junior doctor was inexperienced and at a loss as to how to deal with a patient who didn't seem to want his attention.

'I don't need stitches, I just want you to stick a dressing on it so I can go home.' The man was in his late thirties and was dressed in filthy overalls. His clothes were not just filthy because of the blood-stains down the front, but because they had been dirty before that, although the added blood didn't help.

'It needs cleaning at the very least,' the doctor told him firmly and picked up a sterile swab from the suture trolley he had next to him.

'Well get on with it then and stop asking me stupid questions.'

'It is best if we know how this happened, Mr Jenkins,' the doctor said and looked at Alison for help. She picked up the patient's treatment card from the holder on the wall and briefly read the notes on there.

'Mr Jenkins, did you lose consciousness at all when you. . . walked into an open cupboard door?' she asked.

'No.'

'That's not what—' the junior doctor tried to interrupt but a glower from Jenkins stopped him. He was still holding the swab, having not yet dared to get close enough to the patient to clean the wound. Alison looked at the doctor's name tag.

'Okay, Dr Khan, let me take a look.'

Alison put on some sterile gloves and moved the hair

from the deep cut on the top of Jenkins' head. It wasn't easy because his dark brown hair was thick and quite curly.

'Ow!' He winced as she prodded the tissue either side of the wound.

'It needs to be sutured to stop the bleeding,' she agreed with the doctor.

Mr Jenkins sighed. 'Fine, if you really have to. Just hurry up and do it so that I can get out of this place.'

'And you ought to stay in overnight for observation,' she added.

'That's not going to happen.'

'Mr Jenkins—' the junior doctor started again, but was stopped by another look from his patient.

'And he can stop giving me lectures on things he knows nothing about.' He nodded at the doctor but aimed this at Alison.

'He's doing his job,' Alison said firmly and then turned to the younger man. 'I'll finish up here, Dr Khan,' Alison told him, pulling a plastic apron from the dispenser and putting it on. With a final glare at Jenkins, the junior doctor left. 'And he shouldn't have to put up with patients shouting at him while he does it.'

Jenkins looked taken aback.

'I don't like hospitals,' he explained rather than apologised.

'No one likes hospitals,' she told him firmly, although that wasn't strictly true. She liked hospitals, but then, she'd never been in one as a patient and she imagined it was very different under those circumstances. Satisfied she had covered as much of her clothes as she could with the flimsy apron, Alison checked the suture trolley. She would have preferred to be wearing hospital scrubs like the junior doctor, as she certainly didn't want to get blood on her business suit, let alone any of the grease and dirt that the patient seemed to be covered in, but she wasn't going to leave him while she got changed, as he would probably take himself home if she did. She opened a fresh dressing pack, making sure all the equipment she needed to suture the wound was open and ready before putting on a new pair of sterile gloves.

She talked to her patient while she worked, and took a long hard look at him as well as his wound. His dark brown hair was in need of a cut and his stubble was more than a day old, she was sure, but he had kind eyes, a sort of light hazel colour and with laughter lines at the edges. Not that he was laughing, or even smiling now, but it told her that he did, sometimes at least.

'Why are you so keen to get home?' she asked.

'Things to do,' he replied, unhelpfully.

'Little prick,' she warned him as she injected the local anaesthetic. He glared at her, seemingly unsure if she was referring to him, or the injection.

'Can you feel this?' She prodded the area to the side of the wound, once she had injected all the anaesthetic.

'Yes, no, well, I can just feel a bit of pressure,' he said.

When she was sure the area was numb, she started suturing.

'How did you do this?'

'Not the way that first doctor seemed to think, that's for sure.'

'And what did he seem to think?'

'That I was drunk and got in a fight.'

'To be fair on him, most of the injuries he sees at this time of night are alcohol-related.'

'I can believe it, but I've not been drinking.'

'That's good to know.'

Jenkins said nothing more as she finished tying the last knot and dabbed the wound, making sure there was no further bleeding.

'What's so important you can't stay in overnight?'

'The only way you'll get me to stay in this place is in a box,' he said, swinging his legs round to get off the trolley.

'Mr Jenkins, you might have concussion. I strongly advise – oh!'

Jenkins had tried to stand and wobbled, grabbing the dressing trolley to steady himself, but it shot away from him, clattering and spilling equipment and clipping Alison's hip as it passed. The force of it pushed her over and as she fell, Alison grabbed the curtains, pulling them down.

There was a thud as Alison landed followed by a searing pain in her hip, and then silence as everyone in the department turned to stare, patients and staff alike, frozen for a moment as they wondered what on earth was going on.

Alison tried to move and cried out in pain.

'Stay still,' a male nurse said but hung back, obviously fearful. As Alison looked up from the floor she could understand why. Jenkins was still looming over her, dirty, dishevelled and with a blood-stained shirt.

'Get back!' someone shouted and Jenkins looked up, confused. 'Get away from her!'

Alison turned and saw Eliza, almost running across the department towards them,

'It's okay,' she started to say, but Eliza was already pushing Jenkins back, away from her. Now that she had intervened, a nurse and one of the doctors stood behind her, ready to back her up if needed.

'Someone call security,' Eliza shouted 'and clear the area.'

Alison tried to sit up, but was prevented by a nurse, who slid her back into the corridor and away from the cubicle.

'Don't you touch me,' she could hear Jenkins shout, getting angry. She looked up and saw him batting Eliza's hands away as she attempted to push him further from Alison.

Once the nurse was happy that Alison was clear of the ruckus they both turned to watch.

'It's okay, I'm fine,' Alison tried to say, although she wasn't yet sure that she was all right. 'It was an acci—' Before she could finish, two burly security guards came rushing into the room and headed for the cubicle where

Eliza had Jenkins pinned against the wall with the same trolley that had hit her.

'No!' Alison said, but it was too late, they had taken in the scene at a glance and as Eliza moved out of the way, tackled the patient to the ground.

Despite the protestations of the nurse, Alison pulled herself up to standing. Jenkins was pinned on the ground by the two guards.

'Stop!' she said to them. 'Get off him.' They seemed reluctant to do that and, to be fair, Jenkins was still struggling. 'Keep still, Mr Jenkins, and they will let you up.'

She smiled reassuringly at the staff and patients who were still hovering in the background, unsure what they should do, worried that this was a violent man attacking a woman.

Jenkins was still and the guards stood up and yanked him to his feet.

Eliza was still standing between them, smaller than Alison and much, much smaller than Jenkins, but she still looked ready to take him on if he showed any signs of aggression. To Alison's dismay, she could see that his wound was bleeding again.

'Let's all just calm down, shall we?' Alison said, trying to sound calmer than she felt. It was important that she took charge, despite being the injured party. She was leaning against the wall, trying to keep the weight off her injured hip. She was pretty sure nothing was broken, but it was very painful. 'Mr Jenkins, please sit down on the chair.' She indicated a chair and he did as he was told. 'Eliza, can you check his stitches for me please?'

Neither of them seemed happy with that, but Eliza moved forward and he let her take a quick look.

'They're fine, the bleeding's stopped again,' she reported.

'I'm sorry, I didn't mean for that to happen,' Jenkins said to Alison. 'Are you okay?'

'I know you didn't, and I'm fine.' Alison dusted herself down and took off the apron. 'No damage.' She turned to Eliza. 'It really was an accident.'

Eliza backed away a little, still unsure, but people were returning to the jobs they had been doing before the disturbance, relieved it wasn't anything major. Just another drunk kicking off, they thought, it happened all the time.

'Honestly, I didn't push that trolley into you deliberately,' Jenkins explained again.

'I know, you had a dizzy spell, which is exactly why you need to stay in overnight, Mr Jenkins.' Alison tried to keep the cross tone from her voice, but despite her protestations to the contrary, the incident had shaken her, and she longed to go home.

'I just stood up too quick, I'll be okay now.' He seemed understandably embarrassed.

'Is there anyone at home, who can collect you and keep an eye on you overnight?'

'No,' he replied shortly.

'Then I must insist you stay, it's for your own good.'

'No way.' He shook his head to emphasise his point.

'I'm sorry, but I'm going. If you want me to sign anything so you don't get the blame, I will, but I'm going out of that door. Now.' He pointed in the direction of the main entrance to the emergency department.

'Dr Khan?' Alison turned towards the junior doctor, who had been treating Jenkins earlier and was still watching, from a safe distance. 'Could you organise the paperwork for Mr Jenkins to sign himself out against medical advice?'

'Of course. Come with me, Mr Jenkins, I have the form in the office.' And he ushered Jenkins away, keeping plenty of space between them and nodding to the two security guards to stay nearby in case. Alison may have said he wasn't dangerous, but no one seemed to believe it.

'Are you really okay?' Eliza asked Alison.

'Fine. Honestly, I'm fine.' She rubbed her hip. 'Might have a bit of a bruise tomorrow, but nothing serious. Biggest casualty was my dignity.' She smiled.

'Don't need to worry about that, we've all landed on our arses in here at one time or another.' Eliza made to lead her away. 'I'll make you a cup of tea in my office.'

'I'd really rather go home.'

'Soon as you've filled out an incident form. Sorry, but it's hospital rules.'

Alison sighed. She knew that it was, and that Eliza would want to keep an eye on her for a while as well, just in case there was any damage that was being masked by the adrenalin.

'And thank you for rushing to my rescue,' Alison added as they walked, in her case rather stiffly, to Eliza's office just outside the department. It hadn't escaped her notice that the small middle-aged nurse was the only one who had done so, everyone else holding back cautiously.

'No problem, I know Mike Jenkins and he's harmless deep down, but he's had a few problems recently.'

'How do you know him?'

'He's a local, born and bred. His mum died in the hospital a couple of months ago.' She sighed as she prepared tea and filled the kettle that lived on a tray by her desk. There were mugs, sugar and even a biscuit tin on the tray, making Alison smile. Everything you needed to comfort a distraught relative or a member of staff. It seemed the chief nurse was the first port of call for anyone in distress.

'It was a bit sudden,' Eliza continued, ' and, to be honest, he took it hard. Blamed the hospital, which was ridiculous, but he was angry.'

Alison nodded.

'So that was why he didn't want to stay.' It all made much more sense now.

'Yes, I'd hoped he was over it, but it seems not. Now I'll just pop out and get the incident book while the kettle boils and you can get home in no time at all.'

It occurred to Alison that she was talking to her in exactly the way she would a particularly fragile old lady but, she admitted to herself, she felt a bit like one, so perhaps that was for the best.

CHAPTER SEVEN

Alison was slow to get moving the next morning as she really hadn't slept very well. The bruising to her hip where the trolley had hit was much worse than it had been the day before, and more painful, so she took a couple of Ibuprofen. Despite the painkillers, she was still walking with a slight limp as she made her way up the stairs to her office.

'Are you all right, Dr Wilson?' Mary was all concern as she passed her desk in reception. 'Only I heard you were assaulted by a patient last night.'

So, it had got around the hospital already. Alison wasn't surprised; a hospital was always a hive of gossip, she should know.

'I'm fine, Mary. It was nothing, an accident, that's all.'

Alison turned to go to her office but Mary called her back.

'Oh and Mr Dunsmore wanted to know why you cancelled your meeting with him?'

'I didn't cancel it, he must be mistaken. Could you give him a call and ask him to come and see me later today as arranged?'

She didn't wait for an answer and hoped that Mary hadn't taken offence, but she really needed to sit down. She might have told Mary she felt fine, but she didn't. It was just bruising, she told herself as she sat down at her desk gingerly, and put her laptop onto the docking system. She typed in her username and password when prompted and, as she waited for it to sync, she saw that the docking station was slightly askew, so she straightened it. It still didn't seem quite right, and then she realised that the whole desk had been moved, just a little, turning it slightly away from the window. Pulling it back into position caused a spasm of pain and Alison sat down. Perhaps it was more than a bruise. Maybe she should get it checked out.

There was a knock on the door and an anxious man who looked to be in his fifties, with a neat grey moustache and wearing a white coat, came into the room.

'Dr Wilson?' he asked tentatively.

'Yes?' There was no doubt the pain in her hip was making her irritable, but she quickly realised she shouldn't take it out on other people. 'I'm sorry, can I help you?'

'We have a meeting booked, I think? Mary said you hadn't cancelled.' He ventured forward, holding out his hand. 'Colin Dunsmore, Head of Pharmacy.'

'Mr Dunsmore, of course, do come in. Please forgive me for not standing,' she held out her hand to shake his, 'only I had a bit of an accident last night.'

'So I heard,' he replied. 'Are you all right?'

'Just a bit bruised,' she said, hoping that by making light of the incident, the interest in it would die down.

'It must have been very frightening, but it really isn't common here, not like it must be in London.'

'Thank you so much for coming to see me, Mr Dunsmore,' Alison changed the subject quickly. She had never been injured by a patient in London, and nor did she personally know anyone who had, but felt it better not to say anything. Last night had been an accident after all. 'I'm trying to speak to all the heads of departments, so that I can get to know them better and get to know what their priorities are.'

'Yes, of course and I wanted to see you because of a particular problem I have. . .' He hesitated.

'And that is?' she encouraged him.

'It's about the controlled drugs going missing.'

Alison was shocked. She had expected him to tell her about doctors over-prescribing expensive medications, or not prescribing cheaper alternatives. That was the usual complaint of pharmacy heads trying to keep within their budgets, in her experience.

'That's a very serious matter, Mr Dunsmore. I need more information. What exactly is going missing, and how many?'

'It's all itemised in my email to you,' he told her, surprised that she didn't already know.

'Email?' Alison queried and looked at the emails on her laptop. 'I don't seem to have anything from you.'

'I sent it last week, and again yesterday.' He clearly didn't believe her.

Alison glanced at the hundreds of unread emails in her inbox, and sighed.

'Could you tell me what you said in the email and I'll look for it later,' she suggested.

'Small amounts of diamorphine, one or two packs of ten amps seem to go missing fairly regularly. Pretty much weekly.'

'That would be about what you would expect if someone was taking it for personal use.'

'Yes, exactly.'

'When did it start?' she asked him.

'A couple of years ago.'

'That long?' She was surprised.

'Yes, but. . .' he hesitated once more. 'We thought we had solved the problem when Dr Atkinson left.'

She looked at him in surprise.

'You mean he was the thief?'

'Well, that's what we thought, but it can't be him now, can it? He no longer works here.'

Alison thought for a moment.

'Why did you think it was him?' she asked.

'We put a hidden camera in the pharmacy. There was no doubt it was him that took the drugs then.'

'And are you absolutely sure it's still going on, even though Dr Atkinson has left?'

'I am.'

Alison believed him.

'Do you think we should tell the chief exec?' He wiped his moustache repetitively and seemed very anxious at the thought. 'Someone else has to be involved if the drugs are still being taken.'

'Or Dr Atkinson still has access,' Alison said thoughtfully. 'Perhaps you should get the locks changed, in case he copied the key to the cupboard.'

'We did that already, and he'd need a pass to get through the door as well.'

'I'll check with security that he handed his in when he left,' she told him, 'and we may have to consider using a hidden camera again if all else fails. Don't worry, Mr Dunsmore, we'll get it sorted,' she said reassuringly as he went out, seemingly happy to have passed his problem on to someone else.

Alison sat back in her chair and thought about the drugs and Dr Atkinson. The fact that no one had come out and told her exactly why he had left made sense now. Drug abuse wasn't that uncommon amongst doctors and nurses because they handled them daily so the opportunity was there. Injecting a patient with water while keeping the good stuff for yourself was something that was hard to prove, provided it didn't happen often, but this was on another scale. The amounts going missing suggested someone who was addicted and the risks involved were huge. The hospital could have chosen to report the matter to the police, but she wasn't overly surprised that they preferred to deal with it themselves as it was hardly good publicity. No wonder Dr Atkinson had not just been asked to leave the medical director post but had been forced out of his cardiology consultant post as well. No one would want to trust a drug-addicted doctor with their heart, would they? And the hospital wouldn't want the possibility of a law suit.

Alison sighed and leant back in her chair, this was an added complication she really didn't need.

After a very busy outpatient clinic and another hour or two of paperwork in her office, Alison was ready to call it a day. She rubbed her hip as it was aching again and fished another couple of painkillers out of her bag, washing them down with the remains of a cup of tea she had made a couple of hours earlier and which was stone cold. There was a knock at the door.

'Come in,' she called as the door opened and Eliza looked in. She had changed out of the nurse's uniform that she had to wear at work and was now looking relaxed in jeans and a stripy jumper.

'Just finishing?' Eliza asked. 'Only I wondered if you fancied going for a drink and something to eat? Do say if you have better things to do, but I thought it might be nice if I showed you around some of the town's attractions.'

'I would really like that, Eliza, thank you.' Alison was so pleased to have been asked, and it was a much nicer idea than heating up yet another microwave meal. She really needed to get herself more organised on the cooking front. She stood up and let out an involuntary groan. 'I'm not sure I'm up to walking far though.'

'Hmm, we could take your car and park near the marina,' Eliza said thoughtfully. 'There's half a dozen nice places within crawling distance, or,' she grinned cheekily, 'I could always borrow a wheelchair from A&E, if you want?'

'It's not that bad,' Alison laughed. She looked down at what she was wearing. At least she had eschewed heels that morning in deference to her injuries, but her smart trouser suit was still quite formal. She would have preferred something more relaxed to match Eliza's outfit, but it would have to do.

'Don't worry, I won't lead you astray,' Eliza laughed, 'I know we both have work tomorrow.'

'I'm more worried about upsetting my cat if I keep him waiting too long for his dinner,' she laughed.

'Aaah, What's your cat's name?' Eliza asked as they left the office together.

'Paws,' Alison told her as they headed out chatting. They got in Alison's car and she followed Eliza's directions to the marina and found a parking spot. It seemed like an age since she had been out for an uncomplicated evening and talked about things other than work and it was just what Alison needed. They found a lovely modern wine bar with big windows overlooking the moorings and sat watching people walk by as they talked.

'Have you moved down here on your own?' Eliza asked.

'Yes,' Alison replied and hesitated before continuing. 'I'm divorced.' Alison was surprised by the slight break in her voice as she said this. It had been months since the split, after all.

'Sounds recent and maybe still a bit painful?' Eliza looked at Alison and patted her hand. 'Don't worry, Wayleigh's a good place for a new start,' she grinned and nodded at a bunch of young men passing by. 'There are lots of sailors round here.'

'So that's why you've brought me down to the marina,' Alison laughed. They ordered pizza and second glasses of wine, but Alison was taking it slowly, and refused a third glass. She wanted to ask Eliza about what she had heard about Dr Atkinson, but equally, she didn't want to spoil their evening out. It was so rare for her to have this opportunity to relax and laugh with a friend, and she didn't want to spoil it, and anyway, she told herself, Eliza might know nothing about it.

She looked at her watch, surprised to see how late it was. Time had flown by.

'Gosh. I really need to get back, Paws will be very cross with me!' she said although she knew he was used to it. She waved at the waiter to get the bill.

'Are you sure I can't tempt you to another?' Eliza asked, but Alison was firm.

'I have loads to do and poor Paws will be starving, but thank you, I've enjoyed it.' She looked around trying to see if the bill was on the way.

'Don't worry about it, ' Eliza told her. 'My treat, a welcome to Wayleigh.' Alison looked as if she might argue. 'I insist,' Eliza said firmly.

'All right,' Alison gave way. 'Thank you, but next time, it's on me.'

'I'll hold you to that.' Eliza turned as another group of men walked past the picture window. 'I think I might stay for a while, you never know your luck. . .' she said and wiggled her eyebrows. Alison was still smiling as she got back to her car and realised that the pain in her hip had almost gone.

CHAPTER EIGHT

Alison was disappointed not to find the head of hospital security in his office when she came in the next morning. She wasted valuable time while his subordinate tried to locate him, unwilling to discuss this delicate matter with anyone other than the head of department. Keen to get to the ward in time for her morning round, she left him a note, outlining her concerns that Dr Atkinson might still have a way of getting into the hospital and stealing drugs.

Alison finally arrived on the ward, slightly breathless in her rush to get there, and found them all waiting for her.

Joyce tutted in an irritating way and Simon Bayliss flicked his floppy blond hair out of his eyes, smirking.

'How are you feeling, Mr Andrews?' she asked the patient. After a brief discussion about his progress, and that he should be ready to go home in a day or so, once his catheter was out, they moved on to the next patient.

'Good morning Mrs Rossi.' Alison was unable to keep the affection from her voice as she spoke to the large Italian matriarch. 'How's things with you?'

'Never felt better,' Mrs Rossi replied, 'apart from having had a stroke, of course.'

Her husband, a man about half her size, fussed with her pillows.

'Will you stop that!' Mrs Rossi told him in irritation. 'I'm perfectly comfortable as I am.'

The man didn't seem to take offence and indeed, sat down with a smile.

'She can't be that sick if she's complaining,' he explained.

Alison looked down at Mrs Rossi's chart.

'I'm still concerned that your blood pressure is a bit too high.' She looked at the drug details and was irritated to notice that the increase in medication she had asked for had not been implemented. She gave Simon Bayliss a hard stare and he coloured slightly, only too aware that he had forgotten to do it.

'Sorry, Dr Wilson,' he muttered. She nodded and turned back to Mrs Rossi.

'I'll increase your medication and see if we can bring it down, okay?' She made the changes needed to the record herself. She would have words with the doctor later, not here in front of the patients and other staff.

'You do whatever you need to do to keep me well, doctor. My first grandchild is due next week and I need to be out of here to see him, and hold him,' Mrs Rossi said.

'We'll do what we can to make sure that happens.' Alison smiled again and turned to Dr Bayliss. 'Keep a close eye on her BP over the next few days, we may need to add something else.'

He nodded and stifled a yawn. Alison sighed. He really wouldn't have been her choice of registrar, but he was the one she had inherited and she just had to get on with things, complaining would change nothing. They moved on to the next bay.

It was late when Alison got back to her office having had a busy outpatient clinic after the ward round, and everyone had already left. Working alone didn't normally worry Alison, but there was something about the silence here that was unsettling and she had to admit she would have preferred it if at least one of her colleagues was still there. There was a faint smell of cleaning fluid as she walked along the corridor and she realised that even the cleaners must have been and gone.

Once settled at her desk, she fired up her laptop and checked her emails first. Still nothing more from either Colin Dunsmore or the head of security, Tony Grant. It really wasn't good enough, she had been clear in her note to him that it was urgent. She would have to go and see him tomorrow, again. Putting it to the back of her mind, she pulled up the data on hospital performance that she had been working on.

Waiting times in A&E and on the list for cancer referral were always a hard problem to tackle, but she would set up meetings with each of the department heads and try and see what the hold-ups were and whether or not she could help reduce them.

That left the hospital overall mortality rate. It was stubbornly high and Alison had not, so far, managed to get to the root of the problem.

She sighed. Her eyes were playing tricks with her, all the lines of figures on the spreadsheets were beginning to blur. She looked at her watch: nine o'clock, time to go home. She wiped her face with her hands, and then worried that she might have smudged her mascara. Although there was no one still up in the admin corridor, she didn't want to walk through the hospital with panda eyes. It wouldn't be good for her reputation.

A quick look around the room told her everything she needed to know: there was no mirror. She had to concede that it was understakable as her predecessor had been a man. She would have to remember to bring one in, but for now, the cloakroom it would have to be. She grabbed her make-up bag and left her office, closing the door behind her, and hurried down the corridor to the toilets to repair her make-up in the mirror above the basin. She had been right to check how she looked, there was a large smudge of mascara under her right eye. She used a tissue and some water to wipe it away, then re-applied the mascara with a quick swipe of the brush. Looking at herself in the mirror, she thought she looked pretty good for forty-six, apart from the dark shadows under her eyes. She dabbed a bit of foundation under each eye and smoothed it in. What she really needed was a good night's sleep, or a long holiday, neither of which were going to be easy to come by in the near future. Not now she was on her own, with an all-consuming new job. Putting thoughts of holidays she had taken with Ed in the past out of her mind, she put on a fresh layer of lipstick and then, with a quick brush of her neat, blond hair, she was satisfied she looked presentable – well, presentable enough for a quick walk through the main building and out to her car.

She went out into the corridor and returned to her office to collect her things. She paused at the door, pass in her hand ready to unlock it. But the door was not locked, it was just very slightly ajar. She was sure that she had closed it on her way out. It was an automatic action. She thought back; had she heard the door actually click shut? Or had she not pulled it hard enough and it hadn't latched? Although only senior managers and the cleaning staff had access to this corridor, she dealt with a lot of sensitive data and it was second nature for her to close the door behind her when she left, especially given her concerns about passes and the possibility of Dr Atkinson still having one. The hairs on the back of her neck were standing up, telling her something was wrong. But what? Why would he come back to his office? The pharmacy she could understand, but what was there for him here? Revenge perhaps? But that was silly, she had nothing to do with his dismissal. Telling herself off for over-reacting to something that was almost certainly her own fault, nonetheless, she held back, all her senses alert to any sound or smell out of the ordinary, but there was nothing to explain her fear.

She pushed the door open wider so that she could see inside the entire office. The room was empty unless someone was actually hiding behind the open door. She listened, but could hear nothing, not even the sound of someone breathing and there was no sign of anything out of place from what she could see from the doorway. She walked into the office, flinging the door back in case there was anyone behind it, and feeling foolish when there was not. She methodically checked everything was as she had left it. She jogged the mouse and the locked screen came up on her computer, so at least no one could have seen anything there. She checked the rest of her desk. She had no idea if anything had moved. All the papers she had been working on seemed to be in place alongside her phone. She looked at the red leather tote bag she used as handbag and briefcase combined. It was on the floor to the side of her desk. Had she left it there? She couldn't remember. She checked through it. Her purse and keys were in the side pocket and everything else seemed to be exactly as it should be. She put the make-up bag back in it, telling herself she must be sure to check that the door locked behind her in future and not to be so silly. She closed down her laptop and put it in her tote, gathered up the rest of the things she might need and headed out.

As she drove home, looking forward to putting her feet up and spending some therapeutic time with her cat, she remembered that she was out of cat food. She had meant to get some at lunchtime, but had been too busy to go out. She would have to stop at the convenience store near her house and pick some up, if it was still open. She remembered being impressed by the long hours it advertised, but couldn't remember exactly when it closed. A quick look at her watch told her it was almost half past nine. She would have to hurry in case they closed at ten.

She managed to park just by the shop which she could see was still open, thank goodness. She really couldn't face a cross cat on top of a long day, and Paws could be very vocal when he wasn't happy. She just hoped the shop had his favourite food in stock. Inside she quickly found the cat food and sighed with relief. Paws might be angry at her long hours, but at least she would be able to bribe him with his favourite meal.

'Hello,' she said with a smile to Jenny as she put the pouches of food on the counter, along with a microwave meal for herself, and a bottle of wine.

Jenny didn't reply but scowled as she rang up the purchases. It was late and she was likely tired, Alison told herself.

'I'm so pleased you're still open, you've saved my life.' She tried to make conversation, but Jenny just glared at her and pointed to the total.

Alison opened her purse, and went to take out her debit card to pay for everything, but it wasn't where she expected it to be. Stilling a moment of panic, she took a deep breath and quickly searched through her purse, anxiety mounting when she couldn't find it in any of the card sections. Neither of her credit cards were in there either. Red-faced with embarrassment, she wondered if she had enough cash to pay for her shopping as she hadn't been to a bank recently. As soon as she looked at the derisory five-pound note in there, her heart fell. She wouldn't be able to pay for it all. She would have to put the wine back, but as she pulled out the note and grabbed the wine bottle ready to return it to the shelves, she could see that all her cards were hidden behind the cash. The relief was immediate. She put down the bottle, replaced the cash and held out her bank card to pay. How bizarre! She always put her cards in the same slots in her purse. and she couldn't understand why they hadn't been where she expected them to be. How had it happened? She had to have replaced them herself, surely? But it was several days since she had used any of them, and not all at once, so why were they all in the wrong place? She certainly didn't remember putting them there. Could she have forgotten taking them out? Suddenly aware that Jenny was looking at her strangely, she thrust the card at her.

'Here you go!' Alison said quickly and hurried out as soon as the transaction was complete, calling out: 'Goodnight,' she said brightly to cover her confusion, but there was nothing but a grunt from Jenny. Wondering again what she could possibly have done to upset the woman, Alison finally reached home.

It wasn't until later, once both she and Paws had eaten, that she gave the strange end to the day any real thought. The night had turned chilly and she had lit the logs laid ready in the wood burner in the living room. As she sipped her wine and stroked her very contented cat she went over the bizarre events of the evening.

She started with wondering what on earth she could have done to upset Jenny, but couldn't think of any reason for the woman's sudden rudeness. Perhaps she was just generally antisocial, or had had a row with her partner and her mood had nothing to do with Alison. Somehow Alison didn't think so, but whatever the reason, there was little she could do. And what about her cards? Was she really so forgetful that she had put the cards in the wrong place? All of them? She could not see how that could have happened and her have no memory of it, not unless she was losing her mind, or drinking too much. She looked at the bottle, but she had only had one glass of it. It couldn't be that, could it? With a shake of her head, she poured herself another glass of wine and thought about the events at work and her feeling that there had been someone in her office while she was in the cloakroom. Had there been and had they tried to steal her cards? but if so, why were they still in her purse? Had the would-be thief heard her returning and panicked? But if so, where had they gone? There had been no one in the corridor when she came out and walked back to her office, and if they had been there, how had they got in? Had she failed to close the door properly? She didn't think so. One thing was certain, she had to speak to Tony Grant in security and make sure all passes were accounted for and any that Atkinson might have access to had been cancelled. She sipped her wine. And perhaps she should think about some kind of extra lock, just to be sure, but until then, she should try and make sure she didn't leave anything valuable or confidential, in there.

She thought about doing some work, but she was tired and it was late. Ed had always said she was a workaholic, that she couldn't just sit and enjoy doing nothing. They had argued about it constantly. It wasn't that he wanted her to go out and do things with him, just be there, both physically and mentally, and she knew he was right. Even when they were in bed together at the end of the day, her mind would often wander to things that she needed to do, meetings and presentations and plans. Coming down here would prove that she could sit back and relax. Prove it to herself, at least, even if it was too late to save her marriage to Ed.

Hearing a noise outside, she sat up. What had it been? It had sounded like there was someone in the front garden. She went to the window and looked out but she couldn't see anyone. She opened the front door and went out onto the driveway, the gravel crunching under her feet. That was the noise she had heard, or thought she heard, she realised but there was no sign of anyone there. The only light was from the open door behind her, so there were large areas of shadow where someone could be hiding. She stood still and listened. There was no sound and no movement that she could see. Steeling herself, she walked as far as the gate and looked along the road in both directions. There were pools of light around each streetlamp, but again, there were large areas of shadow that could have hidden a whole army of people. This was ridiculous, Alison told herself. There was no one there. It must have been her imagination. She hurried back into the cottage and closed the door. It was worrying that she felt so unsettled, but understandable after all the changes to her life in recent months.

She closed the curtains and went back to the sofa, clicking on the television so that she wouldn't hear or worry about every noise outside. Grabbing Paws, she persuaded him to sit on her lap so that she could stroke him. It always soothed her, and he seemed quite happy to oblige for once.

There was no one outside watching her, she told herself firmly, either at work or here. She had to get a grip. The feeling of being watched was just a symptom of her anxiety. And she was anxious because she wasn't used to living alone but she had to get used to it, because she was alone now, and that wasn't going to change anytime soon.

I'm loving doing this. Even though I couldn't get close, I could see enough of what was going on. The panic when she thought she didn't have enough money or cards to pay for her shopping, I nearly laughed out loud! But I have to be careful: she very nearly caught me in her office earlier, my heart was in my mouth, I felt sure she had seen something. I had to bite my hand to stop from giving a cheer as I ran down the stairs and knew I was in the clear. I'll have to be more careful, not get so close or take risks like that again. It would spoil everything if she caught me. Maybe I can get someone else to undermine her, put pressure on her. . . In fact, I know just who that should be; he's already wound up and won't take much persuasion to act. Then I'll have to find another way of watching her, of interfering in her work and her life, stop her finding out more. I need to add to the strain, make her feel like she is losing control and losing her mind. I have to make her want to leave here, the town, the hospital, make her run screaming back to London. Because, one way or another, she has to go.

CHAPTER NINE

Alison was treating the senior team meeting as a dry run for the board meeting, a chance to practise what information she needed to get across. She knew that she needed to put in a lot of extra work to make sure that the data was all correct and clearly displayed for them. She wanted to show some of the real improvements that she had managed to obtain, or hoped she had, because that would help to get their cooperation for further changes that she needed to make. The trouble was, whenever she managed to get down to work, someone came into her office to speak to her.

Alison threw her pen down in frustration when there was another knock at the door.

'Yes?'

'Do you have a moment?' Jonathan Selby, the deputy chief exec put his head around the door.

'Of course,' Alison answered between gritted teeth.

'It's about Dr Carrick.' He sidled into the office and perched on the seat opposite her.

'Oh, for goodness' sake! What has he said to you?'

'To me personally? Nothing, but he has made a complaint about you to HR.'

'About me?' Alison was amazed and exasperated in equal measure.

'He says you've been *bullying* him.' Jonathan spoke the word with distaste.

Alison couldn't believe it. This was so unfair; she hadn't been bullying him, she'd simply been trying to change the way the ward was run. The way, *he* ran the ward. She could feel a sudden rush of blood to her face and knew her cheeks would be red. She took a deep breath.

'You'll need to talk to the ward staff, they are all witnesses to what I have been doing,' she told him, at the same time knowing that they would only be able to tell him a part of the story. 'Joyce will be able to. . .' she trailed off, only too aware that Joyce's loyalty would likely be with Dr Carrick. 'He's been very resistant to the changes that I want to make on the ward, to help improve the metrics,' she finished lamely.

'That's as maybe, Dr Wilson, but I have to tell you that this trust has a zero-tolerance policy on bullying in the workplace.' He was being such a pompous prig that Alison had difficulty remaining calm and controlled. What she really wanted to do was shout and scream at him, but that wouldn't help her cause. It wouldn't help at all.

'I didn't bully him,' she said as calmly as she could manage. 'I simply continued to make the changes necessary despite his disagreement.'

'Well, I'm sure the disciplinary committee will take it all into consideration.'

Disciplinary committee? She was shocked that he had jumped to this sort of heavy-handed action so quickly.

'It's a little early for that, surely?'

'Perhaps,' Selby conceded. 'We'll see what HR advises.'

'And meanwhile? Am I suspended?'

'Mr Hargreaves asked me to tell you that he wants to see you this afternoon, one o'clock. He'll be the one to decide on your future.'

Once he had left, Alison put her head in her hands.

She had been at the hospital less than a month and was already under threat of suspension. It had to be a record.

There was a brief knock on the door and Eliza poked her head into the office.

'All right to come in?' she asked, and Alison just groaned by way of reply. She slipped into the room, with her trademark tray of coffee and biscuits.

'You seem to be making a habit of this,' Alison said with an attempt at a smile.

'I see being the tea lady as a promotion,' Eliza said with a much more convincing smile than Alison's effort as she set the tray down and poured two cups of coffee. 'I've heard the gossip, so now, tell me what really happened.'

So Alison did, as fairly and as accurately as she could.

'That man! What is he like?' Eliza exclaimed once she had finished. 'Have another biscuit, you look like you could do with it.'

'I have to see Brian. . . Mr Hargreaves at one,' Alison checked her watch. She had plenty of time yet. She took another biscuit but didn't eat it because she wasn't feeling very well, anxiety had always hit her in the stomach. Perhaps drinking coffee hadn't been such a good idea.

'Well, I don't think you've anything to worry about, he's interviewing the ward staff at the moment, and I'm sure they'll all be telling him the same story as you.'

Alison wondered if they would. After all, Dr Carrick had been in charge of the stroke unit for many years and their loyalties would almost certainly lie with him rather than her.

When Eliza had left, Alison tried to concentrate on paperwork, but her mind was elsewhere. She went over all her dealings with Dr Carrick, again and again. Should she have handled him differently or was this always going to be the outcome? She thought about what might happen, what the outcome of her meeting with Hargreaves might be. Would she be given a warning? Or suspended pending an inquiry? Or even be sacked outright? That would be the end of everything she had worked for, no one ever came back from a sacking like that. She kept going over the possible outcomes of her meeting with Hargreaves, imagining being summarily sacked on the spot. There was no doubt in her mind that that was the outcome that Dr Carrick wanted, and she felt sure he had an ally in Selby too. She had a sudden spasm that had her running to the cloakroom to be sick. Once her stomach was empty, she went to the basins and splashed cold water on her face then rinsed the vomit from her mouth. Never, ever had she felt so anxious as she did now, to the point of being sick, not even when she had been under all that pressure in London. When her whole world seemed to be ending. Career, marriage, everything and she was sure she would never rebuild her life. But she had rebuilt it, her career, anyway. She had made a fresh start and taken the post at St Margaret's. Now it seemed to be falling apart again and she wasn't sure she had the strength to fight it, let alone start all over again.

CHAPTER TEN

The ward, and her patients, had long been Alison's sanctuary. She found it helped remind her of why she had decided on medicine as a career in the first place, so the ward was where she chose to be while she waited for her appointment with Hargreaves as she was far too anxious about what might happen to concentrate on paperwork. She went up to Mrs Rossi's bed and talked to the larger-than-life woman who never seemed to stop smiling, except when she was telling off one of her vast family. She felt calm, and almost happy in herself.

'Carla, you just leave that boy alone, he's no good for you,' Mrs Rossi was telling one of her children, who was quite old enough to decide who she did or didn't leave alone. Carla used Alison's arrival as a chance to escape.

'How are you feeling, Mrs Rossi?' Alison asked her

patient as she checked her blood pressure recordings from the day before.

'Better than you, I think,' Mrs Rossi replied. 'You look as if you have the weight of the world on your shoulders.'

'To be honest, it sometimes feels like that,' Alison answered her, then frowned at the chart.

'My pressure not down then?'

'No, well, a little but not as much as I would like. We'll keep an eye on it for a while longer, but I may need to add something else.'

'Whatever you say, doctor. You worry too much about other people and not yourself. Have a chocolate, go on, live a little.' She held out a box of handmade chocolates with a twinkle in her eye and despite her usual rule of not accepting anything from a patient, Alison took a delicious-looking truffle.

'I really shouldn't,' she said as she popped it in her mouth. It tasted as good as it looked. Mrs Rossi looked past Alison and scowled.

Alison turned to see Joyce hurrying over to her.

'What is it, sister?'

Joyce couldn't help the little smile that hovered on her lips as she answered.

'Mr Hargreaves wants to see you in his office. Now.'

Alison checked her watch. It was only half past twelve. Hargreaves had called her in early, was that a good sign? Or bad?

Alison felt a knot tighten in her stomach as she hurried

off the ward and up to the administration reception where Mary told her to go straight into the chief executive's office. Alison rolled her shoulders in a vain attempt to release the tension as she knocked on the door.

'Come!'

She went into the large, light-filled room that served as Hargreaves' office. He was sitting at his desk, but stood up as soon as he saw her and indicated the easy chairs situated in one corner. It wasn't to be a formal meeting then – Alison felt a small bit of the tension ease.

Hargreaves sat in one chair and she sat diagonally opposite him, a small coffee table in front of them, covered in hospital brochures and NHS magazines.

'I've spoken with the ward staff,' Hargreaves began as soon as she had sat down. 'And to a large degree, they seem to support your story of what has been going on.'

Alison tried not to show the relief she was feeling.

'I have simply been firm about the changes that are needed. Dr Carrick disagrees.'

'Hmm.' He gave her a long, hard stare. 'Well, I am inclined to believe you but it will have to be investigated. HR will want to speak to you later today.'

'Of course.'

'I will also speak to Dr Carrick. I understand he has decided to take a few days off, to. . . think about things. I am hoping I can persuade him to come back quickly and I trust you will be able to cover the ward and the on-call rota until he does?'

'I'll manage.' She sounded more confident than she felt.

'Good.' He cleared his throat. 'I brought you in to do a job, Alison, and I believe you can do it. There is no doubt, as I said at your interview, that you will meet some resistance, and sometimes we have to be firm, as you put it, to get things done. I do know that, but you have to understand our position as well and we cannot get a reputation for bullying, or poor employee relations.'

'I do understand that, Mr Hargreaves.'

'Brian, please.'

'Brian. . . But I am quite clear in my mind that I am guilty only of being firm.'

'Good. I felt sure that was the case! Your character references were stellar, after all, and that was one of the reasons we wanted to give the post to. . . you.'

Alison was in no doubt that he had been about to say, 'give the post to a woman'. She was under no illusions, she knew she had got the job because Hargreaves, and the board, thought that a woman was less likely to resort to bullying techniques in order to implement change.

Back in her own office, Alison tried once again to call the head of security and left him another message. It really wasn't good enough that he hadn't got back to her. Just to be sure he really hadn't, she checked all her messages and emails, but no, there was nothing from him, or Colin Dunsmore from the pharmacy department. She checked with Mary, but no, she had no messages from them either. She really shouldn't be having to chase after the pair of them, but felt she had no choice. Knowing that Tony Grant wasn't answering his phone, Alison decided to start with a visit to the central pharmacy. It would be good to see the set-up and see for herself how drugs might be being stolen from there.

She found Colin meeting with another man and offered to come back later, but he waved her into his office.

'Dr Wilson, this is Tony Grant, we were just discussing the drug situation.'

So this was the elusive head of security. In his forties, tall and bulky, with a thick neck and a ruddy complexion, he seemed to fill the small room. He was very much her idea of an ex-policeman and the antithesis of the precise and pedantic pharmacy lead.

'Please call me Tony,' he said. 'I'm very pleased we've managed to meet at last.' He held out his hand and she shook it. 'I know you are a very busy woman, but I do think it's important we do something about this.'

He was acting as if he had been chasing Alison rather than vice versa.

'I absolutely agree,' she told him. 'Have you checked who has passes, like I asked in my message?'

'Message?' he queried. 'I'm sorry I don't seem to have seen that.' He seemed genuinely puzzled.

'I spoke to your colleague and left you a message and I also left a message on your mobile.' She had also emailed him, twice, but she didn't add this.

'I got the first message, asking to see me and I rang

your office and emailed,' he said to her as he pulled out his mobile and checked before holding it out to her to see. 'No, no messages.'

Alison frowned, wondering if maybe she had called the wrong number, or if he was deliberately avoiding her and had deleted it – but why would he do that?

'Never mind, I'm here now,' she told him and let the pharmacist fuss around moving furniture, so that they could all sit down, even if it meant they were uncomfortably close.

'Colin's been telling me about the missing drugs,' Tony began.

'Good,' she turned to face him. 'I understand that you caught Dr Atkinson taking them last time.'

'That's correct, we used a hidden camera, just above the controlled drug cupboard.'

Alison turned to Colin.

'And he would need not only a hospital pass card in order to get into the pharmacy, but the keys to the cupboard in order to take the drugs.'

'Yes that is correct,' Colin told her.

'And not just any pass card,' Tony added. 'It would have to be one that specifically allowed access to the pharmacy.'

'So a visitor pass or one that had been stolen from another member of staff and not reported wouldn't get the thief into the pharmacy?'

'No.'

'And Dr Atkinson's pass was definitely taken back from him when he left?'

'Absolutely. And I checked as soon as I became aware that drugs were still going missing, it was returned and cancelled the day he was asked to leave, according to the log.' Tony looked her straight in the eye as he said this. 'Either it's not him, or he's got hold of someone else's pass.'

'And keys,' Alison commented.

'Yes.'

'We can of course, narrow down the time the drugs disappear,' Colin said to her, much to Tony's irritation, Alison thought.

'Is it possible to check whose passes were used to access the pharmacy around that time?' she asked.

Colin nodded enthusiastically, but Tony didn't seem quite so happy.

'I'll see what I can do, but it isn't quite as simple as it sounds,' he said. 'People are in and out all the time, and much as we tell them not to let anyone else use their pass, it does happen, if their own has been lost, or left at home.'

'Of course, but at least it will give us a starting point.' She was determined not to let him put her off. 'And if we can't narrow it right down, or if there are several people it might be, we could always do what you did before and put in a camera.'

Alison didn't think it was her imagination, but while Colin was clearly pleased that she was trying hard to catch the thief, Tony was not so happy at all.

CHAPTER ELEVEN

Alison was working late in her office again, pulling together the data for the report she would present to the meeting at the end of the week. She rubbed her eyes. The numbers all seemed to be blurred and, as she typed, she kept hitting the wrong key and having to correct things. She realised that it was because the position of her docking station was slightly off, again. She straightened it and continued with her email but as she typed, she heard the scratching noise that she had heard before. She turned to where she thought the source of the noise was, but as soon as she stopped working, so did the noise. Just like the last time. It really was very strange. Perhaps it was an echo of the sound she made when she was typing?

She started on her report again and sure enough, the sound started up once more, but it was clearly not an echo as it didn't match her keystrokes. The hairs on the back of her neck stood up and she felt as if someone must be watching her, which was ridiculous. The room was empty and her window overlooked the car park and she could see there was no one there.

But still the scratching noise continued. She stopped, it stopped. She started again and it started. She decided to try and catch who or what it was, so she started typing again and jumped up, went round her desk and raced for the door, pulling it open as quickly as she could and checking the corridor. She hadn't been as fast as she would have liked, but it was fast enough for her to see that the fire escape door at the end of the corridor was still swinging closed. She ran along the corridor and caught it before it clicked shut. This was not a door she had used before as it just led to some stairs down to the car park and was simply an emergency escape route. She could hear footsteps running down the stairs and then the sound of the door at the bottom, opening and closing. There was no doubt in her mind that someone had been in the admin corridor and had run as soon as she had got up from her desk. It wasn't her imagination; the door had been open and she had heard the footsteps on the stairs.

She was surprised to see that the stairs went up as well as down although she had thought they were on the top floor. She followed the stairs up to a door, pushed it open and found herself on the roof. She stepped out and walked to the rails that surrounded the edge. She could see little other than the hospital car park from the back of the building. She walked to the front from which she could see most of the town and the lights of the marina which meant that she would be able to see the sea when it was light. At last, she would have her sea view whenever she needed it to restore her. After a few deep breaths of sea air, she reluctantly went back down the stairs to her office and checked the room, she could see nothing. She went back out into the corridor and checked the door to the stationery cupboard next door to her office. It was locked and she did not have a key. She'd have to speak to Mary in the morning and get one. She was quite sure that someone had been in there, and that they were, in some way spying on her, although she didn't have a clue why they would do that.

Now, though, it was late and she really needed to get home and try to get some sleep, although she knew that would be hard to do when she was so wired by the events of the night. The last thing she needed was something like this to add to her worries about the senior team meeting and the complaint against her.

A glass of wine might help, she thought, much as she didn't believe in using alcohol to de-stress, it might actually be necessary in this instance!

That night she dreamed that she was back in London with Ed, in the early days of their marriage when the future had seemed so bright. Two dedicated professionals sure to make their mark on the world, in the time before the arguments started about her working too hard, always putting her career first and not giving her husband enough attention. She had thought he would understand; after all, she had helped support him through the long years of exams to qualify as a neurosurgeon, taking jobs that worked round his placements, helping him study and now it was her turn to make her mark. She had hoped he would understand her need, but Ed hadn't seen it that way at all. They had had a big row, a mega row. In her dream, she was shouting at Ed and when he turned round, it was Dr Carrick she was arguing with and he slapped her. She sat up with a start, instantly awake and switched on her bedside light.

Paws was giving her an unhappy look and she realised that the 'slap' had been him tapping her face. Surely it couldn't be morning already? She could see no light through the curtains, so it must still be dark outside.

'Go away,' she said, switching the light off again and turning over, but Paws was not going to be put off so easily. He crawled over her and began patting her face again, only this time, he didn't retract his claws.

'Ow!' She sat up and looked at the clock. Half past five. She sighed. Maybe the wine had been a bad idea, particularly the second glass, but at least she had had some sleep. Paws was watching her closely, tail swishing to show his displeasure that she hadn't done as commanded already. She swung her legs out of the bed. There was no point trying to go back to sleep, not if Paws wanted his breakfast. As he had already shown, he could be quite forceful if he thought it was time for her to tend to his needs. He didn't understand that she had been up until gone midnight making sure she had the main gist of her report ready for Friday's meeting. It was too early for her to be able to show any real change, she had hoped that she would at least have stopped the downward trend as it would help get the senior team to back her, but there was really nothing to see. She was tempted to massage the figures, very slightly, so that they looked better. In light of the complaint from Dr Carrick, she needed everyone to be impressed by her results so she could get them firmly on her side. It would be easy to make the numbers slightly better, and hard to prove, she was sure, but it was completely against her principles. She wanted the figures to be better because the hospital was performing better, doing a better job for their patients, and not because she had altered the facts. With another groan, she got out of bed. Perhaps it was a good thing he had woken her early. She would be able to have another look at the metrics and decide if she was going to massage them or just hope Hargreaves would understand that this was a long game and give her more time.

Alison had done her best to slap on some make-up to cover the bags under her eyes which were even worse this morning, the result of a poor night's sleep worrying about her future. She hoped she had been successful in making herself look well-rested as she came out of the front door. She turned and looked at the house. It really was a picture-perfect cottage, she thought with a sigh of pleasure. She pulled off the last dead rose bloom from the plant that climbed around the door. It would be beautiful next summer, if she were still here to enjoy it.

A woman Alison had seen around the village was walking her dog past the gate.

'Morning!' Alison called brightly.

'Morning!' came the reply but then the woman stared at the garage, did a double take and hurried quickly away. Alison wondered what she could possibly have seen to react like that and turned to look. Immediately, she saw, sprayed across her garage door in red paint were the words: 'Stay away!'

Alison couldn't believe it. Who could possibly have done it without her hearing anything? The message certainly hadn't been there the night before when she came home, she was sure. And what did they mean? Stay away from what? Or who? Stay away from the village? She was at a loss. What had she done to upset someone so badly that they would do this? It was horrific to feel that someone wanted her to leave so much and she hated to think how many people had seen it already, would know that she wasn't wanted.

Slowly, she walked up to the garage door, and touched the painted words. They were still slightly tacky and her finger came back with red paint on it. It couldn't have been on there long. The noise must have been what had woken Paws so early. Perhaps if she had looked outside when she got out of bed, she would have seen them, known who wanted her to stay away, but it was too late now. The paint was drying fast and would be hard to clean off if she left it much longer.

Biting back tears of anger, she looked down at what she was wearing: beige tailored trousers and a white cotton shirt. Certainly not the clothes she would have chosen if she had known she would be cleaning up red paint. She checked her watch. Did she have time to change? Not really was the answer, and she was guaranteed to get her clothes dirty if she tried to do it without changing, but she had to do something, to try and get rid of those hate-filled words before the whole village saw them. She remembered seeing a hose attached to an outside tap by the side of the garage and quickly went to get it.

Carefully standing well back, Alison hosed the door down, but the words were barely touched. It would need more than just water to get rid of them.

Suddenly, she felt that she was being watched and turned to see a battered Land Rover stopped by her gate. The driver was staring at the garage doors, reading the message. Angry to be the centre of attention like this, Alison threw down the hose and strode towards the stopped car.

'Excuse me!' she shouted and the driver turned and looked at her. She stopped dead. It was Mike Jenkins, the patient who had accidentally hurt her in casualty. What was he doing at her house? Her home? How did he know where she lived? These thoughts rushed through her mind as he looked at her and then, with a scowl, drove quickly away.

Alison stood still, deep in thought and trying to piece together what she had just seen. Could he have been responsible for the graffiti? Was he angry that she was washing it off? And if so, why had he come back? Did he want to see her reaction?

Suddenly aware that her feet were wet, she looked down. She had left the hose on and was now standing in a puddle. Her suede loafers were ruined and there was some mud on the bottom of her trousers, she would have to change before going into work. There was no way she was going to show up at the hospital looking such a mess.

She switched off the water and with a last look at the words that were just going to have to stay, hurried inside to change.

CHAPTER TWELVE

Alison looked at the on-call rota that was pinned to the wall in Dr Carrick's office. There were four stroke consultants including herself and Dr Carrick. One had to be on call at all times to cover for emergencies. With Dr Carrick off, that left just the three of them. Do-able in the short term so long as no one had holidays or went off sick, and so long as none of them had other jobs they were trying to cover, like being medical director.

She would try and find some agency cover, but stroke consultants didn't grow on trees. She looked up as someone cleared their throat and saw one of her fellow stroke consultants, Dr Cheung, standing in the doorway.

'Do you have a moment?' he asked.

'Of course, come in, have a seat.' She noticed that he carefully closed the door behind him. 'How can I help?'

'Ailsa works full-time too and we have three children,

young children,' he explained. Alison remembered that his wife was a theatre sister and knew that it must be hard covering childcare with both of them on rotas. She sighed. She knew there was a limit to what she could put on the other consultant too because they were the most junior member of the team, and still, to a degree, learning. So that meant a significant increase in her own workload. Which, in turn, meant that she would have to rely on her registrar even more than she already did, and she was already beginning to suspect that he wasn't as dedicated as he should be, or as capable as he thought he was. This was exactly what she didn't need. She had to find someone to take Dr Carrick's place, and soon, if she was ever going to be able to take a break.

'I'll do as much as I can,' she assured Dr Cheung, even though she had no idea exactly what she could realistically do. There was a physical limit to how many hours she could work herself, let alone how many hours she could work and still be a safe pair of hands. Perhaps Dr Carrick would only be away for a few days, and would realise that it was not in his best interests from a career point of view to be labelled either as a trouble maker, or as weak. Unless he won. She knew all too well that his only options were to come back and work with Alison, or to make sure she was painted as the villain of the piece, the bully who had forced him out. That way he could get her sacked and himself reinstated. She knew which way she thought he was going to go. She would lay money on it. If he succeeded, then he would be due a significant payout, and she would be out of a job because it was quite possible that she would be suspended as well while the complaint was investigated, which could take months. He would come back, the hero jumping into the breach.

Alison knew that if she was sacked from this job, she might get a post as a stroke consultant again, but no one would dare employ her in a management role. Could she bear it? Getting back to just treating patients? Not being in charge? She wasn't sure she could, not anymore. She hoped the fact that Hargreaves was still backing her meant that sufficient numbers of staff were too, but she was under no illusions. She had to deliver, and quickly, or Hargreaves would drop his support and she would be out.

Telling Joyce that she would be in her office in the senior admin corridor if she was needed, Alison left the ward. Dr Carrick had been due to cover the unit overnight, but as neither of her colleagues were willing, or able to cover it, she would have to do it now. Normally, she would have taken the afternoon off to try and get some sleep before a night on-call, and would definitely have had the morning off after one. There were strict rules about the number of working hours in a row she, or anyone else, could do and she knew she was going to be breaking them, but with the paperwork due by the end of the day and the senior team meeting at nine the next morning, she was just going to have to hope it was a quiet night and she managed to get a few hours' sleep in the on-call room. In London, she would have been able to cover the ward from home, but St Margaret's had not yet invested in the telemedicine infrastructure that would allow her to see CT scans and examine a patient remotely. It was something she hoped to bring in in the future, but for the time being, she had to remain on site when on duty. She didn't want to have massive bags under her eyes at her first senior team meeting, or to be exhausted and struggling to stay awake. That was why she had made sure she was not working the night before the meeting. The best laid plans and all that, she thought.

She spent the afternoon pulling the report into shape. She had slightly massaged the figures, improved them in a way that shouldn't raise anyone's suspicions, but she hoped would buy her the time she needed to make a real difference. After a final tidy up of the charts and graphs that accompanied her report, she emailed a copy to Mary so that she could get the papers printed ready for the meeting set for nine o'clock the next morning. She had also pulled up some financial data that she would go through later that evening while on call, if she had a free moment. Checking her watch, she saw that she had just enough time, if she hurried, to go home and feed Paws, and maybe clean up the last of the graffiti, before she needed to be back for evening round. She knew that Dr Cheung would be covering until then, so it was her last opportunity to get it done. Leaving her laptop on her desk, she hurried out.

'Sorry, no time! I know I'm leaving early, but I'm on call

tonight,' she said as Mary attempted to stop her on her way out and ask a question. She hoped that it was nothing that couldn't wait until the next morning, but she really couldn't spare the time to stop now, even though she spotted the disapproval writ large on Mary's face as she left.

Alison had picked up a large container of white spirit and a stiff scrubbing brush on her way home, but once she was there and Paws was fed, she decided it would be a better use of her time to give him some attention. If she was honest, she was exhausted and Paws was being insistent so the graffiti was no contest. She sat down, intending to only spend a short time stroking him, which she always found therapeutic, but she closed her eyes for a moment.

She woke with a start, to the sound of her mobile phone ringtone. She spotted the time as she answered it. Six o'clock! She had been asleep over an hour.

'I'm so sorry, yes, I'm on my way, if you could just stay until I get there. Yes, I'm so sorry.'

Dr Cheung wasn't happy to stay, and she understood why. He had children to collect from childcare and they couldn't wait. She grabbed on overnight bag and clean suit for the morning and hurried to her car. The evening light was fading fast, but the graffiti still glared at her from the garage door. Even if she closed her eyes, the image of those large, red letters seemed to persist. They were a horrifying reminder that someone didn't want her here, in the place she had chosen as her home, a place that should be a sanctuary from the pressures of her job. Her emotions were threatening to overwhelm her and she told herself not to be so silly. They were just words.

'Sticks and stones,' she said to herself and got into the car. She really would have to do something about it tomorrow, but right now she had to hurry and cross her fingers that there were no emergencies before she got to the hospital.

It was inevitable that there was one. A suspected stroke had arrived in A&E by ambulance while she was still on her way, so she had to rush straight there when she arrived. To add insult to injury, she endured a sharp word or two from the emergency department consultant for her late arrival.

'You're the one always banging on about the importance of speed in the case of suspected strokes,' he quite rightly admonished her and she didn't hesitate to apologise. He was the one in the right and she told him so.

'At least you're here now,' he grunted as he walked off to deal with another patient and left her to examine the potential stroke, which, inevitably turned out not to be one at all. In her opinion, the patient actually had a migraine and once the analgesics she gave them had worked, they were happy to be sent home.

At last, she was able to go up to the ward and check on all the patients there. The nurse on duty had a few queries and some charts that she needed Alison to check.

Once all that was done, there was another call to the emergency department, and then another. It was going to be a long night.

Alison finally crawled into bed at gone midnight, and was asleep as soon as her head hit the pillow. She was called out again at four o'clock for a patient who had become acutely confused on the ward, and then at six for a wake-up stroke – someone who had woken up, confused and with left-sided weakness having had a stroke in their sleep.

There was no point going back to bed after that, Alison decided, so she picked up her tote bag containing her laptop from the on-call room and, after grabbing a cup of coffee and an egg roll from the canteen, she made her way up to the office. She was still dressed in the scrubs that she had pulled on when called out of bed in the night. Experience had taught her that they were much faster to pull on, and even sleep in, than trying to get fully dressed. She planned to shower and get properly dressed after her breakfast, thus making sure that there was no chance of arriving at the senior team meeting with a grease stain on her clothes.

She checked Mary's desk as she went by, but there was no sign of the documents for the meeting. Mary must intend to print them when she got in, she thought, even though it would be tight to get them done in time. Alison decided she would do it herself, just to be sure, and hurried to her office. Once she had logged in, she searched for the documents but couldn't find them. Where had they gone? Had she saved them somewhere bizarre? She wasn't worried because, of course, she had emailed them to Mary, so she could just get them from there, but when she looked, the email from her to Mary had gone as well. It wasn't even in her laptop recycle bin.

Alison sat back in her chair and thought for a moment. Someone must have deleted the email. But had they also deleted it from Mary's computer? Or recalled it? And how could they have done that? As well as removed the documents from her files? She could only think that it had to be someone in IT. They were the only people who could access her files remotely without her passwords.

Making a mental note to contact IT later and find out what the hell was going on, Alison quickly took out a flash-drive. Flash drives were frowned upon by the security guys in IT, even the secure NHS-supplied ones like hers, just in case they introduced viruses into the hospital system. Some trusts blocked their use entirely, but St Margaret's hadn't gone that far and she was just thankful she had copied the paperwork onto one under the circumstances. She saved the documents onto her laptop again and sent them through to the printer. All the financial information she had bookmarked seemed to have gone as well, but she would be able to search for that again later. Meanwhile, she changed her passwords again.

* * *

After the meeting, Alison allowed herself a small smile and a sigh of relief. She had got away with it. Hargreaves had been very enthusiastic about the very small improvements she had put in her monthly report, and, although Jonathan Selby had queried a few of them, she was confident he had accepted them as correct. She had bought herself more time.

After a busy afternoon in outpatients, she was really flagging from the lack of sleep. There had been no further word from Dr Carrick, but no news was good news, as far as she was concerned. Perhaps, after a few days licking his wounds he would come back to work. Feeling more optimistic than she had since she had started at St Margaret's, Alison handed the ward over to Dr Cheung and headed home for an early night. IT would have to wait until Monday morning.

Her good mood was only slightly dented by the young girl who helped out in the local shop.

'Who wrote that stuff on your garage?' she asked as Alison tried to pay for the microwave meal and bottle of wine she had picked up.

'Goodness knows,' Alison replied. 'I'll try to clean it off tonight.'

'It will need a lot of scrubbing,' the girl told her unnecessarily. 'People are so stupid.'

Alison agreed and hurried out of the shop to get the job done. If she didn't want to be the talk of the town, she really should have done it straight away, she scolded herself. Now it was too late, everyone would have seen it and she was probably the main topic of conversation everywhere.

She had intended to spend the weekend tidying up the garden and maybe venturing into the local pub in a bid to start to get to know her neighbours, but she was almost relieved that she wouldn't have the chance. Work, as ever, took priority and despite Dr Cheung being the consultant on-duty, she had agreed to go in and relieve him for the Sunday afternoon so that he could spend some time with family. She just hoped he would be willing to do the same for her when she needed time off. But first, she was going to clean the garage door and then put her feet up for a well-earned rest.

Later, having cleaned as much of the graffiti off as she could, she lit the log burner in the living room and settled down for a quiet evening in with a glass of wine, her cat and some mindless TV. She was still flicking through the channels, trying to find something vaguely interesting when her phone rang. She was surprised to see that the caller was Ed.

'Hello,' she said.

'Hi,' he replied, and then there were a couple of seconds of awkward silence.

'What can I do for you?' she asked eventually.

'Nothing, nothing,' he hastily replied, 'I just rang to find out how you were and how the new job was going.'

'Why?' she asked, wondering if he had heard something on the grapevine.

'No reason, I just wanted to know. I miss you, Alison. I still care about you.'

She was tempted to tell him it was too little too late, that she no longer cared about him, but she wanted to know why he was suddenly calling her.

'Everything's going well here,' she lied. 'How are things with you?'

'Fine, fine, well, I thought you might have heard that I'm, er, not seeing Sara anymore.'

'No, I hadn't heard that, but I'm glad to hear that you've finally come to your senses.' She knew that was a harsh response, but under the circumstances she wasn't feeling too charitable.

'Hmm,' was all he could manage.

'I'm sorry, that came across a little harsh,' she said.

'You have every right to say that,' he responded. He sounded as tired as she felt.

'But it doesn't help.'

'No.' He laughed, a little, and then there was a longer silence. 'Anyway, I heard that there's a post going at Bart's for a stroke consultant and I thought maybe, if you wanted to come back to the centre of things, that would be a good place to start.'

'Thanks, but I already have a job here. Remember?'

'Yes, but I know you, Alison, you aren't planning on staying in some shitty provincial hospital for long, you need to be back in London, finger on the pulse, all the excitement.'

'You can't tell me what I want, Ed, you lost the right to do that when you shagged my registrar, remember?'

'Fair point,' he admitted. 'But I do know you, and I know you want to come back here.'

What really riled her, was that he was right; she did only see the job at St Margaret's as a stepping stone, a way back to where she was meant to be, London. But there was no way she was going to give him the satisfaction of saying it to him.

'If you think I'm going to come rushing back to London just because you are feeling a bit lonely and want someone to warm your bed for you, you are very much mistaken, Ed Wilson!' Alison terminated the call and leapt to her feet, startling Paws. She was livid with him, with his arrogance in assuming she would go back to him, that she wanted to go back to him after what he had done to her. Her relaxed evening was over. She needed to work off her anger. She needed a brisk walk, she decided and, grabbing her coat and keys she went out, leaving her phone behind in case she was tempted to answer any more calls.

Night had fallen and it was dark outside, very dark. She was so used to lights everywhere in London, but the streetlights in Wayleigh were few and far between and many of the side roads had none at all. Wishing she had brought a flashlight with her, or her phone, she made her way towards the local hub where there was the shop, a hairdresser's and the pub. At least that area was well lit.

The shop was still open and she could see Jenny behind the counter. She didn't want to go in there and face more antagonism, she had quite enough at work and with Ed. The hairdressing salon was closed, so that left the pub, but did she want company? Particularly the company of strangers?

She walked a bit further on, to the very edge of town, but the pavements ended and she didn't want to walk along the road and have to dive into the bushes every time a car passed. She turned and started to walk back to the pub. There was a tall, thin man walking towards her and he stopped, as if her change of direction had caught him out. He didn't seem to know if he should keep walking in the direction he had been going, or to turn around as well. He looked from side to side, as if deciding which way to run. Even though it was dark, Alison was pretty sure it was the man she had glimpsed outside the shop, a man she had never actually met but who seemed to dislike her all the same. He was still rooted to the spot as she approached and she wondered if he had been following her.

'I'm sorry, I didn't mean to startle you,' she said. He looked at her and his expression changed from surprise to fury.

'Get away from me!' he said venomously and hurried back the way he had come. Get away from him? It was a public place and he was the one who may, or may not, have been following her. Suddenly she didn't feel quite so safe being out on her own, which was ridiculous – all those years in London and she had never felt unsafe there. She looked at the long, dark route back to her home. She really should have brought her phone with her. How stupid to leave it behind just because she didn't want to talk to Ed. She hesitated by the pub. Maybe they would call a taxi for her. It wasn't far home, but she didn't want to walk alone, and the thought of a glass of wine in a cosy pub while she waited for a cab was very appealing. Before going in, she looked through the window. It was quite busy, and sitting at the bar was Mike Jenkins. He seemed to be chatting up the barmaid. He must have felt her watching him, because he turned and looked directly at her. He looked surprised and stood up, moving towards the door. That made her mind up, there was no way she was going in there and talking to him. There were three people she wanted to avoid: Ed, the batty old man who seemed to have it in for her, and Mike. Yet they were the three people she kept bumping into. She hurried back to the cottage, almost running in her need to get away from everyone. She thought she heard footsteps and someone call to her, but she'd had enough, she wanted to get home.

She fumbled with her keys when she got there, but once she was inside, she locked the door behind her and leant against it, getting her breath back. Why was she running? Why was she so frightened by an old man and the dark? She would buy a torch, or several torches. She went into the kitchen and opened the fridge. She poured herself a glass of wine and went into the sitting room. Her phone was on the coffee table and she picked it up. There were several missed calls from Ed and he had left a voice message. She deleted the calls and the message without listening to it, before going and pouring herself another glass of wine. It would be a while before she could forgive him for what he had done. Not only had he had an affair, but with a member of her team, her registrar. By the time Alison had found out, pretty much the entire hospital knew and must have known for weeks. It had been humiliating. She didn't know what was worse, the people who laughed at her behind her back or the ones who were so sympathetic to her face, telling her that Ed was just having a mid-life crisis. And as for her beautiful young registrar, she didn't even have the good grace to be embarrassed when she knew that Alison had found out. She just shrugged and said perhaps it would be best if they tried not to work together too much. But that was impossible, and she knew it. Day after day, ward round after ward round, they worked together, with every other member of staff watching, waiting for her to crack. It had been torture and it had been all Ed's fault.

She wasn't ready to forgive him. No, she wasn't going to give up on St Margaret's just yet, she thought, and when she did eventually leave, even if she did go back to London, that didn't mean she would go back to Ed.

CHAPTER THIRTEEN

Alison was not surprised to find a sick certificate from Dr Carrick's GP in the pile of mail she picked up from Mary's desk first thing Monday morning. Apparently, he had been signed off for two weeks due to stress. That was exactly the move she had expected from him, but it wouldn't make the forthcoming days and weeks any easier. She had to assume that after this certificate had run out, it would be followed by another, and then another. There was a message from HR as well asking her to come and see them ASAP. Not good news as it suggested that he, or possibly even his union representative, had probably been in touch already. Maybe he had decided to go down the tribunal route and wouldn't be back at work anytime soon. She had been lucky that the weekend had proved reasonably quiet, and she had coped, but for how long would that be the case?

The senior corridor was deserted. It was only eight o'clock in the morning and no one, not even Mary, had arrived at work yet and Alison already felt exhausted.

Going through her emails, she found she had also had a response from the agency that she had contacted with regard to getting a locum. They said they were pulling out all the stops but, reading between the lines, her chances of finding a suitably qualified locum stroke consultant were somewhere between little and none.

She rested her head in her hands. There was no way she could carry on like this, covering both her two jobs and Dr Carrick's one. She had to get some help. She reached for her mobile phone, scrolled through her contacts and called an old friend.

'Dr Faez is unable to take your call at the moment. Please leave a message after the tone and he will get back to you as soon as he can.'

'Hi Anwar, it's Alison,' she said as soon as the tone had finished. 'I heard that you've retired, but. . . look, I need to speak with you rather urgently. Please could you give me a call back?' She tried not to sound too desperate, but at the same time, she did want to hear from him sooner rather than later, and she didn't want to hear that he was loving retirement. In fact, she was fervently hoping he was bored.

Second call of the day was to IT and they treated her as if she was either completely mad or stupid when she tried to explain that she thought someone was tampering with her files and emails. They patiently told her that it was impossible unless she had shared her password, or given people permission to access her files. The more she told them that no, she hadn't given anyone her password and she had checked and no one had access to anything other than her calendar, they just told her to change her password again and this time to make sure she didn't give it to anyone. Finally, she lost patience and went down there to confront them .

'Someone is accessing my files,' she said firmly, 'and it's not me, so it must be you.'

'Me?' the young man almost squeaked.

'Or someone from IT.'

'Why would we do that?'

'I have no idea.'

He looked as if he thought she must be mad, but he did look up her file access records and then showed her, smugly, that only she had accessed them. She looked at the login data. There were multiple times noted in the middle of the night, when she didn't think that she had been working. It was hard to be sure, but then she spotted that at 1 a.m. Friday morning, she had apparently accessed her files and deleted some. She knew for certain that that could not have been her, because she was dealing with a suspected stroke in A&E. Someone else had signed in as her.

'There, that was not me,' she told the young man. 'I was in A&E with an emergency at that time. Can you tell what location I supposedly used to sign in?'

He checked again.

'It was from your laptop.'

'I left it in my on-call room,' she said quietly. Alison tried to work out how on earth this could have happened. 'And there can be no doubt about the time?' she checked. 'I mean, is the clock on the laptop right?'

He gave her a long look. Yes, he definitely thought she was deranged.

'The time the files were deleted is from the central server, and that is definitely right.'

She would be able to check the time she had given the drugs the patient needed as it was recorded, and signed for by herself and a witness. She had no doubt that someone had gone into the on-call room and signed in as her on her own laptop.

'It couldn't have been me,' she said as much to herself as the young man.

'It's easy to get muddled about when you log on and where from,' he said kindly, obviously thinking she was some kind of mad old biddy. He probably thought anyone over thirty was ancient and senile, and to be fair, she was old enough to be his mother.

More in hope than expectation, she asked if there was anything more either of them could do to improve security, but all she got was another lecture on setting a difficult password, using upper and lower case, numbers and symbols and not writing it down or giving it to anyone. As if she would!

Alison was irritated by the patronising attitude of the young lad. She wasn't an idiot, she didn't use her birthday as her password, or the name of her cat or go around telling everyone what it was. In fact, since that first time she thought someone might have accessed her files she had changed it regularly and had no set pattern to the words or number sequences she used. Of course, that meant she was in constant fear of forgetting it. She could just imagine the response she would get if she had to ring and ask him to unlock her computer because she'd forgotten her password!

She was still angry at his attitude as she walked onto the ward and into the office. Her mood wasn't helped by finding Dr Simon Bayliss in there, feet up on the desk, scrolling through his phone.

Alison said nothing, just raised an eyebrow and was gratified that Dr Bayliss jumped up.

'Sorry,' he said. 'Just catching up with—'

'It's okay,' Alison replied. 'We all need to do that sometimes. Now, what's the situation on the ward?'

'It's all fine, as far as I know. No problems, well, none that I can't handle.' He smiled at her and ambled out of the office.

Alison was surprised, she couldn't remember ever being in a position where everything was done and problem free and she was pretty sure the only reason he was saying that was that he hadn't checked them.

For one so inexperienced, he was remarkably sure of himself. Time might change that, she thought, but she honestly couldn't ever remember being quite so relaxed about her work or her patients' well-being. She was always worrying about someone or something that might go wrong. Perhaps that said more about her than Dr Bayliss.

Alison was in outpatients when she got the call from Joyce. A patient had had an allergic reaction to penicillin and she needed Alison on the ward, immediately.

Alison very quickly finished seeing her patient, fortunately the last on her list, and hurried up to the ward, where an anxious Joyce met her at the door and whisked her into the sluice.

'What's up?' Alison asked, she had never seen Joyce quite so upset. 'Is the patient all right?'

'Yes, yes, he's fine, well, got a bit of a rash, but nothing too serious,' Joyce reassured her, 'but Dr Bayliss is blaming me and it was him!' She looked as if she was about to burst into tears.

'Slow down, blaming you for what? Start at the beginning and tell me exactly what has happened.'

'The patient in bay four, Mr Andrews, you know, the man with the catheter. He had a confirmed infection in his wee, so I got one of the junior doctors to write him up for some antibiotics and gave it to him this morning. Then he came out in a rash. '

'Because he's allergic?'

'Yes, and threatening to make a complaint because he says we knew that he was.'

'It was in his notes?'

Joyce hesitated before answering.

'That's the thing, Dr Wilson. I swear it wasn't, but it is now, and dated from when the patient was admitted.'

'Who clerked him?'

'Dr Bayliss, and he insists he asked about allergies and made a note including making sure there was a red flag on the records, but if he had done, we wouldn't have been able to prescribe the antibiotic he was allergic to, would we?'

The electronic patient record system that they used in St Margaret's had a red flag system to try to reduce prescribing errors and interactions. If any doctor tried to prescribe a drug that the patient was allergic to, or that interacted with something they were already taking, a red flag warning appeared asking the prescriber if they were sure. There were times when this might be overruled, but with something so basic as an allergy to a specific antibiotic, it never would be, because there were alternatives that could be used.

'It's okay, Joyce,' Alison reassured the ward sister, 'I'm sure this isn't your fault, I'll have a word with Dr Bayliss, I'm sure he just made a mistake about when he added the note.'

Alison went to the office, where she was sure she would find her registrar skulking and sure enough he was there, busily updating some patient records. She could imagine exactly what had really happened all too easily. Dear slap-dash Dr Bayliss had been told of the allergy by his patient but had forgotten to put it in the notes. Once the patient had had a reaction and was threatening to complain, he had added the allergy and red flagged it.

'Simon, a word please,' Alison said as she went into the office and closed the door behind her. He leapt to his feet with a speed she had never seen from him.

'I'm so sorry, Dr Wilson, I don't know how the nurses could have miss—'

Alison stopped him from saying anything more by holding up her hand.

'Before you continue, Dr Bayliss, rest assured that I will be having the patient records checked by IT so that they can ascertain exactly when the allergy information was actually added.'

His face fell and she could see his mind whirring away trying to work out if that was possible and deciding that it quite probably was. To be fair, Alison didn't know if they could do that, but she was pretty sure she was on safe ground.

'It was a mistake,' he said. 'Everything is too rushed here. The pressure—'

Once again, she stopped him with a raised hand.

'I accept that we are all under a lot of pressure, but patient safety is paramount and this was a basic error on your part, made worse by trying to shift the blame onto the nursing staff.'

'It's not my fault Dr Carrick's off sick,' he said with a snide look.

'No, it isn't, but we all have to pull together and work that little bit harder to ensure standards don't slip. Do you understand me?'

He nodded, but she didn't think he had any intention of working harder.

'What are you going to do about this?' he asked.

'I suggest you apologise to Sister Fletcher for trying to put the blame on her for a start.'

He nodded sulkily then looked at her with a challenge in his expression.

'And?'

'And I'll think about it.' She didn't want to let him off the hook too easily, but, in reality, mistakes like this occurred fairly frequently and she didn't think she could justify further action.

'Well, don't think too long, Dr Wilson, you wouldn't want a second member of staff to go off sick after accusing you of bullying, would you?' he said with a smirk.

Alison would have dearly loved to wipe that smirk off his face, but she knew he was right. She had to let him get away with this mistake. She couldn't afford for him to complain about her, it would be the final nail in her coffin, the proof that she was the one in the wrong, even if she wasn't.

My plan to get rid of the bitch is going well. She's shattered, making mistakes, and spotting the changes she made in the report was a bonus. Who would have thought she'd play into my hands like that? Serve herself up on a plate, so to speak. It was better than I could have expected. But I need to find a better way to see what she is doing, it's too difficult to keep up with all her password changes. I need to find a way to get inside her laptop and I have a plan to do just that.

Meanwhile, on the ward, the staff don't like her and they blame her for them being over-worked. Blame her for the mistakes that are happening, and quite right too. My only problem is that stupid man threatening me, threatening to tell someone about what's been going on, even if it gets him into trouble too. He wants money, of course. Don't we all. Money and power. He doesn't want to have to work for a living, doesn't see why he should, he wants the easy life and he thinks I should pay for it. Some chance! I couldn't believe it when I saw him on the ward and he said he wanted a word. You cannot plan for bad luck like that. I'm going to have to deal with it, with him, of course. If he doesn't want to have to work for his money anymore, that can be arranged, but he might not be happy with the outcome.

CHAPTER FOURTEEN

'Hi,' she said as she poked her head around the deputy chief executive's door. 'Do you have a moment?'

Selby looked up and nodded, so she came into the office.

'I spoke to HR about a new consultant that I would like to start on a short-term contract. I just need sign off and then he can start immediately.'

She had been delighted when her old friend Anwar Faez had finally called her back once he got back from his holiday. He'd said he would happily come and help out at her hospital. He had recently retired from his stroke unit in a major London hospital and had confided to her that he was already feeling bored.

'There's only so much leisure time I can tolerate,' Anwar had told her. It was exactly what she wanted to hear.

'Why is he available so quickly?' Selby seemed suspicious.

'Because he retired six months ago. We worked together in London and when I explained the situation to him, he agreed he could come and work here to help out, but only until we manage to recruit someone permanent.'

Selby thought for a moment.

'That would seem to be a reasonable solution, I'd be happy to ask Mr Hargreaves to sign off on that if. . .' He again paused meaningfully. 'That is, if HR check him out and he's really as good as he sounds.'

Honestly! Who did he think she was? His tone implied she might be trying to pull a fast one.

'I can assure you, he really is that good,' she told him firmly.

'Hmm, much as I don't want to look a gift horse in the mouth, you'll have to excuse me if I don't take what you tell me as necessarily the truth, Dr Wilson.'

'I don't know what you mean,' she told him.

'I studied the report you presented at the meeting last Friday. I studied it quite closely, in fact, particularly the source data, which, shall we say, doesn't exactly match the data you presented.'

The knot in her stomach tightened. He knew she had massaged the figures.

'Really?' She tried to sound unconcerned. 'Did I make a mistake?'

'Oh, I don't think it was a mistake, Dr Wilson, I think you quite deliberately changed them, to make yourself look good and buy yourself more time.'

'I don't know what you are referring to,' she started to say before he waved at her to stop.

'I know what your game is, Dr Wilson, but I haven't told Mr Hargreaves. Not yet, anyway. But be assured that I will be checking your figures very carefully in future.' He smiled as he said this, but his threat was very real. Alison rushed out of his office and along the corridor to the cloakroom. She was going hot and cold; her heart was hammering in her chest and she knew she was going to be sick. Thankfully, she made it to the toilet just in time. She had been so careful to cover her tracks, and nothing that she had seen of him suggested he was clever enough to have spotted her deceit. She had underestimated him and played right into his hands. He had all the evidence he needed to get rid of her, anytime he wanted. Once she had finished being sick, she wiped her mouth, shakily, and went out to the basins to wash her face.

'Eliza!' She hadn't heard anyone come in and was surprised to see the chief nurse there. Had she been in the cloakroom all along, she wondered?

'Gosh, are you all right?' Eliza asked. 'You look terrible.'

'I'm fine, thanks.' Alison gave Eliza a shaky smile.

'Something you ate?'

'Must be. That will teach me not to eat food past its sell-by date.'

'I could get you an anti-emetic from pharmacy, if you like?'

'No, that's fine. I'm okay, really, but thanks. Better out than in, as they say.'

'Of course. Let me know if you change your mind. Can I get you anything else? A glass of water?'

'I have some in my office, thanks, I'll be right as rain now I've been sick.' Alison finally managed to persuade the nurse that she really would be okay, and went back to her office, closing the door firmly behind her and leaning on it for a moment. Her mind was feverishly going over what Selby had said. He'd spotted the changes. But she knew he wouldn't have bothered to check them himself, not unless someone had raised some suspicions, surely? Did one of the consultants notice? But none of them had seen her report, only the senior management team. Perhaps one of them had forwarded it to Dr Carrick and he'd spent the weekend going over it, checking her figures. He could be the one behind this. Could he have hacked into her computer? And why hadn't Selby rushed straight to Hargreaves once he knew? What was his game? She shook her head to clear it. She mustn't let herself get into a spiral of paranoia. It wouldn't help.

She took a few deep breaths and drank some water and slowly began to feel a little better. Her mobile rang and she answered it, Joyce wanted to speak to her about a patient, so, dreading what it could be, she went down to the ward.

'Hello Joyce, what's the problem?' Alison asked.

The sister hesitated, which was unusual for her, and looked around as if checking who was within hearing distance.

'I wondered if I could ask your opinion on Mrs Rossi, and get your advice on what I should do.'

'Of course, do you want to come into the office?' Alison suggested.

'I'm worried about her blood pressure,' Joyce said as soon as they were safely in the office with the door closed.

'Oh? Why?' Alison asked.

'It's not come down.' She brought up a chart on the computer for Alison to look at.

'I thought I ordered additional medication?'

'You said you would, but it hasn't been written up yet.'

They both knew that it was Dr Bayliss' job to have done that.

'Why has he not done it?'

Joyce shrugged, and looked embarrassed.

'I don't think he's had time.'

Alison shook her head in dismay. She would have to have a word with the man himself, it wasn't Joyce's fault. Dr Bayliss always seemed to have plenty of time to hang out with the nurses, and check his phone, so he really ought to be able to find time to do his job.

Having added the medication to Mrs Rossi's list, Alison wanted to get back to her office and see if she could narrow down who might have alerted Selby to her altered figures. As she passed the men's bay she thought she would check on Mr Andrews. Patients could sometimes be persuaded not to make formal complaints, if they felt that their concerns were being taken seriously. As she walked into the bay, she could see that he was asleep, so she decided to leave him be. As she turned to go, something about the uncomfortable way he was lying made her stop. She went closer to his bed and realised that he wasn't breathing. She grabbed his wrist, there was no pulse. She hit the emergency buzzer and pulled the pillows from behind his head, so that he was lying flat. The fact that he was still warm to her touch meant that it hadn't been long since he had stopped breathing so she lowered the bed and started chest compressions, acutely aware that everyone in the four-bedded bay was wide awake thanks to the loud incessant noise from the emergency buzzer. Alison knew that they were all watching the horrifying scene that was unfolding in front of them. She would have liked to close the curtains but didn't want to stop CPR and she could hear shouts and running feet so she knew help was on the way.

Joyce and another nurse quickly arrived with the crash trolley and one of them took over chest compressions from her. Joyce tilted Mr Andrews' head back to open up his airway and was using an ambu-bag to push oxygen and air into his lungs.

'Crash team's on its way,' a nervous-looking junior doctor rushed up and told her.

'Let's make sure we have everything ready for them,' Alison told her calmly and started opening the packs of equipment they would need. The crash team arrived shortly afterwards, a little out of breath having run to the ward, and Alison stood back and let them get on with their jobs.

They were a good team, all with their designated and well-practised roles as they took over from the nurses. One started delivering chest compressions, the anaesthetist was intubating the patient, a nurse got the heart monitor pads in place and another doctor was drawing up the drugs they might need. Alison quickly concluded that they didn't need her there and instead stood back and observed them from the edge of the bay. A nurse had already closed the curtains round the other patients so that they didn't have to witness the distressing scene.

Once the heart monitor was up and working, they could all see that the patient was in fibrillation.

'Stand back!' the anaesthetist in charge of the team ordered and everyone stopped what they were doing and stood back as he applied the defibrillator paddles and shocked the patient. Everyone turned and looked at the heart monitor. There were a couple of normal beats and Alison held her breath, hoping that it would continue, but just as they all thought they had been successful, the rhythm was lost and the trace showed fibrillation again. Chest compressions were restarted while the defibrillator charged up. Only, to the team's and Alison's distress, it didn't seem to be charging up properly. The consultant anaesthetist who was in charge of the team, was clicking switches and checking leads, but nothing seemed to be working. There were some anxious looks between the team as they realised what was going on. Like Alison, they knew another shock might be all that was needed, they had to get a working defibrillator, and quickly.

Alison quickly ran to the unit doors and to the next ward to get their defibrillator.

'Quick!' she shouted at the first nurse she saw. 'Crash trolley!'

The nurse ran to the trolley and Alison grabbed the defib, as soon as the nurse had unplugged it, and ran back to the stroke unit with it. It took only a couple of minutes for her to get back, but she knew that for a patient in fibrillation, just a few minutes could be the difference between life and death.

She arrived, panting, back on her own unit, to see the team were continuing with the CPR while the anaesthetist was still trying to get the defib working. Seeing Alison running up the ward with the new one, he grabbed the machine from her hand. He quickly plugged it in, checked the charge and called for the team to stand back as he once again shocked the patient. There were no normal beats this time, just a continuation of the fibrillation, and then a flat line. Alison knew that much as the team would continue for a while yet, the delay had cost Mr Andrews his life.

Twenty minutes later, with still no response from the patient despite several attempts to shock his heart back into sinus rhythm, the anaesthetist called time and pronounced the patient dead.

It was never easy when a patient died in these circumstances, and Alison could tell from the faces of the crash team that they had taken this one hard. She tried to give them some encouragement, telling them they had done everything they could, thanking them for their efforts but her words were little comfort. Eliza was there, talking quietly to the nurses along with Joyce, telling them that if they needed to talk, anytime, then they were there for them.

'It would have helped if we had decent bloody defibs!' the anaesthetist said bitterly to Alison as he passed her. Alison knew from her examination of the equipment accounts, that the hospital had quite recently spent a large amount on some very expensive equipment, but perhaps he had other ideas.

'Do you have time for a quick word?' she asked him. 'In the office?'

He nodded and headed towards the small room behind the nurse's desk. As Alison followed she noticed Mrs Rossi gesticulating from the next bay and went over.

'Is it urgent, Mrs Rossi?' she asked. 'Only I have to speak with the anaesthetist.'

'I need to tell you something, Dr Wilson. . .' Mrs Rossi seemed quite insistent and upset about something, so Alison went over to her.

'I saw—'

'Dr Wilson!' The anaesthetist called from the office doorway interrupting her, he was in a hurry and not prepared to wait for her while she spoke to someone else.

'I'll come and speak to you later,' Alison assured her patient, 'I promise, Mrs Rossi.' Then she hurried out of the bay.

'Is there a problem with Mrs Rossi?' Joyce asked as Alison passed her and the group of nurses.

'Don't worry, it's probably nothing,' Alison assured the ward sister as she hurried to the office. 'I'll speak to her later.'

CHAPTER FIFTEEN

'The man died of an acute cardiovascular event,' she explained to Hargreaves the next day. 'Exacerbated by equipment failure.'

He frowned and Selby looked a bit alarmed.

'I trust that won't appear on the death certificate,' he answered.

'Well, it should,' she replied although she understood exactly why the CEO wouldn't want that on the record because he wouldn't want the hospital sued. But if the defibrillator failing to charge was relevant, she, as medical director would want it known, if only to make sure that she prevented it from happening again. 'We will have to wait for the post-mortem results. If it was a second stroke, which is the most likely, then there wasn't really much we could have done anyway. I'll look into all his treatment and results and make sure there were no warning signs we overlooked.'

'Like being given the wrong antibiotics?' Selby asked.

Hargreaves looked at him and then back at Alison.

'Is that right, Dr Wilson?'

'He had an allergic reaction to an antibiotic he was prescribed, but it was stopped and it was not a factor in his death,' she said firmly, hoping she was right and wondering how Selby knew about it. The man clearly had a very good source somewhere on the ward.

Hargreaves' frown was getting deeper. He didn't like what he was hearing. Selby was rubbing his hands and shifting his weight from one foot to the other, looking like a schoolboy in need of the toilet. He was clearly worried, too.

'Yes, please do look into all the factors and I trust you will find there is no blame attached to this death,' Hargreaves told her.

'I will look at it closely, I promise you that.'

There was no way she was going to brush this under the carpet if someone, or some equipment was at fault, even if only partly. She owed that much to her patient.

'I'm sure I don't need to remind you that I brought you in to improve care, not make it worse.'

'And I'm trying my best to do exactly that, but I'm not being helped by a lack of staff due to Dr Carrick being off for goodness knows how long. Did Jonathan ask you about Dr Faez? An extra pair of hands would make a significant difference and free me up to work on the other areas that need improvement.'

Hargreaves sighed.

'I do not appreciate you trying to hold me, or the hospital, to ransom, Dr Wilson, particularly as it is entirely your fault that the unit is short-handed.'

Alison didn't know if it was better to stay silent or add to her plea. She glanced at Selby, but got no help there. In the end, she couldn't stop herself from speaking out.

'I'm not trying to hold you to ransom, Brian, but it would make a significant difference if Dr Faez was able to come and help. There's just too much for me to do without him.' She hoped the sincerity of her request would win the day and was relieved when it did.

'All right, Dr Wilson, you can present your case to the board tomorrow, but there must be no mention of this patient's death, do you understand me?' He straightened the papers on his desk as he gave it some thought. 'Don't think I'm going to fund unlimited extra staff, let alone more expensive equipment. The trust is in the red enough already. And please make sure the report into the patient's death doesn't leave the trust open to criticism, or further action.'

It was a threat, Alison knew – a subtle one, but still a threat. His continued support depended on her not blaming the hospital in any way for the patient's death, and if she did, not only would she not get the help she needed, but she had no doubt that they would shift the blame onto her, one way or another. But at least she had permission to put the case for Anwar Faez to come and work as a temporary consultant to the board, as well as the extra therapy staff. She was sad to have lost a patient, especially under these circumstances but at least some good might have come from the death.

'Oh, Dr Wilson?'

She turned to see Selby behind her having followed her out into the reception area, closing the door to Hargreaves' office behind him.

'Yes?'

'I'll be looking closely at the data you present to the board tomorrow.'

'I'm sure you will.'

'And I'll be interested if you can show any signs that things are improving.'

'Which I certainly can, just small improvements, but we all know these things take time.'

He nodded.

'Of course. You are creating quite a stir here,' he said. 'An unwelcome stir. I'll say one thing for Dr Atkinson, we never had any problems with his work and he never asked for more staff.'

'Well, if he had, you might not be in such a mess with your ratings,' she replied crisply. The man really was a turd.

She worked on her report at home until nearly midnight getting it ready for the morning's board meeting. It felt quite cosy sitting in the cottage, laptop on her lap, glass of wine by her side, with the bottle within easy reach, and Paws curled up at her side. She was confident that, as she had told Selby, she could show modest improvement, in some areas at least, and she hadn't needed to massage the figures this time. Jonathan Selby could examine the report all he wanted, she was confident they would stand up to scrutiny.

But right now, the numbers and graphs were swimming before her eyes. She looked at the wine bottle, it was empty. Had she really drunk the whole bottle? She really couldn't go on like this, working long hours, using alcohol to keep her going. She just hoped the board, and Hargreaves, were happy with her report and that they approved her request to employ Dr Faez as a locum to help cover the loss of Dr Carrick. With a final sigh, she copied the report to her USB stick and then emailed it to Mary to print copies for everyone first thing. With a last check that the doors and windows were locked, she switched off the lights and went, unsteadily, upstairs to bed.

I watch the lights go off downstairs and then one goes on in the room I know is the bedroom. She stands at the window, looking out. It seems like she's looking straight at me, and I shrink back, pressing further back into the bushes I'm using for cover. But she can't see me, not in the dark. Now more certain I am safe where I am, I crane my neck to watch as she closes the curtains.

Left to my thoughts, I can't help but berate myself. I was in such a hurry to get rid of Andrews that I had made a mistake. That bloody woman had seen something, I'm sure, or heard him cry out in pain as the drug tracked up his arm. It was unfortunate that she must have realised that I had no reason to be there, to be doing anything to him in the first place. I should have been more careful and now I have to stop her speaking to the Wilson bitch, telling her what she thought she saw. I have to get rid of her, get rid of them both. And I need to buy myself more time. That's why I'm here now, outside her house.

The light goes off upstairs. The house is in darkness. How long should I wait? How long before I can be sure she is asleep?

CHAPTER SIXTEEN

Alison woke up the next morning, momentarily confused. She had slept unusually heavily, she supposed she had the bottle of wine to thank for that, and had been dreaming about the last holiday she and Ed had taken together. They had decided to go away after a particularly bad row about her working late. They had both taken time off from work and gone to Portugal. For the first time in years, she had switched her phone off and didn't allow work to interrupt the whole two weeks of warm evenings and long relaxed meals on the terrace accompanied by Vino Verde. The streets were lined with jacaranda trees and they walked, arm in arm, on a carpet of purple blooms. It had been magical as was the dream and, when she woke, it took her a few moments to recognise where she was: the cottage, in Wayleigh, alone except for her cat. All the hope and happiness of her dream disappeared, leaving a crashing feeling of disappointment before the anxiety returned and took over.

Pushing her fears to the back of her mind, Alison set about feeding Paws, making tea, showering and dressing, ready for the day ahead. It was easier not to think when you were busy, it was only in the moments when there was nothing happening, nothing to do except relax or sleep, that the anxiety really kicked in and she went over and over everything that had happened. It was in those moments that it was easy to lose perspective, to think the smallest thing was the end of the world. She knew that, from experience. That's why she kept herself so busy. Always busy.

A shower refreshed her, got rid of the muzzy feeling that was all that was left of the alcohol and as she drank a second cup of tea, she told herself firmly that today was going to be a good day, a day when she would show the board what she could do. All her new protocols were in place now and beginning to work, to show small but significant results, and today she would persuade them to finally approve a new locum consultant, Dr Anwar Faez. HR had run some checks and found that her old friend was, unsurprisingly, eminently qualified to take up the post. He was one of the best, she knew, and she was lucky he had answered her call for help. Once he had settled in, he would be able to take some of the strain off her, and allow her to concentrate on her medical director role and finding a more permanent replacement for Dr Carrick.

Yes, today was going to be a good day, she repeated to herself as she left Paws licking the last of his tinned salmon breakfast from his paws and closed the front door behind her. She would be positive.

The moment she saw her car, she realised something was very wrong. She had backed into the driveway, leaving the car facing out towards the road ready to leave. The front seemed to be dipping to one side. As soon as she walked to the front end of the car, she could see that the driver-side tyre was completely flat. She wondered if she had driven over a nail on her way home the night before and just hadn't noticed. Like most modern cars, there was no spare, so she had no choice but to call out the local tyre service and wait for them to turn up. Fortunately, there was one listed in Wayleigh, quite near to where she lived and she called them. That done, she went back into the cottage, much to Paws' surprise, and put the kettle on. It was a bind but she still had plenty of time, the board meeting wasn't for another hour and a half, and if it took a long time to get her car sorted, she could always ring for a taxi. She might as well have breakfast herself while she waited, but first she had something to do.

'Mary?' she said into her mobile once the secretary had answered her phone. 'I've been held up; my car has got a flat tyre. I need to organise for the tyre to be changed and then I'll get a taxi in. Can I ask a big favour? Could you make sure you print the documents I sent last night, the ones for the board meeting this morning? Yes, that's right, a copy for everyone please.'

Once she had checked that Mary had got her report and the message to print it for her, she settled down to her coffee. There was a toot and she looked up, surprised to see an ageing grey van with 'Wayleigh Motors' and a telephone number on the side, pulling into the drive.

'You were quick,' she said as she came hurrying out of the house. A man was bending down by the front of her car. He stood up as she walked over to him.

'Oh!' she said in surprise because she could see that it was Mike Jenkins. He was dressed in dirty overalls, with a greasy rag poking out of a pocket.

'Seems like you've really upset someone,' he said with a frown.

'What do you mean?'

'Your tyre's been slashed.'

She bent down to take a closer look, there was a clear tear in the side wall of the tyre. She reached out and touched it, suddenly acutely aware that he had crouched down beside her and their faces were very close. She stood up, abruptly.

'How do you think that could have happened?' she asked him. He was still crouched by the wheel, examining the damage.

'A knife, or screwdriver more likely, pushed into the side wall and then wiggled about a bit to make sure it was obvious.'

'Why would they want to make it obvious?'

'To send you a message,' he explained and looked at the garage where the graffiti of the week before was still faintly visible despite all her efforts with white spirit and a scrubbing brush. 'Like I said, you've really upset someone.'

The question Alison asked herself, as she left him to get on with changing the wheel, was who? The only person she could think of was Dr Carrick. He certainly had a motive to get rid of her. He wanted to get his job back and regain control of his ward, but he was doing that through official routes already. He might well succeed with his plan as well, unless she proved her innocence or made herself so invaluable to Hargreaves and the board by improving the figures to such a degree he would have to defend her. There was also Dr Atkinson, her predecessor. Did he blame her even though she had nothing to do with his leaving?

'That's done.'

She was startled to realise that Mike had managed to change the wheel in what seemed like no time at all.

'That's fantastic, thank you so much. What do I owe you?'

She reached for her purse and pulled out a credit card.

'Sorry, I don't take cards outside of the garage. Don't have a mobile reader. Can you transfer the money?' he said and as he stood up, she was surprised to see him wiping some blood off his hand.

'Of course,' she replied. 'Did you hurt yourself?' she asked him.

'No, it's the cut on my head.' He pointed to the wound she had dressed before.

'Is it still bleeding? Here, let me take a look.'

She moved up to him and he raised a protective hand to his head.

'And keep those filthy mitts away from it,' she said sharply and was pleased that his hand dropped immediately.

'Hmm, that needs a good clean-up, it's infected,' she said after a cursory examination of the wound.

'Could you do it here?' he asked.

'No, it needs a proper clean-up, not just a swoosh with some sterile water, and you need antibiotics, which, before you ask, I can't prescribe outside of the hospital. I don't have the right sort of prescriptions to do that, and I haven't got any hospital ones here, either.'

'No way am I going into that place,' he said darkly, and she remembered what Eliza had said about him blaming the hospital for his mother's death.

'You need to, this isn't something that can be done at home, or in the local pharmacy. There's infected tissue in there and it needs cleaning properly, which will not be pain free unless you have a local anaesthetic.'

He still looked as if he was going to refuse.

'Look,' she touched his arm gently, 'I'm the doctor, okay, I know about these things, just like you know about cars. I wouldn't come to you for advice on my health any more than I would advise you to come to me for anything car-related.'

He smiled at this and she pressed home her advantage.

'If it helps, I can do it in the treatment room on the stroke ward. You don't even have to go into A&E.'

'You'd do it?' he asked. 'Not anyone else?'

He was looking at her with an intensity she found unsettling.

'If that's what it takes to get you to have it done, then yes, I'll do it.'

After a pause, he nodded assent.

'Right,' she said, 'two o'clock on the stroke unit, just ask for me and to make sure you come, I'll pay you when you get there.'

She opened the car door and was relieved to see him smile.

'You're a hard woman, Dr Wilson.'

'That I am,' she agreed and got into the car and drove off. When she looked in her rear-view mirror, he was standing there shaking his head, but still smiling.

Alison didn't bother with going to her office, she rushed straight to the board room where Mary was busy preparing the coffee for the board members who would be arriving soon. A picture board stood in the corner of the room with photos of all the board members which Alison thought was very helpful, and she went over to put names to faces. Inevitably, the medical director was still listed as Dr Richard Atkinson under his photograph. Alison leant forward for a closer look. His face was faintly familiar, but she was pretty sure she had never met him. Perhaps she had seen him at a conference somewhere, or in another context.

'I'll have to get that changed,' Mary said, as if it was Alison's fault for making more work for her to do. 'Your papers are there, I got them ready for you,' she added, pointing to the table where packs of papers were out ready for everyone.

'Thank you, Mary,' she replied and rifled through the papers to find her report in amongst them. Having found it, she flicked through just to make sure she had remembered all the key points. It all seemed to be in order, but then something caught her eye. One of the graphs was not how she remembered it. She looked closer.

'No!' she almost shouted as she felt her stomach tighten. It couldn't be right. She went through the document more closely. Someone had changed her report, of that she was sure. She felt her pulse race, and a flush hit her cheeks. She put out a hand to steady herself.

'Did you change anything, Mary?' she asked the secretary.

'Of course not, Dr Wilson, I know better than to do that.'

And Alison knew that was true. Apart from anything else, Mary would no more have been able to alter the graphs than fly to the moon.

'Quick! I need all the copies of my report,' she said, going through each pack of papers set out neatly, ready for the board members to pick up with their coffee and took her report from each one. Mary looked at her as if she had finally lost it, as Selby came over to find out what was going on.

'Is something wrong, Dr Wilson?' he asked as Alison grabbed the last copy of her report and hurried from the room, almost knocking over the board chairman as he came into the room with Hargreaves.

Alison could hear Hargreaves and Selby apologising for her as she ran to her office.

Closing the door behind her, she had a moment of panic. What on earth had happened to her report? Had she imagined it? Leaning against the door frame, she opened it up again. No, the figures were definitely wrong. They were good, much too good. On two key areas, where there had been little change, the figures were suddenly better, much, much better. But when she did the report last night, she felt sure she had left them as they were. She hadn't changed them, had she? She knew that she had been exhausted, and when she finally finished, she had been surprised that she had drunk almost a whole bottle of wine, but if she had done something so obvious, wouldn't she remember doing it? The board would be delighted but it was so obvious, too obvious. It had to be a mistake. She just couldn't believe she would have done this, not after the warning she had been given by Selby. Not even drunk would she have thought it was a good idea, she would have realised that it was career suicide. Selby would be sure to check her figures and she knew he would not hesitate to report her for gross misconduct if these figures went to the board.

She leant her head against the window, and let the panic overtake her for a short moment. She needed time to calm down and collect her thoughts as it all threatened to overwhelm her. Her pulse was racing and her breaths were coming in short bursts. The glass was cold against her forehead as the rain tracked down the outside of the glass, and a sob escaped from her. How had she got herself into this mess? What had happened to her charmed life in London? Her marriage? Her career? She knew that this report would be the end of her time at St Margaret's if it went to the board. She would be out on her ear and would never get another job as a medical director. She would be lucky to get another job ever again. She would end up in a satellite unit somewhere in the suburbs, working with the homeless or elderly. She let the despair wash over her.

She slowly got her breathing under control and lifted her head. She couldn't let it happen. Now wasn't the time to give up. She hadn't put those figures in, had she? No. The report had been changed by someone else, someone who wanted her gone so badly they were prepared to ruin her. But she could fight this, this person, whoever they were. This person who was trying to sabotage everything, even if it was herself.

Quickly setting up her laptop, she went back into her documents saved onto her data stick rather than on the system, checked that it contained all the correct data and sent the report to the printer. She prayed the printer would behave itself and not choose this moment to run out of paper or ink or just break down on her.

She was in luck, the printer behaved and printed and collated the copies. She grabbed them again and hurried back to the board room. She stopped and made sure her breathing was under control, and then opened the door.

'I'm so sorry,' she said as she entered the room which was now full of people. 'This report needs to be added to your papers.'

She saw Selby look up in surprise and then frown, making her wonder if he was behind the sabotage as she handed round the new copies of her report.

'This is the new medical director, Dr Alison Wilson, now if we could get started?' Hargreaves flashed a look at Alison to show his displeasure at having been kept waiting.

Alison took her place and shuffled her papers together. She ran her hand through her hair and hoped she didn't look a mess, she hadn't even checked her appearance in the mirror, something she always did in case her hair was a mess or she had food caught in her teeth. She surreptitiously wiped a finger under each eye in case her mascara had smudged when she cried. Mary put a cup of coffee down beside her, spilling some in the saucer as she did so. Alison turned to smile her thanks, but the older woman had already hurried to her place beside Mr Hargreaves and was readying herself to take the minutes.

As the meeting started, Alison went to pick up her coffee, but with the danger of drips and the way her hand was shaking, she decided she could do without. She didn't want to add coffee stains on her shirt to the dishevelled hair, panda eyes and late arrival. The board would already be thinking that the new medical director was a bit of a mess.

To her surprise, the meeting went without a hitch. She managed to put on a cool and collected front, despite the panic that had threatened to overtake her only a short while earlier. She watched Selby closely as she presented her figures, expecting him to be angry that they were not the ones that had been in the report only a short while earlier, but there was not even a flicker. Either he was a very good actor, or he wasn't the person who had changed them.

Once the meeting had ended, she took herself up to the roof and felt the cool breeze on her face. As she had thought, from here she could see across the town to the sea. It was a view that none of the patients ever saw, but Alison believed that was a mistake of the hospital architects. She was in no doubt that the view was healing and she could feel it work its magic on her now as she took deep breaths. Her palms no longer felt moist and her hands had stopped shaking. She had got through it. She hadn't given in to her anxiety by crying or shouting, or running from the room. She had presented her data, answered the questions and made a good case for the addition of a temporary stroke consultant to her team. There had been some awkward questions, which she had expected. One particular board member, a non-executive director and an ex-military man, had pressed her repeatedly about why Dr Carrick had felt unable to work with her and she got the distinct impression that he and her colleague were either friends, or that he had been lobbied to ask those questions. She was grilled by the finance director about the case for Dr Carrick's temporary replacement when they were still having to pay him while he was on sick-leave, but she had held her ground, insisted it was necessary or they would lose more staff, and she was hopeful she had won. She would find out later, she supposed.

She turned away from the sea and walked to the other side of the roof, which overlooked the car park. There were cars driving around in circles waiting for a spot to come free. In time, she thought, she would have to make a case for a multi-storey car park, probably partly financed by some big parking company. Parking was always a problem area and had been at every hospital she had ever worked in. There was never enough, it was too expensive, the grumbles and moans from patients and staff alike never stopped and all complaints were taken into consideration when the CQC came to visit and rate the hospital. A new car park could improve their complaint numbers more than improving care, depressing as that was, and the board were more likely to give the okay to a new car park than a new member of staff, particularly as car parking fees increased the hospital revenue.

She took a deep breath, closed her eyes and crossed her fingers, hoping that the board would decide in her favour and allow Anwar to join her at St Margaret's, even if only until Dr Carrick returned or they were able to recruit a permanent replacement. It would be good for her sanity, if nothing else.

When she reopened her eyes, she saw that one of the cars that had been circling, a distinctive blue sports car, had found a space, but the driver wasn't getting out. Perhaps he was waiting for someone to come out from an appointment, she thought. The car seemed vaguely familiar. Had she seen it in the village? Or maybe it belonged to a regular here and she had seen it in the car park before, in which case, she hoped the person they were waiting for was not someone frail and elderly, because the car was not an easy one to get into. Or perhaps she was just imagining things and she had never seen the car before. She was about to turn away when a man got out of the car. He was tall and thin and wearing a suit that must have fitted him once but now hung off him, testament to the weight he had lost. He turned towards the hospital and looked up. Alison ducked behind an air-conditioning vent and then told herself off for being so silly. She came out from her place of hiding and saw the man hurrying towards the hospital entrance. In the few seconds that he had looked up, Alison had recognised him as the man who had frightened her so by following her when she walked near her home. She had also realised that he was Dr Atkinson. A thinner, less well-cared-for Dr Atkinson than in his picture on the board, but recognisably the same man. So, what was he doing at the hospital?

How had she spotted the changes I had made to the report? I had hoped that by making sure she was running late it would mean she had no time to see the report before the meeting. It had been so easy to make those changes and I had made them so obvious no one could possibly have missed them. That was the point. If that report had been shown to the board, the bitch would have been out on her ear in seconds flat. How had she got to work so quickly? How had she managed to check the report and change it all back in time? She will be on her guard after this and I have no choice now. I can't let her speak to that interfering woman on the ward, she would know immediately that something was wrong. I can't take that risk. She had sealed her patient's fate and I had no choice but to act. On her head be it.

CHAPTER SEVENTEEN

Alison showed Mike into the treatment room. She hadn't been certain he would show up, but was pleased when he did, on time and in fact, a little early. He had changed out of his filthy overalls, and had even scrubbed most of the grease from his fingernails. He was wearing a clean shirt and jeans and looked surprisingly good. There was no doubt that Mike scrubbed up well.

'Take a seat,' she said, pointing to a chair next to a stainless-steel trolley. Once he had sat down, Alison leant closer to look at the cut on his head and smelled the subtle scent of a musky aftershave and not a cheap one at that. He had certainly made an effort.

The next few minutes were taken up with Alison hunting through the various cupboards looking for the items she needed.

'You can tell I don't often do this,' she told him, trying to put him at ease because he looked distinctly uncomfortable. 'I should have asked one of the nurses to prep a dressing trolley.' But she hadn't wanted to do that, because that would have led to awkward questions, like why was she dressing a head wound on the stroke ward, or anywhere else for that matter. The fact was, she wasn't sure why she was doing it herself, but it needed doing and Mike had been adamant that he wasn't going to allow anyone else to do it. And he had helped her by coming so promptly to change her tyre.

At last, she had the equipment ready and washed her hands. She opened the sterile pack and put on gloves.

'This is going to sting a bit,' she warned him before she put in the local anaesthetic but he still winced.

'Ow!'

'All done. I'll give it a moment or two for the anaesthetic to work and then get it cleaned up.' She rearranged the items on the trolley, ready, then started to clean the wound, cutting dead skin and debris from it until she could see clean, healthy tissue.

'Hmm,' he grunted.

'I'm sorry, did that hurt? The anaesthetic must be wearing off.'

'No, it's fine, just get it done, okay?'

She could tell by his irritability that he was in pain, but that was fine, the wound was as clean as she was going to get it.

'All done. I'll just put a dressing on and get you a

prescription for antibiotics.' She stuck the dressing in place and reached for the prescription she had prepared before his arrival. 'You have to take the prescription to the hospital pharmacy, I'm afraid.' She held it out.

He scowled at that, but took it all the same.

'I suppose I'll have to.'

'Make sure you take the full course, okay? And I'll transfer the money for the tyre into your business account, now that you've let me do that.'

He stood up.

'Thanks,' he said, then paused. 'I mean that, it was good of you to do this.' He ducked his head to indicate he meant the dressing.

'And I'm grateful you sorted my tyre out so promptly.'

He nodded at that.

'Did you report it to the police?'

'No,' she admitted. 'I didn't really have time.' She could have made time, of course, but what would they have done? Asked around the neighbours, perhaps? Check if anyone had CCTV?

'Do you know who might have done it?' he asked.

'Not really.' She didn't say that she suspected Dr Carrick, it certainly wouldn't help her case if she accused him without any evidence.

'Have you at least thought about getting a camera or something, so that if they do it again you'll know who it is?'

'It's not my house. I only rent.'

'The owners can't be happy to have their garage graffitied, I suspect they'll be more than happy to let you put up a camera to act as a deterrent, if nothing else.'

'I'll give it some thought and speak to the owners,' she promised him.

'Good. I can always put it up for you, you know, if they agree.'

'You don't have to do that.' She was taken aback by this kindness.

'You helped me, it's the least I can do.'

'Well, thank you but—'

'Someone needs to do something about this bastard hospital and the goings on here, and I'm hoping you agree.'

With that, he left.

Alison thought about what he had said as she set about clearing the trolley. She knew there were problems at the hospital such as poor care, low morale and a high staff turnover. You only had to look at the state things had been in when she arrived to know that, but Mike had seemed to imply there was more to it than just a lack of leadership and money. 'Goings on' was a strange way to describe a badly run hospital. Was that what he meant? Or was there something more sinister behind it? And if so, was he right?

Alison finished clearing up after doing Mike's dressing and came out onto the ward just as the emergency buzzer went off. Joyce rushed out of the office and almost bumped into her as they passed the main desk. A staff nurse was on the phone, making the call that would bring the crash team to the ward. Another nurse had grabbed the crash trolley and was wheeling it quickly towards the women's section of the ward. Alison followed her, her heart sinking as she realised that the emergency was in Mrs Rossi's bay. Was it wrong that she hoped against hope that it was one of the other patients who had arrested, not Mrs Rossi? When she turned into the room, she could see through partially open curtains that a nurse was already working on her patient who was lying on the floor next to a commode.

'What happened?' Alison asked crisply as she pushed the commode out of the way and felt for a pulse while the nurse paused. Mrs Rossi's skin felt cold to her touch and there was no pulse.

'I left her on the commode, with a buzzer, but she didn't ring.' The nurse was almost in tears. Joyce put an ambu-bag over Mrs Rossi's mouth and squeezed. Alison looked at Joyce and their eyes met; they both knew this was not going to work.

'How long ago did you put her on the commode?' Alison asked as the nurse resumed pumping Mrs Rossi's chest.

'I don't know. A while ago.' She looked guilty. 'Ten minutes?' But she didn't sound sure and Alison knew it could well have been longer than that. They could hear the noise of the crash team arriving on the ward and being directed to them and she stood to one side as they attempted to resuscitate Mrs Rossi. Alison and Joyce watched, both knowing that it was too late. Mrs Rossi had been dead for a while and it wasn't long before the crash team came to the same conclusion.

'Asystole,' the consultant said once the cardiac monitor was up and running, waving to everyone to stand back and stop. Mrs Rossi was beyond resuscitation and there was nothing more to be done. Alison was surprised to feel tears prick her eyes and turned away. Patients died, she knew that, but she had felt a genuine connection to this one and she would miss her. Once the time of death had been called and the team had left, two porters helped the nurses to get Mrs Rossi onto the bed and Alison stepped forward to pull a sheet over the body, her hand resting gently on the woman's chest as she said a quiet prayer. She wondered what Mrs Rossi had wanted to say to her yesterday and wished that she had not been distracted by the anaesthetist and then by the need to get her report sorted. She should have found the time to speak to Mrs Rossi as she had requested but it was too late, and she would never know now. Alison hoped the woman she had liked so much and who had seemed so alive only yesterday, was at peace now.

It was never easy speaking to the relatives of a patient who had died, but it was doubly hard when it was a patient that you cared for as much as Alison had cared for Mrs Rossi. Alison knew that she needed to try and be professional, but feared that she might shed a tear as Joyce showed the family into the office. They had said goodbye to the matriarch of the family in the chapel of rest and then had come up to the ward to collect her personal belongings. They were openly crying and hugging each other, her husband, two daughters and one son. Joyce fussed around them, making sure they all had seats, asking if they wanted tea, coffee or anything else. All refused, but the questions gave them time to get themselves under control. Joyce was experienced and good with relatives so Alison was relieved to have her there. Although, she would have preferred the ward sister to sit with her at the desk, two professionals working together, rather than have her take a seat by the door as she had chosen to do.

'I am so sorry about Mrs Rossi, your mother and your wife,' Alison began, nodding at Mr Rossi.

'What happened?' one of her daughters interrupted, Carla, Alison remembered her name.

'She said she was coming home soon,' the other added between sobs.

'It's not unusual for patients who have had one stroke, to have another, more serious one.'

'But you were treating her, she should have got better,' Carla said.

'Sometimes, even with treatment we can't prevent a further event like this. I'm so sorry, we did everything we could.'

'Why was she left alone on the toilet? Why was no one

there to help her?' Carla asked with a glance at her father. Mr Rossi was still too caught up in his grief to say anything but the son flashed his sister a look of support. Alison could see that Joyce was looking concerned at the back of the room.

'She needed her privacy,' Alison calmly answered, 'and she had the call button with her.'

'Are you sure about that?' the son asked belligerently. 'We know nurses sometimes leave it out of reach.' He turned and glared at Joyce.

Alison thought back to when she arrived at the bedside and remembered seeing the call buzzer on the bed next to the commode when she got there, although the nurse could have placed it within reach after the event. Joyce looked worried behind him as if she had thought the same and wasn't quite sure how Alison would answer.

'Absolutely,' Alison reassured him and saw Joyce breathe out a sigh of relief. 'I saw it myself, and you can rest assured that if your mother had felt unwell, she would have called for help. It must have happened very quickly and she can't have suffered.'

'They already told us all this,' Carla berated her brother and sister.

'Yes, but we also heard that the doctors hadn't put her on the right medication, is that true?'

Alison was taken aback. She looked up at Joyce who was looking anxious again, was it her who had told them that? Or one of the other nurses looking to shift the blame?

'It's true that we decided to increase her medication to try and bring her blood pressure down more, and she had just started on the new drug.'

'Had she?' Carla asked Joyce.

'It was on her chart and she would have started it later today, once it had come up from pharmacy.'

Alison tried not to look annoyed that it had taken so long to get the drug brought up to the ward.

'You see? You could have done more to save my wife!' Mr Rossi said to her, before signalling to his children that he wanted to leave.

'We never got the chance,' Alison started to say, even though it was not strictly true. Bayliss could have prescribed it earlier as she had asked and she should have checked that he had, she knew what he was like, and Joyce could have sent someone to collect the drug from pharmacy and started it straight away. They had all failed Mrs Rossi and she wanted to say something to comfort her family but they had had enough.

'You'll hear more from us,' the son said ominously as they left.

CHAPTER EIGHTEEN

It was Alison's weekend on duty and the ward had been unbearable. Patients and staff alike had been mourning the loss of Mrs Rossi and Alison had spent much of her time trying to cheer them up despite feeling sad herself. Mrs Rossi had been a real character and, with her extended family, had brought a little light relief onto the ward. She would be sadly missed by them all, and not just for the constant supply of cakes and treats she handed out. Alison had taken particular care with the other patients in the bay where Mrs Rossi had died and was relieved that none of them mentioned Mrs Rossi being left on the commode for a long time. In fact, the one patient who had been awake at the time, or for some of it, reassured Alison that a nurse had checked in on Mrs Rossi while she was on there, so it wasn't like she had been abandoned. Alison was pleased to hear that, and she hoped she would be able to reassure the family if they went forward with their complaints against the staff.

After such a sad and heavy weekend, it was a relief to get back to her normal duties and even more so when late on Monday afternoon, Alison heard from Hargreaves that the board had decided to approve her request for Dr Faez to join her but not the extra therapists for now. At least she had won one of her arguments, she thought. At last, she would have an ally.

Monday evening was turning into another late night as Alison pored over the figures for the hospital. She had once again pulled up all the financial data for the last year, to give it a closer look, but she was sure something had changed, or rather, was missing from the data she had looked at before. The numbers were swimming before her eyes. It was time to go home, but, as before, she downloaded the files onto a flash-drive to take away with her. She could compare the data sets later, when she had time.

Grabbing her tote bag containing her laptop, she headed out of her office. Now that she knew about the back way out via the emergency exit, it was a much quicker way to the car park. She wondered why no one had ever told her about it before.

As she went down the stairs, she heard a door bang shut and she stopped to listen. There was no noise, but there was a slight smell of something in the air. She could feel the hairs on the back of her neck standing up, something was alerting her to danger. She stood still and listened intently, but there was nothing to hear. She sniffed, trying to identify the smell, but couldn't, it was something faintly medical, like hand sanitiser. She shook her head. So what if it was? This was a hospital, a public space. If someone had been on the stairs before it wasn't surprising and there were hand sanitiser dispensers everywhere. She needed to get a grip and stop imagining things.

She stopped on the way home, to pick up some supplies from the corner shop. She was disappointed to see that it was Jenny standing behind the counter and not her more helpful assistant, but perhaps it would give her the chance to break the ice and find out what the problem was.

'Hello Jenny,' she said as she put the bottle of wine and a loaf of bread on the counter. 'How are you?'

Jenny didn't reply but concentrated on running the items through the till.

'Have I done something to upset you?' Alison persisted. 'Because, if I have, I apologise.'

'That'll be eight pounds twenty-three pence.'

Alison gave up trying to build bridges and handed over a twenty-pound note. As she started to put the wine in her tote bag, Jenny spoke again.

'In a local shop like this, our loyalties have to be to our regular customers, not here-today-gone-tomorrow types like you, coming here and stealing people's homes and forcing them out of their jobs.' Jenny slammed the till shut, threw Alison's change onto the counter and hurried out to the storeroom at the back of the shop.

Alison was stunned by this outburst and would have responded if there had been anyone there to respond to, but as Jenny had gone, she picked up her change. A fifty pence piece had rolled off the counter and under some shelves, so she left it.

As she rushed out of the shop, embarrassed and furious, she bumped into a man who was just coming in. She dropped her bag as she reached out to steady him, fearing that he would fall into the road.

'I'm so sorry,' she started to say before looking up. The man she had run into was Dr Atkinson. He snatched his arm back as soon as he saw who had stopped him from falling.

'Let go of me!' he shouted and turned to go.

'Stop! Dr Atkinson!' she called to his retreating back and he turned and glowered at her. 'I don't honestly know what I have done to upset you, but I don't appreciate you going around bad-mouthing me to everyone.'

He stood and looked at her, silently, eerily not reacting at all to what she was saying.

'I'm sorry if you feel you have been treated badly, but I had nothing to do with it,' she continued.

Still he said nothing, just stared at her, making her feel distinctly uncomfortable.

'So please just leave me alone and let me get on with my job.'

'Your job?' he hissed. 'It was mine until you came along.'

'Yes, I know, but it isn't my fault you had to leave,' she said firmly, cross that he was still blaming her. 'And you can stop all the things you've been doing to try and get rid of me as well, or I will have no hesitation in reporting you to the police.'

'For what?'

'For harassment, Dr Atkinson, and criminal damage, so leave me alone.'

She bent down to pick up her bag, dismayed to find that the wine bottle had broken and drenched everything that was in there. She just hoped her laptop and the data stick had survived. As she straightened up, she saw that he was still standing there, staring at her.

'Harassment and criminal damage?' he said, incredulous. 'That's nothing compared to what happened to me. You don't know the half of it, you stupid woman. Worse will happen to you, just you wait.' He shook a finger at her as he spoke and Alison instinctively backed away from him, frightened by the intensity on his face as much as the threat. To her relief, she could see that a woman walking her dog was coming down the road. Atkinson saw her too and turned on his heel and hurried away, leaving Alison standing on her own, clutching a tote bag that was dripping wine all down her leg and trying not to shake.

* * *

It couldn't have gone better, the best one, the most satisfying one yet! Mrs Rossi was on the commode when I went behind the curtains. She knew I shouldn't be there, but I had the syringe all prepared and as she reached across the bed for the call button, I was able to inject the potassium chloride into her cannula before she knew what was happening. She cried out, of course, but only that deaf old biddy across the bay was there. I had made sure of that, made sure there were no credible witnesses this time. She tried to snatch her hand away but it was too late. It only takes a short time for the drug to travel to your heart. One heartbeat, or two? No time at all when you are frightened, and your heart rate is fast, and once it reaches the heart? That's it, game over. The thrill of watching the realisation in her eyes as her heart stopped beating was better than any of the others so far. I almost laughed. They were all too stupid to know what was going on. And then it was done. I had to hold her on the commode as her body shook, gave up the last of life and then she slumped, and I propped her up and left her there for someone else to find.

And such a sweet irony to find out that, like Andrews, there were inadequacies in Mrs Rossi's care. It wasn't hard to make sure the family knew. I left an anonymous note in her possessions, ready for when the family picked them up. It said they had a right to know what had happened and that I was only trying to help. There'll be a complaint, I'm sure. It's all adding up against the bitch. A bit more pressure and she'll be gone. I'm sure of it.

CHAPTER NINETEEN

Bumping into Dr Atkinson had, understandably, left Alison very shaken. She had immediately hurried home and checked that the windows and doors were all firmly shut and locked. Fortunately, her laptop didn't seem to have come to any harm, but she was too wired to concentrate on work. Paws had decided to go out and leave her once he'd eaten his dinner and, having broken the bottle of wine when she tried to stop Dr Atkinson falling, she didn't even have alcohol to help calm her nerves and help her sleep. All night, she had tossed and turned, unable to stop thinking about all that had been happening at home and at the hospital: the graffiti, her tyre being slashed, Dr Carrick going off sick, Dr Atkinson threatening her, the complaints against her that were building up, the drug thefts. There was so much going on and she couldn't see how everything was connected, or even if it *was* connected. It wasn't until Paws came in from his wandering just before dawn that she managed to get to sleep, only to be woken by her alarm less than an hour later.

So it was that she was still quite agitated and tired, when she got to work the next morning. She had sent several emails to Tony Grant, the head of security, during the last week, asking how the investigation into the drug thefts was progressing, but, as yet, had had no response. She rang him this time, but got his voicemail.

'Mr Grant, this is Dr Wilson. I need you to get back to me today, please. I need to know where you are in the investigation into the drug thefts as soon as possible, please.' She put the phone down and then picked it straight up again to call Colin from pharmacy. He too was out and she left another terse message.

She was absolutely positive that she had seen Dr Atkinson at the hospital at least once now, and she suspected he was there more often than that. In some respects, it was perfectly natural; he had worked at the place for many years, he lived locally and would have friends in the hospital, but he no longer worked here and should not be hanging around the place, she felt sure. If drugs were still disappearing and he was still a suspect, then he must have a way of getting into the pharmacy. He could have copied the drug cupboard key, of course, but to get into the room he needed a pass that he had either borrowed or stolen.

Despite having no legitimate reason to go into the

personnel files and look for Dr Atkinson's details, Alison did exactly that the first opportunity she had. The comments from Selby that he was better than her, were more than a little irritating and made her want to know more about her predecessor, that and the knowledge that he was stirring things up at home, telling Jenny stories about getting him sacked. She was able to find his current address, which she was unsurprised to see was only a short walk from where she lived.

Alison sat back in her chair and gave it some thought. The corner shop was the nearest one to his home as well as her own, so it was possible he wasn't following her when she had seen him that night or the time when she was out for a walk. He might well have been doing the same as her, just going for a walk to clear his head. She understood that it must be hard for him to see her, day after day, knowing that she had replaced him at the hospital, but that didn't excuse him telling Jenny that Alison had pushed him out of his job. The way Jenny had spoken about her had smacked of someone else's resentment and now she knew whose. Things were clicking into place.

The question Alison had was: did he write the warning on her garage door, and slash her tyre? It certainly seemed to fit with a simmering resentment against her. Did he really think that he would get his job back if she left? She supposed that depended on why he had left in the first place, but if he had stolen drugs, she didn't see how he could. It seemed she was just a convenient scapegoat for his anger.

And if it was not Dr Atkinson, who else had she upset? Who else might want her to leave? There was Dr Carrick, of course; after all, if she left, he would certainly get his job back. She felt a bit guilty as she looked up his records. He lived in a small cottage in a village on the other side of the town. And, while she was checking everyone out, Dr Bayliss lived in an apartment in the centre of town. Feeling that she might as well be hung for a sheep as a lamb, she looked up Selby as well and was surprised to find that he didn't live far from her either, but that wouldn't necessarily stop any of them from finding out where she lived and carrying out the vandalism or the hacking, after all they all had access to the hospital system, and cars. Knowing where they lived had not helped eliminate anyone, but it had left her with a nasty taste in her mouth. She had invaded their privacy and it had been no help at all.

And Mike? She knew he had something against the hospital, what if it extended to her? She didn't think it was the case, but, if she was honest, she didn't really know him.

All in all, she felt Atkinson was her best bet as the person behind everything. He had threatened her, or at least, acted in a threatening way. And if it was him, what was she going to do about it? There didn't seem much point in going to the police when she had no proof that he was the perpetrator, but it would be a different matter if she had him recorded on CCTV. She needed to get it installed. If she had proof it was Atkinson, then she could go to the police, but would she? He was clearly a troubled man, so it might be better if she went to see him, in the daytime, and told him that what he was doing would never get him his job back and could stop him from getting one anywhere else into the bargain? Or would that just make things worse?

In the end she decided to wait and see. If there were any further attacks on her home, she could confront him about it, or she could involve the police as Mike had suggested, but that was a route she was loath to take for petty vandalism as it really would end any hope he might have of working again. No, she wouldn't involve the police unless he upped the ante, she decided.

Having decided to take no action against Dr Atkinson, for now at least, Alison put it out of her mind and did her usual head-in-the-sand act, and buried herself in work.

She had requested the order history for defibrillators from procurement, wanting to find out why they had so many failures and she had also been working her way through all the patient deaths for the last five years. There were a lot. This was a hospital, after all, and a proportion of patients were expected to die, but not quite as many as seemed to be doing so. She had made an appointment to speak with the hospital pathologist. Equipment failure wasn't mentioned as a cause of death anywhere, but she wanted to get his opinion on whether it could be a factor in more deaths, as the head of the crash team had intimated.

On top of her concerns there, it had to be said that the other areas that she was trying to make improvements were not responding as well as the stroke ward. Which added to her concerns.

She worked her way down the list of people who hadn't responded to her emails requesting information or meetings. She then tried to speak to the head of procurement as she was the first to admit that she wasn't best qualified to interpret financial data. Unfortunately, it seemed that he was on holiday. Not wanting to bring such a delicate matter up with his deputy, Alison decided to leave it for now.

Finally, she got a call back from Tony Grant.

'I expected you to get back to me sooner than this, Mr Grant,' she told him sternly.

'I rang as soon as I got your message,' he replied and sounded surprised.

'I meant I expected you to get back to me last week about whether or not any passes were missing.'

'But I did,' he sounded bewildered. 'No passes are missing and only appropriate passes have been used to get into the pharmacy. I asked if you wanted me to set up a camera, but haven't heard back from you.'

To say Alison was surprised, was an understatement.

'I've had no messages, either by phone or email,' she told him, quickly searching her email folder to make sure. There was nothing from Tony in her inbox. She went to the spam folder, but there was nothing there.

'I have sent you three emails,' he insisted. 'I'll send them again now.' He sounded irritated and she could almost see him rolling his eyes at the end of the phone.

As she waited for his re-sent emails to come through, she checked her deleted messages and there was one from him, sent several days earlier and deleted almost immediately. How had that happened? Could she have done it accidentally? Or forgotten she had done it?

'I've got them,' she said once the new ones had arrived. She read them quickly.

'Have any more drugs gone missing since I spoke to you last?' she asked. 'I saw Dr Atkinson in the hospital last Friday,' she told him.

'Really?' He looked surprised. 'Well, yes,' he told her, 'they did. Just like before. I checked with Colin before ringing you, I'll have to check again and see when they went missing, see if it was Friday.' He paused. 'You know, the hospital is a public place and we can't stop people from coming here.'

'I am well aware of that, but I thought you should know, because if he was here at the same time as the drugs went missing. . .'

'Yes,' he sounded thoughtful, 'it's unlikely to be a coincidence.'

'I think we probably need to set up a camera,' she told him. 'How long will it take?'

'A day, maybe two. I'll have to source one and then set it up, somewhere he won't think to check.'

'Good, please do that, and Tony?'

'Yes?'

'Please communicate with me by phone or text, I seem to be having problems with my email.'

'You need to speak to IT.'

'I have,' she assured him, not adding that they were absolutely no help at all.

After a quick tour of the ward, and handing over to Dr Cheung, she decided against going back to her office. It was late and time for her to go home.

Taking the coward's way out, Alison stopped at the supermarket on the outskirts of town to shop for a few essentials like cat food and a ready meal for dinner. It was bad enough that work was something of a war zone, she didn't want her home to be one too, and calling into the local store when Jenny was there was beginning to make her feel like it was. Things were fine when her assistant was behind the counter, but she could hardly hang around outside and check who was behind the till before going into the shop.

Once she had parked the car on the drive she went inside and unloaded her shopping. Paws was winding his way round her legs expecting food and almost tripped her several times as she put her purchases away. One day she would fall, or tread on him, and he would learn a lesson the hard way. She fed him and then looked at the microwave meal she had bought for herself. It really wasn't appetising. Her hand hovered over the meal and the bottle of wine beside it.

'Sod it!' she said and grabbed her handbag. 'The pub it is then.'

The Jolly Sailor pub looked very inviting that evening. The old, brick building, had colourful plants in pots around the small front garden. They were looking a little worse for wear now that autumn had well and truly taken hold, but there were still a few blooms battling against the elements. Despite being a confident woman in so many respects, Alison still had an underlying anxiety about entering a pub on her own. While a man could pop in for a pint and no one would think he was signalling anything more than that he wanted a drink and perhaps a chat with his fellow men or the barmaid at a push, a woman on her own was sometimes assumed to be 'on the pull' and therefore fair game. It all depended on the people who frequented any particular pub, Alison knew, and the only way to find out what they were like, was to go in. Alison always checked a pub out before going in by looking through the windows. Did it look friendly? Welcoming? If she couldn't see in, she never went in, that was her rule. Naturally cautious, she would never willingly walk into anywhere completely blind. She looked through the windows of the Jolly Sailor, and she saw a well-lit space, with tables scattered around, a log-fire burning in the grate with an elderly dog asleep on the rug next to it. There were a few people in there – a young couple, two elderly men playing cribbage, a smattering of others in small groups, some with women. So not primarily a man's pub then. She saw nothing off-putting at all and in particular, she didn't see Dr Atkinson. She really didn't want to come face to face with him again.

Alison pushed open the door and walked in. If she had expected a concerted intake of breath and everyone turning and staring at her, the unwelcome stranger in their midst, she was disappointed. No one so much as batted an eyelid.

She approached the bar and the barman, a man in his early twenties with a ponytail and an armful of tattoos, turned to her while still polishing a pint glass.

'What can I get you?' he asked with a cheery smile.

'A medium glass of Pinot Grigio,' she replied. 'And the menu please.'

He put the pint glass back on the shelf and picked out a bottle of wine from the refrigerator.

'The menu's in the holder at the end of the bar and the specials are on the blackboard over there.' He nodded back in the direction she had come in and sure enough, when she turned, she could see a long list of specials written on a board just inside the door.

'But the kitchen closes in twenty minutes, so don't take too long deciding,' he advised her as he poured her wine.

She took her glass and picked up the menu and gave it a quick once over as she walked over to the specials board.

It didn't take her long to decide on fish cakes and salad, and once she had paid for her meal and drink, she looked around for a free seat. That was when she saw him.

'Mr Jenkins!' she said in surprise and walked over to a small table in the corner where Mike Jenkins sat alone, a pint of lager, half-drunk, in front of him.

'Dr Wilson, how are things? You've had no more trouble I hope.'

'No, the car's fine, thanks. I'm so pleased I saw you, I wanted to say thank you.'

'It was no problem.' He looked embarrassed. 'It's my job and thank you for this,' he waved at his head.

'And that's my job,' she said, even if they both knew that wasn't strictly true. 'Do you mind if I. . .' She indicated the empty chair at the table.

'Of course, yes, do sit down, Dr Wilson.'

'Alison, please.'

'And Mike, then,' he replied, running a hand through his thick, curly hair.

She sat down and looked over at the bar. The barman was clearly more interested in a couple of young women who had come in, full of giggles and chatter. In fact, as Alison looked around she realised that no one was paying them the slightest attention. *That's what happens as we get older*, Alison told herself, *we become invisible to the young*.

'How is your head?' she asked Mike.

'A lot better, thanks.' He ducked his head, showing her that it was, indeed, much better, and healing fast.

'Good,' she said, glad that it wasn't going to be a problem. They chatted a little about how she was settling in, both taking care not to mention the graffiti or the vandalism of her tyre. 'So, come on, give me the lowdown on this place.'

'How do you mean?'

'You've lived here a long time, I take it?'

'All my life.'

'So, tell me about the people in here, like those two.' She nodded towards the two old men playing cribbage.

'The two Kens,' he told her. 'One's a widower, on his own, the other's got a wife at home, but she doesn't like pubs. They come in every night at six and play a few games of cribbage and drink two pints each. Never more, never less. Then they go home. You could set your clock by them. Only time they ever missed was when the first Ken's wife died and even then, they only stopped away one night.' He smiled affectionately at the two old men.

'They're like an old married couple.'

'Yes, I reckon if one of them goes, it won't be long before the other follows.' He glanced at their two glasses, both nearly empty. 'Can I get you another?'

'Thank you, yes, a medium Pinot,' she watched him as he went up to the bar.

'Fish cake?' a middle-aged woman asked, holding a plate of food.

'Yes, thank you,' Alison replied.

The woman went to fetch cutlery and sauces as Mike returned with their drinks.

'All right then, Mike?' the server asked with a grin. She looked as if she might have given him a nudge and wink if she hadn't been worried he might spill the drinks. As it was, he just blushed as he set her drink down.

'Thank you,' Alison said once she had swallowed the first mouthful of surprisingly hot fish cake and took a quick gulp of wine to cool it down.

'I'll let you eat,' he said still holding his pint.

'No, no, sit down, please, otherwise I'll feel like I've driven you out of your seat.'

He sat down.

There were a few moments of slightly awkward silence as she ate and he couldn't think of anything to say.

'So, carry on,' she said. 'Telling me about the locals.'

'I don't know everyone in here,' he protested with a laugh.

'But I'll bet you know most of them.' She looked at him with a twinkle, safe in the knowledge that the Jolly Sailor was too far off the beaten track to get many tourists.

Mike then proceeded to work his way around all the people in the bar as she carried on eating.

'So, the barman is Jake, he's the son of the landlords, John and Ellie. That was Ellie that brought your meal out. She does all the cooking. Very good, she is too.'

'Got to say, this is just what I needed,' Alison agreed.

'They bought the lease five years or so ago, done wonders with the pub. Believe me, you wouldn't have wanted to eat here when the previous owner had the place.'

Mike continued to give her a potted history of everyone in the pub that he could see.

'Over there, behind you is Linda and her husband George, they had a B&B on the sea front but sold up and bought a place down the road when they retired. Then there is Matt, he's a primary school teacher and a Satanist by night, and Helena who is a dominatrix and has a dungeon in her garage.'

'Wait, wait,' Alison stopped him, laughing. 'You are making this up, please tell me you are making this up.'

'Of course I am, I haven't a clue who half these people are and even when I do, you'd be bored to tears by what little I know about them. This is a very ordinary boring little town, not like London, you know.'

'Yes, well, forgive me for pointing out that one or two things are just like London, like the vandalism and the cliques. Do you know that Jenny in the shop can hardly bear to be civil to me? I went in there to buy cat food and she accused me of stealing people's homes and jobs!'

'Ah,' he said, as if something had clicked into place.

'Ah what?' she asked.

'Dr Richard Atkinson,' he explained, his mouth puckering as if he had a bad taste in his mouth.

'Yes, I've seen him around,' she admitted, reluctant to say more about their encounters. 'I know he's a local, and I have taken over his job, but I didn't push him out of it.

He resigned,' she told him, leaving it at that because she really didn't want to go into the reasons.

'That's not the way he tells the story round here,' Mike explained to her. 'And, of course, you're living in his family home as well.'

'What?' She was astounded by this piece of news. 'But I'm sure that's not the name on the rental agreement.' She tried to remember what the name of the owners had been.

'No, he sold it a few months back, moved into a smaller place, but he didn't want to have to sell up and you could see it hurt.'

It was all beginning to make a horrible sort of sense to Alison. Dr Atkinson had lost everything, and she seemed to have unknowingly inherited it all.

Having finished her dinner, Alison insisted on buying Mike a drink in return for him having bought her one. She was surprised by how much she was enjoying his company, but she had decided she would go home after her third glass of wine, which she made a small one as she had to be fresh for work the next morning. He was also being cautious about drinking, asking only for a half pint of bitter.

'My doctor says I shouldn't drink too much when I'm taking antibiotics,' he explained with a smile and she had to accept that his doctor was probably right. Once they had finished their drinks, she was surprised when he insisted on walking back with her.

'Just to be sure Dr Atkinson doesn't jump out of the bushes and shout at you,' he explained, half-jokingly.

She shivered. She ought to be more careful when she walked around the village at night and she was very glad she had Mike to see her safely home.

'What happened with your mother?' Alison asked as they walked along the narrow road towards her cottage.

'She had a fall and broke her hip and they didn't really want to have to take her for surgery because of her heart problems. Anyway, I made a fuss, she was in pain, her condition was deteriorating every day, and finally they decided they didn't have a choice; she might die under the anaesthetic but she was definitely going to die if they didn't do something.'

'So, they operated and she died anyway.' Alison took his arm in what she hoped was a supportive way. 'That's sad.'

'Yeah, but not during the operation. She had a heart attack the next day and they couldn't get her back. If they'd operated earlier she might not have been so weak, might have... I don't know, maybe she wouldn't have had the heart attack.'

'She might have, or she might not. You know, it's very hard to know what to do for the best sometimes,' Alison rubbed his arm. 'Doctors don't always get it right. Believe me, I am one.'

'I understand that, and God knows, we all make mistakes, but later, the anaesthetist said to me that she'd got through the operation fine, they had all thought she would make it, but then her heart just stopped. It was a surprise to them all. The thing that's really stuck with me though, is that he made a comment about when they tried to get her back. He said the defib failed just when they needed it. I mean, I know mechanical things can go wrong, but not something like that, not if it's been properly maintained and serviced surely? It makes no sense to me.'

Another one? Alison was shocked. This wasn't one that had come up when she was looking at the data. There could not have been any mention of defib failure as a cause of death. How many people had died because of these problems? She was going to have to take it seriously, investigate what was going on.

'Makes no sense to me either,' she admitted to Mike. 'Look, would you mind if I looked into it? Tried to find out what went wrong?'

'Of course not! I've been campaigning for exactly that but I just keep getting these drivelling apologies and reassurances from official channels, like Atkinson. Believe me I was very happy to hear he'd resigned.'

They had arrived at her cottage and Alison felt Mike stop.

'Shit!' he almost shouted and hurried up her drive.

Alison turned and saw 'You are next' scrawled on her garage door.

She joined Mike as they stood and looked at what was written there.

'What do you think it means?' she asked.

'Whatever it means, it's a threat. Have you reported any of the incidents to the police?'

'No, not yet.'

'You need to do that. Now.'

'In the morning,' she said, pulling out her keys and going to open the front door.

'No, now.' He took the keys from her hand and opened the front door, going into the cottage first, checking each room as he went into the house.

The first thing that struck her was the strange smell in the house and then the fact that Paws hadn't welcomed her. She hurried into the kitchen and there he was, curled up in the armchair by the range, a favourite spot of his, but as she approached, he didn't even raise his head.

'Paws!' she shouted and rushed to him. She lifted his face, and simultaneously saw that there was a pool of vomit on the cushion. He was barely conscious and she continued more softly as she tried to examine him as best she could, knowing that she was no vet. It was clear that the cat was seriously ill. 'What's wrong, sweetheart?' She picked him up, gently.

Mike had rushed into the kitchen behind her as she shouted.

'What's up?' He took in the sick cat and the tears on Alison's face, then looked around the kitchen, trying to piece together what had happened.

'Is there a twenty-four-hour vet round here?' she asked him as she wrapped Paws up in a towel and picked him up. A faint mew of protest was his only reaction. 'I haven't even registered him locally yet.'

He nodded.

'It's not far,' he replied, and, using a piece of kitchen towel, picked up the remains of a piece of salmon that was beside a pool of vomit under the table.

'Did you feed Paws before you came out?'

'Yes.' She looked at what was in the towel. 'But tinned salmon not fresh.' Where had the piece of fresh salmon come from? She looked over at his feeding bowl and could see that it was almost empty.

Paws mewed pitifully and she stroked him and made soothing noises.

'Where is the vet?' she asked Mike.

'I'll take you,' he said and walked to the front door.

'But you've had too much to drink,' she told him as she followed him out, cradling her cat.

'I'm fine, two and a half pints over three hours, and I didn't even finish the last one. My Land Rover's just along here.'

She hurried behind him to the battered old car and he held the passenger door open and helped her climb in with Paws.

As they drove to the vet's, she cradled her cat and talked to him, trying to let him know that he was loved, wondering if he could hear her. But he didn't respond, not even mewing when they stopped outside the vets. After all that had happened, she couldn't bear to think of losing him, and she couldn't stop a tear from falling on his soft fur. As Mike pulled up outside, she rushed to the door and rang the bell, willing them to come quickly and was relieved when in no time at all she was handing over the cat, and the salmon Mike had brought with them to a veterinary nurse, explaining her fear that he had been poisoned.

It had been a very long night by the time they got back from the vet's. Paws was being kept in for observation, but the vet seemed to think he was over the worst; being sick had probably saved his life. The salmon had been sent off for analysis, but it was the vet's opinion that her pet had definitely been poisoned. Mike insisted on coming in with her once they got home. He checked all the doors and windows were locked before agreeing that she could leave calling the police to the morning, which wasn't that far away now.

'What you need is sleep,' he said as he went into the kitchen and put the kettle on the stove.

'Oh, no, I don't want a hot drink,' she said.

'That's for me,' he said. 'I'll sleep downstairs on the sofa,' he told her. 'Make sure nothing else happens.'

'You really don't. . .' She started to tell him it wasn't necessary for him to stay, but stopped, there was no doubt she would feel safer and sleep sounder, for what was left of the night, knowing he was downstairs. She was surprised that a little bit of her would have liked him to be upstairs, with her. She knew the rules about patient/doctor relationships and it might be seen as overstepping the mark, even if he wasn't really her patient, strictly speaking. So she contented herself with a: 'Thank you,' and went up to her cosy room alone, wishing Paws would come and curl up on the end of her bed as he usually did. Knowing that he wouldn't and that he might never do that again, she cried herself to sleep.

CHAPTER TWENTY

She woke to the smell of coffee wafting up from the kitchen. Hurriedly grabbing a dressing-gown and tying it around her, she ran a brush through her hair. As she came down the stairs to the kitchen, the smell of bacon was added to the coffee, which was strange, because she knew she didn't have any bacon in the house.

She went into the kitchen to find Mike standing over a frying pan. He looked up.

'Tea or coffee?' he asked.

'Tea, please.'

He nodded and poured boiling water from the kettle into a teapot.

'I thought you might be a morning tea person,' he explained.

'It takes a while before I can face coffee. I take it you are a coffee in the morning person.'

'I need it,' he admitted. 'Mostly to counter the alcohol from the night before, although not today.' He placed a mug of tea on the table, where he had laid a place for her. 'And now you're going to tell me you don't normally eat breakfast, aren't you?'

'Well, yes.'

'But this morning, you are going to need it. You've got the vet and the police to call before you go into work.'

She knew he was right and was surprised at how hungry she felt as he placed a plate of bacon and eggs in front of her.

'I could only find brown bread,' he said sadly as he put a plate of toast on the table. His expression made her laugh.

'Next time you stay the night, I'll be sure to get some white bread in for you,' she said and blushed as she realised what she had said, made worse by the twinkle in his eye that said he hadn't missed it. She quickly turned her attention to her breakfast instead.

Once she had eaten her breakfast, she picked up her phone and rang the vet's first. She was pleased to hear that they were confident that Paws was going to recover but that they would keep him in for another twenty-four hours just to be sure everything had settled before he came home.

'They must have left some poisoned salmon out for him, although I don't know how they could be sure to get him and not any other wildlife,' she said to Mike.

'I think they must have put it through the cat flap,' he told her. 'I found a bit more that your cat hadn't eaten on the mat just below it. I've bagged it for the police.' She looked at the cat flap and shuddered. It was a good thing she had fed her cat before going out. If he had been hungry he would have wolfed down all of it and probably be dead.

Her second call was to the hospital to explain that she was going to be late in. It was already later than she normally arrived and apart from anything else, she needed to stop at the vet's on the way into work and let Paws know that he was loved – and reassure herself that he was going to be all right.

Alison had been putting off calling the police, but with Mike refusing to budge until she had done so, she finally rang them on the non-emergency number.

'Hello,' she said. 'I'd like to report that someone tried to poison my cat last night.'

The call seemed to take an age as she was passed from person to person, as she explained about the previous incidents as well and had to go over and over everything until she was finally told that someone would come to speak to her, but probably not until late afternoon. She explained that she'd be at work, and it was finally agreed that it would be in the evening.

'Right, now I really need to be getting ready to go to work,' she told Mike. 'And I'm pretty sure you have a job to go to as well.'

He smiled.

'Yes, I do but I'll try and keep an eye on this place during the day, and you should ring the owners, see if you can put up cameras and security lights.'

'I will, I promise.'

She couldn't help thinking, as she drove into work, that Mike Jenkins was a kind man, and she was very glad that he had been with her last night.

'I'm so sorry I wasn't here to welcome you, Anwar,' Alison told Dr Faez as she brought two mugs of coffee into the office on the stroke unit.

'That's quite all right, I understand you have a lot on your plate at the moment.'

'Er, yes. That's something of an understatement,' she told him, not yet ready to go into details about all the problems she was having, and unsure if he would be insulted to think that she had prioritised a sick cat over him. 'I hope Eliza showed you round?' She handed him one of the mugs.

'Thank you. She did yes, along with Joyce and they gave me a better understanding about what has happened here.'

'Oh.' Alison was taken aback. She sat down abruptly and put her mug down on a coaster that seemed to have been taken from a pub. One step up from one telling her that she didn't have to be mad to work here, but it would help, a mantra she had seen on more than one coaster and a mouse mat around the hospital. 'What exactly did they say?'

'That your Dr Carrick had left in a huff, was off sick with stress and had made a complaint about you bullying him, is that right?' He didn't seem worried by this story. In fact, he seemed serene and unruffled as he sipped his coffee.

'Er, yes, that about covers it,' she said ruefully.

'You? A bully? I suppose he just objected to you trying to improve care here.'

'Exactly that. This was his world, his domain, if you like.'

'And you came crashing in, with your fancy London ways and tried to change things, is that it?'

'I'm afraid so.'

'Poor man!' Dr Faez said with a smile. 'I fear you might not have been as tactful as you might have been, were you?'

'Possibly, but I had to make those changes, Anwar.'

'Of course you did. You are much too committed to your patients to allow them to receive poor care, and I told the nurses that, but I can't see you as a bully, Alison.' He laughed. 'The very idea!'

Alison blushed and said nothing. Anwar had been retired for six months and clearly hadn't heard any of the gossip about why she had left London and found herself another job – a new start.

'And how is Ed?' Anwar asked next. 'Are you managing to get up and see him at all?'

Alison looked at Anwar's kind and twinkling eyes and felt guilty that she hadn't even told him that she and her husband had split up.

'Not much, no.'

'Well, perhaps now that I'm here you'll be able to find the time. Marriages take hard work to maintain, Alison. Like roses, you must tend them carefully.'

Alison had the grace to blush at this. She would have to find time to talk about her ex-marriage with him, but maybe not just now, she decided. Right now, she had too many other things to tell him.

When Alison turned into her driveway, she was surprised to see a small Fiat car parked in her space, and a young woman in conversation with Mike on the doorstep of her house. She pulled up beside the Fiat and got out.

'Dr Wilson, I presume?' the young woman approached holding out her hand. 'I'm DC Cresswell.'

'Of course, thank you so much for agreeing to come in the evening.' Alison walked to her front door where Mike was busy fixing a new doorbell on the frame. He stood back to let her open the door. 'Everything all right, Mike?' she asked.

'Just fitting a video doorbell,' he explained. He had rung during the day, to check she had spoken with the owners, which, of course, she hadn't. 'I didn't think they could object to that.'

'I was saying, they're a great idea,' DC Cresswell added, following Alison into the house.

'Can I get you anything? Tea? Coffee?' Alison called over her shoulder as she led the DC through to the kitchen.

'A cup of tea, please, if it's not too much trouble.'

Alison filled the kettle and set about making tea for them both. After a moment's hesitation, she added a mug for Mike. What she really would have liked was a glass of wine but she didn't think it would look good for her to be drinking at this point, especially as she might have to move her car to let the police detective out.

Tea made, Alison took a mug out to Mike, who merely grunted his thanks due to having a screw held between his lips. She sincerely hoped he remembered to remove the screw before drinking the tea, she could do without having to take him back to A&E.

Once she and DC Cresswell were settled with their drinks, Alison spent a lot of time going over what had happened again with her, all the while acutely aware of Mike working at the open front door, and then shortly afterwards, at the back door.

'This is the salmon we... *I* found under the cat flap,' she corrected herself with a look at Mike and handed the young woman the plastic bag with a small piece of salmon in it.

'I'll get that sent to the lab,' she said as she tucked it in her bag. 'And you've no idea who might be behind these events?'

'Not really, no,' Alison replied, hesitantly.

'Are you sure? You don't seem certain. Is there something you want to tell me?'

'Well, I don't want to say something when I have no real proof.' She looked up at Mike again, but he was busy marking where the video bell should go on the back door.

'Don't worry, we won't go barging in and accusing anyone, but if you have an idea of who it could be, it might help us.'

'I recently took over as medical director at the hospital and the man who had the post before me, also used to own this house. The locals seem to think that I took his job and his home, pushed him out.'

'And if they are saying it, he's the one who probably told them that. Does he still live locally?'

'Yes, I believe so. And I didn't push him out, he resigned and sold the house before I even came to the area.'

The DC nodded, but they both knew that it didn't matter that Alison hadn't actually done what she was accused of doing, what mattered was what people believed had happened.

'What's this man's name?'

'Atkinson, Dr Richard Atkinson.' Alison reluctantly told her as the DC made a note and stood up.

'Right, I'm going to get a forensic team round here tomorrow, to check for fingerprints on the back door and cat flap, so if you could try not to touch the obvious areas and don't wipe them down.' She flashed a look at Mike who had a cloth half-hanging out of his pocket.

'I have to go to work tomorrow,' Alison said. 'I have clinics and meetings booked. I really can't be here.'

'That's okay, it's the outside of the door we're interested in, there's no suggestion anyone got into the house, is there?' she checked with Alison.

'No, no, definitely not.'

'You might want to get the locks changed, just in case, particularly as this doctor once lived here.'

Alison realised that Dr Atkinson might well have keys left from his time at the house if the new owners hadn't already changed them. She gave an involuntary shiver as she thought that he could get into her home at will, just like he seemed able to get into the hospital pharmacy. She realised that both DC Cresswell and Mike were looking at her strangely.

'Of course, I'll check with the landlord that it's okay and get it done as soon as possible.'

DC Cresswell nodded her approval.

'It's a good idea, having those video doorbells, front and back. I also pointed out some places where you might want to put up some motion-activated lights to your handyman.'

Alison tried not to react to hearing Mike described as her handyman, although, when she thought about it, he certainly was handy to have around.

'Like I say, I'll have to check with my landlord as this place is only rented,' Alison explained as they walked to the front door.

'Well, you can tell him that the police have advised it for your safety and the security of the building. He'll find it hard not to agree to it after that.'

They shook hands and Alison checked that she could get her car out before going back to the kitchen.

'I'll just show you how to use these,' Mike said as she opened the fridge and pulled out the bottle of wine chilling in there. She held the bottle up to him.

'I don't suppose you've got any beer?' he asked.

'Sorry.' She shook her head. 'I'm not really set up for visitors.'

'Or handymen,' he said with a smile.

'No,' she agreed. 'Is that who you told her you were?'

'It seemed the easiest explanation.'

'Thank you so much for doing this, Mike.'

'It's not a problem. Anyway, I have to go, so let me show you how these video bells work.'

She hadn't been able to persuade him to stay for a glass of wine. She'd offered to buy him a beer at the pub, but he wasn't sure that was a good idea, not two nights in a row, and she had to admit, he was probably right. There was quite enough gossip going around about her amongst the locals already and she still hadn't fully resolved the doctor/patient issues in her mind. Was it acceptable for her to start a relationship with him? Did she want to? The answer to the second part was probably a yes, so she needed to be clear in herself that it would not be crossing a line.

So, she drank her wine and ate her dinner alone after she had called the vet's. Paws was much better and would be well enough to be collected the next day which was a relief. Strange as it sounded, the house seemed empty without him and Alison had to admit, she felt just a little bit lonely.

Checking all the doors and windows were securely locked, she went upstairs to bed.

The cat should have died. She should have been left all alone, with alcohol her only friend, then she might finally have broken. I've been dropping hints at the hospital, warning them that she has an alcohol problem, suggesting it might be the cause of her erratic behaviour. I had high hopes that killing the cat would finish her off but instead she seems to have found someone to lean on, to support her. Someone who believes in her and that won't do. It won't do at all. I need to do more to get rid of her. I have another trick up my sleeve thanks to a friend in London. Another way to suggest she isn't up to the job. It is time to use it. I NEED HER OUT OF THE WAY!

CHAPTER TWENTY-ONE

It had been a satisfying day, overall, Alison thought. Anwar was settling in remarkably well, both with his colleagues and the patients as she knew he would. The ward sister had taken a particular shine to him and her pointed remarks about how Dr Carrick would have handled things, or what he always told them to do, had stopped, which was a great relief. Alison didn't want to belittle the man when he wasn't there to defend himself, but some of his practices were very out of date and needed to be changed. Fortunately, Anwar agreed. It was due to his gentle persuasiveness that he seemed to have been successful in making good progress on all fronts. Perhaps Alison could learn something from him, she admitted to herself, about people management, at least.

Feeling that she could safely leave the ward in his hands, she had spent much of the day catching up with her role as medical director. She had requested information from a number of departments in her quest to find out where the hospital funds were going, if they weren't going on the equipment that they were supposed to be spent on. She also did some digging into the exact causes of St Margaret's high mortality rate. She just hoped her requests had got through. If she didn't get responses quickly, she'd have to try telephoning them, to make sure no emails had gone astray again.

She got Mary to organise meetings with both the head accountant and also the head of pathology and add them to her calendar.

'And if I could ask you to give me a written note of them as well?' she added.

'Of course, Dr Wilson,' Mary couldn't keep the triumph from her voice. 'Dr Atkinson could teach you a thing or two, couldn't he? Belt and braces?'

Alison chose not to respond to this because she was in a rush to leave work early, so that she could collect Paws on her way home. She was just closing her office door, when Jonathan Selby appeared.

'I'm so sorry, did you need to see me? I'm in a bit of a hurry,' she said.

Selby looked at his watch.

'A bit early, isn't it?'

'I have to collect my cat from the vet's,' she explained, 'and don't worry, I have plenty of work I can do at home.' She patted her tote bag.

'I trust you're not taking anything confidential home with you?'

'I adhere strictly to all privacy and security rules,' she told him firmly, with her fingers crossed, although she could also point out that she suspected there had already been a security breach and the source was probably his own IT department. 'Was there anything else, Jonathan?'

'I was talking to someone yesterday. Someone who had heard about you leaving London. It seems you left in quite the hurry. . .' There was a little smug smile on his face that seriously irritated Alison. In fact, his whole demeanour irritated her.

'Believe me, you don't know the half of it,' she told him. 'Now if that's all you've got to say for yourself, I have to go.'

'So why *did* you leave in such a rush, Dr Wilson?' he called after her.

She turned around. 'Personal reasons.'

'Personal reasons?' He shook his head. 'What on earth sort of personal reasons could make you leave such a good job?'

'It's not easy trying to work when your husband is having an affair with one of your junior colleagues and you are the talk of the hospital,' she said and was rewarded by a shocked expression on his face.

'Oh, I thought. . .' He looked genuinely surprised, confused even. 'I heard something different.'

'What did you hear?' she asked but he had turned and walked away.

She could believe he had heard something different. Even though she had left before Sara could make a complaint, and there was no mention of the incident on her record, the gossip would still have said she had been made to resign. If he knew someone in London, that's the story he would have heard.

Ignoring his dig about leaving early, she headed out to the car park, silently calling him all the names under the sun at the same time as wishing she could take back what she had said about Ed's affair. Now everyone here would know about her humiliation and she would be the subject of gossip, just as she had been in London.

Furious that she had let the man get under her skin, she sat for a few minutes in her car, resting her head against the steering wheel. How had he found out about her sudden departure?

When Alison had found out that Ed was having an affair, she had been so angry, but prepared to forgive him if the affair ended.

'How could you!' she had screamed at him.

He had had the good grace to look ashamed.

'She was there, she made me feel, wanted—'

'Don't you dare! Don't you dare tell me it's my fault,' she had said, but that didn't stop her from thinking that it was, just a little bit, that if she had been there for him, it might never have happened.

That night, once she had calmed down, they had talked about it, and she had asked him, begged him to stop seeing Sara. They had to see each other every day, she told him, and she didn't think she could do it. Even thinking about it was humiliating, but he had told her it was too late, they were in love. He couldn't give Sara up even if he wanted, and he didn't. He told her she would just have to find a way to live with it.

'I'll move out. After all, I can't expect you to leave under the circumstances,' he had said and gone upstairs to pack a bag. She hadn't hated him in that moment, but she had hated Sara. All those little smiles when Alison had told her registrar that she had ended up working late again, so poor Ed was on his own all evening, suddenly made sense. Oh, how she had hated her, and of course, Alison wasn't able to stop that from spilling out of her, when they next met.

'You need to leave my husband alone,' Alison had told her quietly. 'Let him come home to me.'

They were in the end office on the stroke unit, behind the nurse's desk, not the ideal place for a confrontation, but Alison couldn't help it, couldn't help herself.

'And why would I do that?'

'Because with you it's just an affair, he'll tire of you in time, then come running back to me anyway. I'm just saving you from that humiliation, letting you take control, end it now on your terms.'

'He loves me.'

'That's what every mistress thinks.' Alison was shaking as she said it.

'Well, this mistress is going to be wife number two, just you wait and see.' Sara had left the office then and Alison was suddenly aware of the ward sister standing by the door and looking at her with pity. It was too much for Alison and she rushed from the room and locked herself in the staff toilet, weeping for all that she had lost.

Thinking about it now, Alison found herself sobbing again as she sat in her car in the dark car park. After a few, deep, calming breaths, she fished in her bag for a tissue and blew her nose and wiped her eyes, looking around to make sure no one had seen her break down. That would only make it all worse. Alison was relieved to see the car park was almost deserted. As she leant forward to start the car, she saw a man come out of the fire escape door that she used to come down from the administration corridor. As the man turned to let the door softly close, she saw that it was Atkinson. She went to open her door and confront him, but he was hurrying, almost scurrying to his car and she could see that she wouldn't catch him before he left, so she waited and watched as he drove away. There was a moment, as his headlights washed over her car that she was sure he must have seen her. She couldn't see him in the driver's seat, but the car seemed to hesitate and then sped up again, speeding away with a screech of protest from the tyres.

CHAPTER TWENTY-TWO

Alison arrived at the hospital early the next morning, nursing a hangover and a slightly guilty conscience. Before leaving home, she had locked the cat flap so that Paws couldn't get out, and more importantly, poisoned food couldn't be posted through to him. Paws was not happy about being shut in the kitchen like this, needless to say. Alison had left a cat litter tray for him, knowing that he would much rather go out and explore the world but there was no way she was going to risk a repeat event. The vet's bill had been astronomical, but it wasn't that, it was because Paws was more important to her than money.

As always, she was in before Mary and most of the other senior staff members, even after stopping by the ward first, so she docked her laptop and switched it on before heading to the small kitchenette and setting up the coffee maker. She needed a stronger caffeine hit than her early morning tea before starting work. Mary could at least be relied upon to ensure there was fresh milk, for which Alison was truly grateful.

Once armed with her coffee she returned to her office and began the business of the day. She sent a text message to the chief pharmacist and Tony Grant, telling them that she had seen Dr Atkinson at the hospital again the night before and asking if any more drugs had gone missing. She hoped they had managed to set up a camera in time, but suspected it would be too early for that to have been arranged. She checked her calendar for times and locations of any meetings booked. She knew she was due to meet the chief pathologist that morning to discuss the persistently high mortality rate but when she checked, the meeting was not in her diary. She scrolled through and saw that several other meetings had disappeared, including those with the head of finance and the lead anaesthetist.

As soon as she heard the sounds of Mary's morning routine – dumping her bag on the desk, rummaging around in it to find her lunch box and the stomping footsteps as she walked the short distance to the kitchen to place it in the fridge – Alison hurried down to speak to her.

'Good morning, Mary,' Alison said.

'Good morning, Dr Wilson.' Mary straightened up and grabbed the kettle. She always had a steady supply of tea on the go as she worked.

'I know I had several appointments for meetings today and later in the week with the head of finance, the pathologist, oh and the lead anaesthetist, but they all seem to have been cancelled.'

'Well, I didn't cancel them,' Mary said crossly. 'Look, here are the notes I made for you, see?' As Alison requested Mary had written down the details of all the meetings. 'If they've gone from the calendar, someone must have cancelled them.'

'It wasn't me, so I have to assume that they all did. Perhaps none of them want to talk to me.' She smiled to show she was joking, but she didn't think humour registered with Mary.

As Alison made her way down to the ward, her phone buzzed and she saw that Colin had replied to her text. Some drugs had indeed gone missing and no, the camera was not yet in place. Diverting from her usual route to the ward, she went to Tony Grant's office instead and found him at his desk. She briefly knocked and went in. He quickly turned away, hiding what he had been doing. When he saw who it was, he was relieved and turned back.

'Good morning,' he said.

'Did you see my text?' she asked him.

'Yes,' he replied, holding up the box he was holding. 'Just got this, so I'll speak to Colin and once everyone has gone home we can set it up.'

Alison looked at the box he was holding. It was for a small surveillance camera. He pulled out the contents of the box to show her.

'This bit is the lens, almost impossible to see and then

we can put the rest of it behind some boxes of pills. No one will know it's there.'

'You're enjoying yourself,' she said.

'It's good to have something to get my teeth into, something other than drunks in A&E and opportunist thefts from changing rooms. This is more like the old days, when I was in the job.'

'And you will put it in place tonight?' she asked.

'No reason not to.'

'Good,' she said, 'because I understand some more drugs went missing last night.'

'And you saw Dr Atkinson again, yeah, it's just too much of a coincidence, isn't it? Mind you, it'll probably be a while before he comes back, if he's got any sense.'

'I know. Look, I'm not sure, but I think he saw me, I was in my car when he came out of the fire door, so maybe he won't risk coming back at all.'

'If there's one thing I've learnt about junkies after all my time in the police, it's that when they get desperate they'll do anything, no matter how stupid, in order to get their hands on more drugs.'

She knew he was right, but she also hoped that Dr Atkinson wasn't so far gone down the road of addiction that he returned to steal again. She knew that if they caught him, there would be no coming back from it, they would have to prosecute him and he would almost certainly be struck off.

* * *

Once the ward round was over, Alison went to the head of finances' office and reorganised her meeting with him, but told his secretary not to send a meeting invite to her or Mary. She would have to remember important meetings herself or go back to having a paper diary, something she hadn't done in years. That way, if the appointments were not in her calendar, no one could cancel them without speaking to her personally. Perhaps she should get a personal organiser like everyone used to have in the Eighties. It might make her look a bit behind the times, but she could live with that.

'Try and interfere with that!' she challenged whoever was behind the sabotage with a satisfaction she realised she hadn't felt since she had arrived at St Margaret's.

Throughout the day, her phone had chimed as her new doorbell informed her of the postman delivering her mail at home, and then someone posting a leaflet through her door during the afternoon. At eight o'clock, when she was just about to finish up for the day, her phone chimed again. Looking at it, she could see a man who looked remarkably like Ed at her door. He moved back a bit and she could see it really was Ed.

'Ed,' she said through the doorbell app, 'What on earth are you doing down here?'

If he was startled that she was talking to him in this way, he recovered fast.

'I just happened to be passing and thought I'd drop by, are you still at work?'

'Yes.' As Wayleigh was a good two-hour drive from London or anywhere he was likely to be, she couldn't believe he was just passing. She regretted giving him the address so that he could forward any post, she certainly hadn't expected him to visit. She was tempted to just tell him to go away again, but she was curious to know why he had come all this way. Was he the source of Selby's information about what had happened in London? Perhaps he wanted to apologise. If so, she wasn't in any rush to accept it. In fact, she wanted to give him a piece of her mind. 'But I was just leaving.'

'Will you be long? I can find somewhere to wait.'

'There's a pub down the road, if you want to go there and I'll meet you in about twenty minutes.'

'That's great. I'll see you later,' he said awkwardly and walked away from the door. Alison quickly changed her password for the hospital system and her email, again, and then closed her laptop down and packed it up to take home with her. As she hurried to the door down to the car park, she was surprised to hear it click shut. Someone must have just left this way, but she was sure that she was the only person left on the corridor. They had all gone home hours ago. Alison almost ran down the stairs in the hope of catching whoever had left just before her, but when she went out into the car park, once again, there was no one in sight. She looked for Dr Atkinson's car, but couldn't see it anywhere either.

* * *

She saw Ed as soon as she walked into the Jolly Sailor. He was sitting at a corner table, doing *The Times* crossword, a glass of red wine, barely touched, in front of him. Alison waved a hello when he looked up and went to the bar to get herself a drink. She looked round as casually as she could and was relieved not to see Mike lurking anywhere. She wasn't quite sure why she felt better not seeing him in the pub, or rather that he wouldn't see her there with Ed. There was nothing going on between them after all, and regardless of the fact that Ed was very much her ex.

'Large Pinot,' she said to the barman and once served, carried it over to the corner table. Ed stood up as she put the glass down and went to kiss her, but she turned her head to the side so that his lips merely brushed her cheek. It was an awkward moment.

'You surprised me with the video doorbell, you've never been one for security measures like that before.'

'I live on my own now.' She didn't want to go into the reason why she had had it installed. Not with Ed. Not now.

'Of course. Very sensible.'

'Anyway, what brings you down here? Is there a problem with finalising the divorce?'

'No, everything's fine. Moving forward. I. . . well, I just came to see you of course. See how you are settling in.'

She refrained from asking what business it was of his how she was settling in. 'It's good. I love being by the sea, even now that summer's over. It's quieter now that the tourists have gone home.'

'I'm surprised you find time to go to the beach. That's not the Alison I know and. . .' he trailed off awkwardly, reluctant to actually say 'love'.

'I don't. Not often, anyway, but you can see the sea from the roof of the hospital,' she continued, hurriedly trying to cover up his awkwardness. 'I go up there sometimes to relax and think.' *And cry*, she didn't add.

'And how is life as medical director of a provincial hospital?' He sounded very snobbish and that irritated Alison.

'Not every hospital can be in London, Ed, and it doesn't necessarily follow that they can't be as good in the provinces as any big city hospital. At least I'm trying to do something about it, trying to improve things here,' she chastised him and he had the good grace to look abashed.

'I'm sorry.' He played with his wine, she hadn't seen him take so much as a sip since she had arrived, and she was surprised to see that her own glass was nearly empty. She must slow down, she needed to be in control.

'You have no plans to come back to London then?' he asked.

'None at all,' she said firmly. 'There's nothing for me there.'

She was pleased to see that this barb had hit home and that he did take a gulp of wine as a result.

He cleared his throat in preparation for saying something – his real reason for coming all the way to Wayleigh, she hoped.

'As I said, I'm not seeing Sara anymore,' he finally told her.

'Congratulations.'

'She left when they appointed an outside candidate to the... vacant consultant post.'

Her vacant post he meant, but she was ridiculously pleased that they hadn't given it to Sara.

'Has she gone elsewhere then?'

He nodded.

'She's taken a job in Australia.'

Alison raised her eyebrows at that. Sara had moved as far away from him as she could possibly get.

'Wow, that's... far.'

'Don't you see what it means though, for us?'

'No, I honestly don't, Ed. All I see is that you don't like being alone, and that you think I am the easy answer to that problem.'

'It's not like that at all, Alison.' He tried to take her hand, but she moved her hand away. 'I'm really sorry for all the hurt I caused you, caused us.'

'Really? Or are you just here because she dumped you?'

'She didn't dump me, it was mutual.'

'It makes no difference, Ed.'

'Of course it does. I realised it was a mistake. *She* was a mistake.'

'I think everyone could have told you that.'

'I know. We weren't suited, it was just a moment of madness.'

'Moment? It went on for months.'

'I know, I know, but it's over and I want you back, Alison. We can stop the divorce before it becomes final.'

'Do you honestly think it's going to be that easy, Ed? You waltz in here out of the blue and ask me to go back with you and I'll just drop everything and follow you back to London like a good little wife?'

'Of course not. But I spoke to Harry Querrick and he says there's a stroke consultant post at UCH coming free, you could come back and—' He stopped as he saw the two bright spots burning on her cheeks.

'I am not coming back.'

'But you can't want to stay here! Not with everything that's going on!'

'What have you heard?'

'Nothing,' he said but she could tell he was lying. Someone had spoken to him, told him that the job wasn't going well.

'Who did you talk to?'

'I really can't, it wasn't anyone you know, there was just a rumour they said.'

'Saying what?'

'That you were going to be sacked, just like before.'

It was like a slap in the face and she closed her eyes.

'I wasn't sacked, I resigned. I hope you told them that, this mysterious person.'

'Sacked, resigned, you know as well as I do that it's the same thing. Come back, Alison, I know it's not you, it's just the stress of the job. You need to take some time off.'

'You betrayed me,' she hissed.

'I know, and I'm truly, truly sorry, but it wasn't serious and it's over.'

'No!' she shouted and banged the table and he looked round anxiously, making sure they weren't attracting too much attention. Alison looked up as well and saw the barman quickly go back to polishing a glass that didn't seem to need it. He was probably wondering if he was going to have to intervene. 'It *was* serious. You blew up my life, Ed. And not just because of the affair,' she continued in a more even tone. 'You betrayed me when you sided with her, believed her over me, believed that I had threatened her with the sack, when I hadn't. I was innocent then, and I am innocent now, that's why I can't go back to you.'

Alison stood up and left the pub quickly. She was intensely aware of the looks of everyone in the pub – and to her mortification, one of them was Mike. She wondered how long he had been there and how much of the argument he had witnessed, but she didn't stop, she went straight out of the door and hurried home.

CHAPTER TWENTY-THREE

Alison knew it was bad from the look on Joyce's face when she arrived on the ward.

'What is it, Joyce?'

The ward sister had followed her into the office and was standing by the door.

'I heard from patient liaison that the Rossi family have lodged a formal complaint against the ward.'

Alison slumped in the desk chair. This was all she needed on top of everything else.

'Do you know exactly what they are complaining about?'

'Well, apparently there are two things, firstly they say their mother's blood pressure was never adequately controlled and secondly that she had been left on the commode for too long.'

Alison groaned.

'I wish I could say they had no cause for complaint.'

Joyce nodded. 'It was good of you to say you had seen the buzzer within reach, Dr Wilson, when the family were here.'

'It's the truth, and I spoke to the other patients in her bay and a nurse did come and check on her, so I don't think you have anything to worry about there.'

Joyce came and sat down, she looked puzzled.

'It must have been one of the other nurses then, because Shelley, who was down to look after her, admitted she forgot all about her and went for her break.'

'She should thank her colleagues then, for getting her off the hook.'

'And me, so thank you for telling me that. It's good of you to stand up for the nursing staff.' She hesitated and seemed to soften slightly, before looking pointedly at Alison. 'That just leaves you with the matter of Mrs Rossi's blood pressure, and we all know whose fault that was.'

'Yes, indeed, thank you, Joyce,' Alison concurred. 'I need to speak to Dr Bayliss and work out how best to play it down.'

'Good luck with that,' Joyce smiled at her as she stood up to leave. 'I know we didn't get off to the best start, Dr Wilson, but I wanted to say, that I know that you are only trying to improve things for patients and that I do appreciate what you are doing.'

She went out, leaving Alison speechless for a moment. It was good to know that she had a new supporter, and such an influential one on the ward as well. It was a shame about the complaint though. She sighed and rubbed the spot on her temple where she could feel a headache brewing.

The headache only got worse after she had been to see Tony Grant. Alison was stunned when he showed her the camera footage from overnight.

Alison could see a woman in nursing uniform come into the pharmacy. Because of the angle, she could only see the top of the nurse's head.

'I always put the camera up high, because people don't look up although it makes it hard to identify people sometimes. Look here. . .' He paused the tape, and Alison saw the nurse feel along the highest shelf. 'You can see her checking the place we put the camera previously, but I put it in a different place, just in case the thief knew how we'd caught Dr Atkinson.'

'Which she must have,' Alison said sadly.

'Yes,' he agreed, 'but not because anyone said anything from my end.'

'Well, how she knew about it doesn't really matter at the moment,' Alison told him. 'What does matter is that we can see her quite clearly taking a packet from the cabinet.'

'But. . .' Tony fast forwarded the tape, so that the thief moved jerkily, stopping and turning as if she heard something, then quickly putting the packet back in the cupboard and locking the cupboard door. By the time the second person came into view, the pharmacist on duty that night, the nurse was looking at the controlled drug register. As they spoke together, the nurse turned and her face was revealed. Alison took a sharp intake of breath as she saw Eliza wave as she left the pharmacy.

'But she didn't take anything,' Alison was surprisingly relieved.

'Not that time, no, but only because the duty pharmacist came in.'

'What should we do about it?' Alison asked him. 'It's a bit of a dilemma, isn't it?'

'I agree, it's tough, but either we wait it out until we get definite evidence against her, or we take what we have to the top.'

'Hmmm, I think I'd rather just have a quiet word with her, see if I can get to the bottom of it,' she said.

Tony didn't look happy at that idea.

'But. . .' he began, but Alison put up a hand to stop him.

'I appreciate your concern, Tony, but I know my staff. She's a good nurse, and I don't really think we have enough evidence to be throwing accusations around, so in this instance, I'm going to have to overrule you.'

She remained firm despite Tony's protests. She wasn't going to be rushed into condemning anyone. Besides, to lose the medical director because of a drug theft was one thing, but to lose the chief nurse for the same crime, would be catastrophic for the hospital. Not to mention that Eliza had been her biggest help in trying to improve things at the hospital. To lose her now would make the job so much harder.

'What's going on?' Eliza asked as she came into Alison's office.

'Sit down, Eliza, please,' Alison said and the tone of her voice warned the chief nurse that all was not well.

Eliza sat and Alison composed herself for a moment, thinking carefully about what she should say.

'I wasn't aware when I came here that Dr Atkinson was asked to resign because he was caught stealing opiates from the pharmacy. Were you?'

Eliza hesitated. 'I heard rumours,' she finally admitted.

'It was assumed that the thefts would stop when he left, but it was reported to me recently that drugs were still going missing despite Dr Atkinson having . . . moved on. So, we installed a hidden camera, in a different spot from the previous one, in case whoever was taking the drugs knew where the last one had been,' she told Eliza, who visibly paled when she heard this. 'I admit we were expecting to catch Dr Atkinson again but last night it caught you going into the controlled drugs cupboard, remove a box of diamorphine ampoules, and then put them back when the duty pharmacist came in.'

'I was just checking that the register was up to date and correct.'

'And yet you didn't count how many boxes were in the cupboard.'

'I could see them.'

'You know you are not supposed to check the controlled cupboard on your own, and it's the job of the pharmacists to check them, anyway.'

'As you said, drugs have gone missing in the past, so I was just keeping an eye on things, making sure.'

'Eliza . . .' Alison shook her head. 'You have to know that this puts you under suspicion for the thefts. You have to stop lying. You know as well as I do that this doesn't add up.'

Eliza sat there, fiddling with her fingers.

'Also, you weren't even on duty last night, so why were you here in the hospital, let alone checking drug stocks at half past ten at night?' Alison pointed to the time stamp of the footage.

'I was helping out, it was manic.'

'Who asked you to help out?'

'The. . . night sister.'

She was lying, Alison could tell.

'Who was on last night?' Alison hated that she was badgering Eliza when she could see the nurse was panicking, but she had no choice. 'And don't forget, I can and will check that she asked you as well.'

Eliza's head hung even lower; she was running out of explanations. She sniffed and Alison pushed a box of tissues towards her and waited while Eliza blew her nose and got herself more under control.

'Now why don't you tell me the truth, Eliza,' Alison gently coaxed. Eliza didn't respond for a while, then sighed and gave a final blow of her nose.

'Okay, I *was* thinking about taking a box of diamorphine last night.'

'And you have done this before?'

'No.'

They both knew she was lying.

'Why? Why were you thinking about taking the diamorphine? Do you take drugs?'

'It wasn't for me.'

'Who was it for?' Although Alison was pretty sure she knew the answer to that.

'Richard, Dr Atkinson.'

'And have you let him use your door pass and the keys himself? At other times?'

'I may have left them on my desk, turned a blind eye when he borrowed them,' Eliza admitted, reluctantly.

'Why did you do it for him?' she asked.

'He's a good man, really he is,' Eliza explained. 'He's been using, just small amounts, for years and it never, ever affected his work.'

'And you knew this? You knew he was a drug addict?'

'He told me when I caught him taking some from a ward. I told him it had to stop, that I couldn't cover for him if he continued to steal it and I thought he had stopped, but he'd just found other ways of getting hold of it. Forging prescriptions, things like that. And then he was under more pressure, which made him use more and he was finding it harder and harder to get enough, so he started stealing from the main pharmacy.'

'And got caught.'

'Yes.'

'Like you last night.'

'Yes, but I was only doing it for him because he was so desperate, because he begged me. You've no idea what losing his job, his wife, his home did to him. He's lost everything.'

Much as Alison wanted to be sympathetic, she found it hard.

'It was his choice, Eliza, and by helping him to get drugs, you aren't really helping him, you're just enabling him to remain an addict.'

Eliza looked as if she was about to protest but Alison held up her hand to stop her.

'Oh, I know you are going to say the drugs never affected his judgement, that he was fully functioning, but are you sure? This hospital has a higher than average mortality rate, not to mention the poor rating it was given at the last CQC inspection. To me, that indicates a medical director who had taken his eye off the ball.'

'I know, but it wasn't just his fault, the whole hospital is to blame and he got punished for it.' She was openly crying now. 'Please don't do the same to me, make me resign or report me to the police. I promise I won't do it again, it was just that I was worried he'd kill himself if I didn't.'

Alison paused before replying.

'It can't go on, Eliza. If I smooth things over with security and Colin in pharmacy, explain what happened—'

'They know it was me?' Eliza looked horrified.

'Tony brought me the footage, so he knows of course. Colin just knows that we put a camera in at this point.'

Eliza sobbed.

'And it is perhaps better if he doesn't know it was you we caught.'

'Please, please I'll do anything you say if you just let me stay here. I've been at St Margaret's all my working life, I can't go anywhere else. I know the staff, the patients. You know what it's like in a place like this. If I have to go, if you sack me, or make me resign, I won't be able to stay here, in the town, because everyone will know.'

'If I were to let you off—' She held up her hand to stop Eliza butting in again. '*If* I were to, there could be no more thefts.'

'There won't be, I promise you.'

'Tony, Colin and I will all be checking stocks regularly and if there is any discrepancy, for anything, ever, you will have to go. I'll be keeping this recording and I will have no compunction about using it if the thefts start up again.'

'They won't. I promise you that.'

'And I want you to stop enabling Dr Atkinson. Go and speak to him and get him the help he needs to stop using. If he chooses not to take that help, then that is his choice, do you understand?'

'Yes, if course, I'll tell him. Thank you, so much. Thank you.'

'You're a good chief nurse, Eliza and you have been a good friend to me. To be honest, I don't know where I would have been without you these past few weeks, and I need you if we are to turn this hospital round,' she tried to reassure her colleague, her friend.

'I'll do everything I can to help you,' Eliza vowed.

'It will be okay, Eliza, we can do this.' And she really believed it. 'I'll speak to Tony and assure him that the thefts have stopped.'

Alison truly hoped that this would be the end of it.

CHAPTER TWENTY-FOUR

It wasn't nearly as easy to persuade Tony and Colin to let the matter drop for the time being. Colin was still unaware of exactly who the culprit was – Tony was keeping that quiet not wanting to make things too awkward for Eliza to continue working at the hospital, but Colin clearly thought it was Dr Atkinson, using someone else's pass and that it had to be someone quite senior in order to have access. They both understood her reasoning that now was not the time for another scandal, and reluctantly agreed to wait and see what happened going forward. They would leave the camera in situ, she agreed, and Tony had a copy of the camera footage so that action could be taken should any more drugs go missing.

Alison's other problem was that she had come to rely on Eliza, but now she felt that she should try and distance herself from the nurse, in case she needed to take action against her further down the line. She knew, only too well, that you shouldn't mix work and friendship.

It had been another long day and Alison's head was throbbing. She decided to check on her patients one last time before heading home.

She was surprised to find Anwar Faez on the ward. He was in the office, sipping an herbal tea and checking medication charts, making sure his junior colleagues had done everything correctly.

'Hello?' Alison said as she came into the office. 'Still here?'

'Just keeping an eye on things,' he replied. 'What about you?'

'Same,' she answered simply and came into the room, pulling up a second chair. 'You heard about the complaint from Mrs Rossi's family, did you?'

'I did, yes. It is unfortunate.'

'To say the least,' Alison agreed, and hesitated before continuing. 'Do you get the feeling that things aren't quite right here sometimes, Anwar?' she asked him.

'Very much so,' he replied, 'but I can't put my finger on what is wrong.'

'Me neither.'

'There's a lot of anger,' he told her. 'Amongst the staff.'

'I know, and I think they have cause to be angry.'

He looked at her, surprised.

'Why do you think that?'

She told him of her suspicions that high-quality equipment was being paid for, but that low-quality equipment was being supplied and that it was possible that patients were dying as a result.

'The overall mortality rate is high but the number of deaths that seem to reference equipment failure are not that many.' She hadn't forgotten that at least one, Mike's mother, hadn't mentioned it when it should have. 'But there has been at least one since I arrived here and one from before that I have heard about,' she told him.

'You must contact NHS Counter-Fraud, if you think that. They will be able to conduct a proper investigation, find out if it is true.' Anwar seemed quite rightly indignant that someone could do such a thing.

'I agree, but this could well be a problem from the past. My predecessor was forced to resign because of, well, let's just say stock irregularities.'

'So that would explain it. But if he has already left, I don't see what the problem is with reporting it.'

'Yes, but while he may have been behind the original fraud, I don't think he could have done it alone. And there are still some pretty strange things going on even though he is no longer here, you agree, don't you?'

Anwar gave that some thought.

'Yes. You are right, but I think many of them can be put down to poor leadership in the past. I am sure you will put them right in time. As to the fraud, perhaps someone from procurement is involved?'

'It seems the most likely place to start. I want to get enough information to prove it though, and I don't want to tip them off beforehand, give them a chance to cover their tracks.'

'Surely if you can get hold of the invoices, you can do that.'

Alison told him of her problems – that someone seemed to be able to hack into her computer, almost at will, and that they changed data and cancelled appointments. 'It feels as though I can no longer trust anything,' she said.

'But then I must help you, Alison.'

'Thank you, Anwar,' she smiled with relief. 'I knew you would be the right person to ask.'

Alison and Anwar sat in the office and discussed the information that was needed in order to build a case to take to the counter-fraud authority. Alison would pursue the details of equipment orders and costings from the finance and estate departments, and make sure she backed it up on data sticks and the cloud rather than just her laptop, and they would both try and get photographs of the actual equipment in use around the hospital. Anwar would also talk to the consultants in charge of each of the medical and surgical departments, to try and get them to make statements about any incidents that had occurred as a result of equipment failure and that could then be investigated.

'You don't think you should go to the chief executive with this?' Anwar queried.

'Absolutely not,' Alison told him vehemently. 'He

already thinks I'm a bit flaky and if I'm right, even if he isn't involved, he won't be able to remain in charge. The scandal would be too big, not to mention the legal cases that will inevitably follow.'

'You think he would stop you investigating because of this?' Anwar was horrified. This was a very alien concept to him, a man who had spent his entire life trying to improve the care of his patients and who would never do anything that could harm them.

'Yes,' Alison said simply. She had far fewer illusions than her friend, 'I am sure he would do his best to cover it up. Which is why this has to be done quietly, Anwar.'

He nodded slowly.

'And what does Ed think about all this?'

'Ed's not here with me, Anwar. He stayed in London.'

'I know but—'

'We're getting divorced.'

Anwar didn't seem to be as shocked by this revelation as she had expected.

'Even I had heard a rumour,' he admitted, sheepishly, 'but I hoped. . .' He shrugged. 'And you haven't seen him at all?'

In that instant, Alison realised that Ed and Anwar must have spoken and that he knew that Ed had come down to ask her to go back to him. In fact, she suspected that the whole thing had been Anwar's idea.

'He came down to see me, as you probably know,' she said, trying to hide her irritation at this. She knew Anwar must have only been trying to help when he spoke to Ed, and she needed to keep him onside. 'But I'm not ready to go back to him yet, and, if I'm honest, I'm not sure I ever will be.'

He patted her hand.

'These things take time.'

'Yes, and I can't think about it with all this on my plate.'

'So.' Anwar stood up decisively. 'We will get this sorted, and I am thinking, that if you are right and the fraud people get the evidence, you might have to leave here. You will make many enemies.'

'I already seem to have plenty of those,' she admitted with a sigh, knowing that he was right. Being known as a whistle-blower might make it impossible to stay at St Margaret's. 'But that doesn't mean I will go back to Ed, Anwar.'

He smiled. He clearly didn't believe her, and she wasn't so sure about it herself.

Why is she still here? Why has she not left with her tail between her legs, branded a bully just like she was before? She seems to be made of Teflon, everything I throw at her she comes bouncing back, interfering and poking her nose into places I don't want her to go. She's a fighter, I'll give her that. It was a close call, I'll have to be more careful, but I need to do something, something that will show her it's not worth staying here. What can I do? It has to be final. She has to do something that means she is summarily dismissed. Then everything can go back to how it was. How I want it. But first, I have another problem to deal with, and it's a hard one.

CHAPTER TWENTY-FIVE

She woke in the night with a start. In her sleep, she had thought she heard a noise outside. Sitting up in bed, listening, she was suddenly aware that the security lights at the front of the cottage had come on. Mike had placed them in strategic positions, front and back, when he changed the locks, once she had permission from the cottage owners. Telling herself it was probably just a cat, or a fox, she shifted Paws, who had no intention of moving from his comfortable spot lying across her legs, and went to the window. Without turning on the light in the bedroom, she moved the curtain out of the way and looked out.

She could see someone was by her car which was parked in its usual place. The person was dressed in dark clothing, with a cap pulled down low and a scarf around the lower part of their face so that it was impossible to identify who it was. The figure seemed to throw something at her car, but she could not see what. Some sort of liquid perhaps?

Grabbing her phone and pulling on a robe, she raced down the stairs. At the front door, she hesitated. She wasn't sure what she should do. She didn't really want to go outside. Should she leave it until morning? That would be the sensible thing to do, she told herself, but she knew she wouldn't be able to go back to sleep if she left it. Perhaps she should go out and see what had happened? The lights had gone off now, so she looked out of the window next to the door. It was hard to see anything in the darkness, and she couldn't be sure someone wasn't still there, hiding, and keeping still so as to not trigger the security lights. In the end, knowing that she would be unable to sleep if she didn't check, Alison pulled the robe tightly round her and went out to inspect her car and see if there was any damage to it.

As she walked across the gravel driveway towards her car, she was acutely aware of the crunch of her footsteps. Try as she might, it was impossible to walk silently on gravel. With a start, she realised that it was this noise that had woken her. When she got closer to the car and the security lights had come back on thanks to her presence, Alison could see that there was some sort of liquid on the bonnet. She went to touch it but pulled her hand back when she noticed that the paint underneath was bubbling. It must be some sort of acid, she realised. She went quickly back inside to ring the police.

* * *

It was a long night, sitting in the living room, with a very disgruntled Paws on her lap while she waited for the police to arrive. Dawn was breaking and she had drunk several cups of tea by the time they were there. They looked at the car and the footage from her video doorbell and asked her if she knew who might have done this. She once again told them about Richard Atkinson and asked if anyone had been to see him following the last attack on her. They didn't know but promised to let DC Cresswell know and took a copy of the footage away with them.

Alison sighed as she saw them out and decided that as it was too late to go back to bed, she should get dressed. She would have to leave her car, again, so she called for a taxi. She was just waiting for it to arrive when DC Cresswell swung in through the gates and parked next to the car. She got out and went straight to look at the damage.

'Good morning. I'm afraid I'm expecting a taxi to take me to work any minute,' Alison explained.

'That's okay, I just wanted to take a look, if you don't mind. I saw the footage you sent in with my colleagues.'

'Good, you just carry on.' Alison grabbed Paws who was trying to make an escape, and put him back inside before closing the door quickly. She was still keeping him locked in, frightened that he would not survive another poison attack, and he was still objecting strongly to this imposition. When she turned back, DC Cresswell was photographing the damage to the car and Mike was standing next to her, clothes dishevelled, his brown, curly hair standing on end and his face looking like thunder. Alison walked over to join them both.

The damage to the car looked worse in the morning light. The paint had blistered and dulled over quite a large area.

'Have you been to see him then?' Mike asked the policewoman belligerently.

'Not yet, no,' she admitted. 'But I'm going to.' Having taken her photographs, DC Cresswell nodded to Alison and took her leave, before Mike could have a go at her.

'Bloody useless,' Mike said as he watched her back out of the driveway.

'How did you know about this?' Alison asked him, waving at her car.

'Can't keep things quiet round here, it's the talk of the shop.'

Alison shuddered; she hated the thought that she was the main topic of local gossip.

'Can I show you the footage from the camera?' she said to him. 'See if you think it's Atkinson? I've seen him around here and at the hospital a couple of times but other than that, I've only seen a photo, and just a head shot at that. You probably know him better.' She didn't want to tell him about the time she had thought Atkinson was following her, or elaborate on the times she had seen him at the hospital as Mike was already wound up about him.

'Yes, of course.' He looked down at her phone as she played it for him. 'I don't know,' Mike said, shaking his head. 'It could be him, I suppose, he's quite tall and thin, but it's hard to be sure. You get the feeling it's someone younger than him, somehow, from the way they move.'

'That's my feeling as well,' Alison answered.

Mike thought about that for a moment.

'He was always quite fit, but he looks older now, since well, since his wife left. He used to be quite smart too, but now he looks a bit grubby, if you know what I mean.'

'Yes.' Alison remembered how she had wondered if he was a down-and-out when she first saw him, and he certainly hadn't seemed to move easily, like the person in the video.

'You shouldn't have gone rushing out like that though,' he said. 'Even if it is Atkinson, he could have hurt you.'

'I don't think he would, I mean, it's just vandalism.' She was trying to convince herself as much as Mike.

'Poisoning the cat wasn't vandalism and he could have chucked any acid left over at you.'

He was right, she thought. She shouldn't have rushed out, and she shivered as she thought about what the acid could have done to her skin if that had happened. Mike moved closer, a pained expression on his face.

'Promise me you won't do anything that risky again,' he said.

'I did wait until the security lights had gone out,' she told him, but knew that could just mean whoever had been there was lying in wait. 'But you're right, I should have waited.'

'Or called me.'

He was standing so close, she could have reached out and touched him, and she wanted to, wanted him to hold her. She had never been a woman who wanted to be protected, to feel safe, but then, she had never been threatened in quite this way. She reached out to him, but then had second thoughts and drew back, frightened by the intensity of her feelings.

'I can't drive it like that,' she said.

Was it her imagination or did he look disappointed?

'I can drive it to my workshop and get it cleaned up, if you want,' Mike suggested, in a slightly thick voice. 'You'll need a respray though.'

'Whatever you need to do, Mike, and thank you for coming around, it's really kind of you. I don't know what I'd have done without you.'

'No problem,' he replied and once more took a step towards her. 'I worry about you, you know.'

'That makes two of us,' she said and attempted a smile, and lifted her head as he bent forward to kiss her. She closed her eyes, ready to feel his lips on hers but jumped back when there was a loud crunch on the gravel driveway as the taxi arrived.

The driver got out and came over to the car.

'That's not nice,' he said, shaking his head and looking at the damage.

'No, it isn't,' Alison agreed, unable to keep the irritation out of her voice. Having grabbed her bag from the hallway and checked the door was firmly shut, she walked towards the taxi, before pausing. 'Thanks Mike. I really appreciate all your help.'

'No problem,' he said. 'I'll see you tonight.'

'Yes, I'd like that.' She nodded and got in the taxi. Trying not to think too much about Mike and the near kiss, she focused on Dr Atkinson instead. It seemed from what Mike said that he was going downhill, and not just because his wife had left him either, she thought. He was getting deeper into his addiction with no one there to stop him. Without work to keep him at a still functioning level either, he would continue to get worse. Particularly as Eliza had been helping to keep him stocked up with drugs. Well, that was going to change rapidly now she could no longer do that. He was going to need to go cold turkey, or find an alternate source of drugs and Alison knew, as Richard Atkinson would too, that there were risks attached to that. He'd been getting a definite, measured and tested strength of clean drugs, but anything purchased illegally would be of unknown strength and quality and might well have contaminants added. She could only hope he would take the removal of his comparatively safe source as the impetus to give up altogether, but having known and worked with a number of addicts over the years, functioning and chaotic alike, she knew they were rarely successful in getting clean. She had no illusions about it at all.

She thought about it all the way into the hospital, shutting out the endless stream of chit-chat from the taxi driver, but the more she thought about it, the more she feared there might be some awful climax to Dr Atkinson's drug addiction. One last act of violence towards her, or himself.

CHAPTER TWENTY-SIX

'Ah, Alison,' Dr Faez said as soon as she came onto the ward. He ushered her into the office and closed the door. 'I have put together all the photographs of defibrillators that you sent me with the ones that I photographed,' he told her as he rapidly opened a file on his laptop. 'Here.' He turned it around so she could see. 'I think we have them all between us. And I printed out the list of all defibs bought by the trust in the last five years from the procurement file. All top of the range models you see.'

'And where are they located?' she asked.

'You tell me. They are not in any of the locations we have found, and some of these,' he indicated the photographs, 'are supposedly quite new, but I think they are refurbished models.'

'Second-hand?' Alison was horrified.

'It isn't that uncommon, some firms specialise in supplying refurbished equipment.'

'But not when the hospital has paid for new.'

'No,' he agreed.

Alison looked at the evidence in front of her.

'Can you send it to my personal email, Anwar? I think I have enough here to take this to counter-fraud.'

He did it straight away.

'Done,' he said, 'and I've copied it onto a data stick for you.' He handed a flash drive to her just as Joyce knocked on the door and opened it.

'Can I talk to you about a patient, Dr Faez?' she said. 'If you have a moment.'

'Of course,' Anwar said, and once he had checked Alison had everything she needed, he hurried out after her.

Up in her office, Alison found a pile of old notes that she had requested. She had trawled through the mortality data for the last six months and requested the notes of any patient where she felt the causes of death listed suggested they had died unexpectedly. The lead anaesthetist had given her three names of people whose resuscitation had failed, including Mike's mother and Mr Andrews, and she had added Mrs Rossi to the list. Mr Andrews and Mrs Rossi both had electronic records as they had been patients after the hospital changed over to a paperless system. Alison couldn't help remembering that Mrs Rossi had wanted to speak to her but that she had never got around to finding out what her patient wanted to tell her. It was too late now, but it still made Alison feel guilty that she hadn't found out what was worrying her.

There were three boxes of notes, and with a sigh, Alison started going through them, making her own notes on a pad, rather than her laptop as she read.

It was getting dark by the time she had finished, but she had whittled her list down to five patients. The three from the anaesthetist, Mrs Rossi and one more.

Two were failed resuscitations before she had started at the hospital. One, the first on her list, had been a patient in cardiology. He had probably had a second heart attack. His arteries were certainly badly affected, according to his post-mortem but there was no definite cause of death and he had two stents inserted that seemed to be working well. The anaesthetist had included him because the defibrillator had failed. The new patient she had found was a member of staff as well as a patient. Dennis Oldham had been a porter at St Margaret's for many years, but had been taken unwell while at work and seen in A&E. The notes suggested that he probably had simple gastroenteritis, but then he collapsed and died. Attempts at resuscitation had failed. A subsequent PM had not found any clear cause of death, but he had some signs of heart disease, so that was put down as the primary reason he had died.

She was interested to see that in the cases of Mike's mother and Mr Andrews, there was no clear evidence either. In each case, heart disease was cited as the primary cause, but to Alison's mind there was nothing much to back it up. She went to Mrs Rossi's notes, and wasn't surprised to see that no PM had been done yet. Armed with the details of the five patients, she checked her watch and hurried out. If she was quick, she just might catch the pathologist still at work.

She went down the back stairs two at a time and out of the main hospital building. The pathology department was in a separate building across the car park and as she walked towards it, she felt as if someone was watching. Unnerved, she turned around quickly, but couldn't see anyone nearby. She looked up at the main building. There were so many windows, and many had blinds or curtains, so she could have no way of knowing if anyone was watching her from there. Her eyes went higher and there was a flash of movement on the roof. She stared harder, but it was hard to see, the bright lights of the hospital put the roof in deep shadow. Had someone really been watching her? Heart beating fast, she hurried on towards the lights of the pathology building. She wanted to be somewhere with people round her, which was ridiculous: why would anyone be watching her here? She quickly looked around the car park, but Dr Atkinson's car was nowhere that she could see. With a shake of her head, she walked briskly on. It was probably someone who had gone up to the roof for a sneaky cigarette and was worried she had seen them. There was no point going up to the roof to check, whoever it was would be long gone.

Alison found the chief pathologist in his office, fiddling with an elaborate coffee machine, he obviously took his caffeine seriously.

'Dr Martens? I'm Alison Wilson, the new medical director.'

'Yes, of course, I wondered when you would get round to visiting us here. Do take a seat.'

'I'm so sorry to drop by unannounced like this,' she said as she sat down.

'Not at all, visitors are always welcome here. Coffee?' He indicated the machine.

'Thank you, yes, just an espresso, black.'

'Oh, very good.' He seemed pleased with her choice and Alison hoped it wasn't too strong or she would never get to sleep.

As he fussed with his coffee machine, it gave Alison the chance to assess him, and the office. He was in his mid-to-late forties, hair disappearing fast but he looked as if he kept fit. His hands reminded her of Ed's, long and slim with well-manicured nails, and in complete contrast to Mike's battle-scarred, grease-stained fingers. She smiled as she thought of Mike and his good honest, working-man's hands, Ed would have been surprised, and even horrified, that she found them attractive. It was a moment or two before she realised that the pathologist had spoken to her.

'I'm so sorry? I was miles away,' she explained.

'I just asked if you took sugar, Dr Wilson?'

'No, thank you, and do call me Alison.'

'Then I am Malcolm,' he said.

Alison smiled her agreement.

'Now,' he said once they were both settled with their drinks. 'What can I do for you?'

'I wanted to ask you about the mortality rate here at St Margaret's and also about some specific deaths that I am concerned about.'

'Concerned? In what way?' he asked.

'There have been several deaths, three for certain, and, having spoken with some of my colleagues possibly two more in the last six months, where the feeling is that they were unexpected to say the least. I have pulled the records for those that were here when the hospital still used paper records.' She placed the folders on the desk. 'These are cases that people were able to tell me about, and I have the details of the more recent ones here so that you can look up their electronic files.' She pointed to a note clipped on the front of the top file. 'There was a post-mortem in each of these cases, apart from the most recent, Mrs Rossi. Do you know when you will be doing her PM?'

'Mrs Rossi?' Malcolm checked on his computer. 'No, I thought not. No PM was ordered for Mrs Rossi.'

'No PM?'

'No, it was requested originally but overruled.'

'By whom?'

He looked at his computer again and hesitated, then cleared his throat before answering. 'Yourself, Dr Wilson.'

He turned the computer so that she could see her name and code were next to the action.

Deciding that now was not the time to tell him about her mysterious hacker, she moved on.

'Has a death certificate been issued?' she asked.

'Yes.' He peered at the screen. 'By a Dr Bayliss. Cause of death is down as cerebrovascular accident, no further details.'

Cerebrovascular accident, or stroke, was, Alison had to admit, the most likely cause of death and an acceptable answer, but a post-mortem would have made sure of that. While Alison might have liked there to have been a PM, just to be sure why Mrs Rossi had died, Dr Bayliss would want the death tidied away with as little fuss as possible given that he might be partly to blame, and she knew that Hargreaves would agree with that. But had either of them used her code to overrule the PM decision? Or someone else entirely and if so, why?

'And if I were to say I had changed my mind and asked you to do a PM?' she tentatively asked, knowing that she was unlikely to be successful.

'The body has already been moved to the undertaker's, so . . .' He shrugged his shoulders and she understood what he was telling her. It would cause a great deal of work to try and get the body back from the funeral director's, and Malcolm wasn't keen to do that. Not without a very good reason. 'And the process of embalming might already have begun which would complicate matters further.' He pressed home his point. Malcolm was not going to try and retrieve Mrs Rossi's body, not unless she was absolutely certain there was something to find, her hunch that there was something wrong with Mrs Rossi's death was not enough.

'Well,' she said decisively. 'Can I ask you to look at the rest of the cases? See if you have any concerns about their deaths? Anything out of the ordinary?'

'Of course.' He nodded as she stood up, but Alison had no great belief that he would do as she asked. After all, if he did find a problem with any of them, the person who would be blamed would be himself, for missing it in the first place.

As Alison walked towards her car, thinking about the deaths and feeling guilty about not speaking to Mrs Rossi before she died, she couldn't resist looking up at the roof. It seemed empty now and she didn't feel as if she was being watched. It must have been her imagination.

She went to the spot where she usually parked her car.

'Damn!' she exclaimed.

'Got a problem?'

Alison turned and saw Eliza.

'I stupidly forgot I didn't bring my car with me this morning, I'll have to call for a taxi,' Alison told her, with a rueful smile.

'I can give you a lift,' Eliza told her.

'Oh no, I couldn't put you to all that trouble,' Alison replied. 'I know you don't live in my direction.'

'It's not out of my way at all. I'm going to see Richard, see how he's getting on. I've got some information about rehab centres I wanted to give him, so I'm going quite close to where you live. Come on.' And she hurried over to a small hatchback, with Alison following. It would save having to wait for a taxi, after all, and give her a chance to talk to the chief nurse about her predecessor.

It wasn't a long drive back to her home, so Alison launched into her questions a little abruptly, partly to distract herself from the speed at which the nurse was driving.

'Do you know where I live?'

'Richard's old house, isn't it?'

Of course, Eliza would know that if she was still in touch with Dr Atkinson.

'Yes, I believe it is. I didn't know that when I first rented it, of course.'

'He was gutted when he had to move out after the divorce.'

'I'm sure he was, it's a lovely cottage.' Alison just hoped they got there in one piece. 'Did Richard ever confide any concerns about the hospital metrics to you?'

'All the time, he was desperate to improve them, but nothing seemed to work. He was always pleading for extra staff, but that wasn't going to happen, not with the hospital's financial situation.'

Alison held onto the grab handle as they rounded a corner a little faster than she would have liked.

'What about the mortality rate?'

'I don't think he ever mentioned that,' Eliza said thoughtfully as she braked sharply when a car pulled out of a side-turning in front of them. Alison braced herself against the dashboard, mentally telling herself not to accept lifts from the chief nurse in the future.

'Is it worryingly high?' Eliza asked.

'I think so. It's certainly higher than it should be, mainly due to some sudden and unexplained deaths that I want to take a closer look at, see if I can find a pattern. Oh!' Alison almost swore as Eliza turned into her driveway without braking and sprayed gravel onto the lawn as she did an emergency stop. Thank goodness Paws was safely inside the house, and Alison's car was obviously still at Mike's garage, or they would have collided with one or both of them.

'Thank you so much for the lift, Eliza,' Alison said breathlessly as she hurriedly climbed out of the car. As she bent down to pick up her tote bag, she saw Eliza grinning.

'Sorry, everyone always tells me that my driving is appalling, but I do like to go fast.'

'That's okay. It's good of you to have given me a lift, and I hope you manage to persuade Dr Atkinson to take up your suggestion.' Eliza looked confused for a moment. 'Of rehab,' Alison clarified.

'Oh, yes, well he doesn't have a lot of choice now I'm not helping with his supply.'

'And you won't let him badger you into doing it again, will you?'

'Absolutely not.' Eliza looked her straight in the eye as she said this, making Alison believe it was true. 'I promise.'

Alison nodded and walked towards her front door as Eliza reversed out of the drive, with another spray of gravel onto the lawn and a squeal of her tyres once she hit the tarmac road.

Alison was making herself a cup of tea, when she heard the sound of car tyres on her gravel driveway again. She really didn't need the alert on her phone, but it was reassuring to hear it go and know that she would be warned even if she was asleep. Looking out of the living room window, she could see her own car was back and Mike was getting out of the driver's seat.

'Oh, wow,' she said as she came over and inspected the car, 'you would never know it had been resprayed. That's amazing!'

And it was true, there really was nothing to show that the paintwork had ever been damaged.

'It was really only the bonnet and a couple of splashes on the driver's door, so it didn't take as long as I expected.'

'Well, I am very pleased, thank you.'

'Let's just hope no one decides to do anything else,' he said, bringing her back down to earth with a bump.

'Yes, I worry about that too.' She shook her head to dispel such an unpleasant thought. 'It's a relief to have it back too, I really need this car for work. I had to rely on a lift home from the chief nurse this evening, and I really don't want to repeat that. She drives like a demon.'

Mike frowned his disapproval and she sighed.

'I know you have concerns about the hospital, and so do I, but she's a good person and an extremely good nurse.'

He didn't look convinced.

'Look why don't you stay for something to eat? I warn you I'm not the best of cooks, but I threw a few things in the slow cooker before I left this morning and I'm hoping it's magically turned into something edible.'

'How could I refuse an offer like that?' he said with the slow smile that made her stomach flip. She turned away quickly hoping he hadn't seen the expression on her face and went inside, leaving him to follow her.

Alison and Mike were both pleasantly surprised at just how well the stew had actually turned out, with Mike even having second helpings.

'That was great,' he told her once he had finally finished eating. 'Maybe I'll have to get myself one of those things.' He waved in the direction of the slow cooker.

'Do you normally cook for yourself?' she asked, knowing first-hand how hard it was working up the enthusiasm to cook for one.

'Yes, but I'm really only a short-order cook, you know, eggs, bacon, steak, fast food basically.'

'And don't think I haven't noted the lack of vegetables in that mix,' she teased.

'Baked beans, tinned tomatoes,' he grinned. 'You'll have to give me the recipe for that stew.'

'Recipe? As if,' she replied. 'Like I said, I just chucked the meat and veg in, added some water and a packet sauce mix and switched it on. Comes out differently every time I do it. This was one of the better ones, but believe me, I am not a good cook.'

He laughed and helped clear the table.

'I've been thinking about the things that have happened,' he continued as he loaded their plates in the dishwasher and she filled the kettle. 'Have you heard back from the police at all?'

'That DC Cresswell, you know, the detective that was here before, well, she called me earlier and said that they had been to Dr Atkinson's and spoken to him but that he had denied it all, apart from perhaps a bit of bad-mouthing around the locality and was very upset when she mentioned what happened to Paws and said he would never hurt a cat.'

'Well, he would say that, wouldn't he?'

'Exactly.' She handed him a mug of tea and led the way through to the sitting room. 'And her going to see him has probably only made matters worse. God knows what he'll do next, I've a good mind to go around and have a go at him myself.'

'I really don't think that would be a good idea,' Mike sounded genuinely concerned that she might.

'It's all right, I know that.' She smiled and then, after a

moment of hesitation, added: 'and neither would it be a good idea for you to go, Mike,' she told him. 'I saw that look on your face. This is my problem and you've already done so much with the lights, locks, doorbells and fixing my car every time it gets trashed.'

'All right,' Mike nodded, 'so long as you promise me that you won't go rushing outside if you hear any noises in the night again. Just call me. I can be round here faster than the police.'

'It's a deal,' she agreed.

He put down his mug and stood up.

'I should. . . go,' he said. 'Let you get on.'

'You don't need to go just yet, do you?' She stood as well and touched his arm. He turned and she leant towards him, head tilted up, hoping that he would make a move and disappointed when he didn't. He just stood there, so close she could smell him and then turned abruptly.

'I have to go,' he said huskily and went out of the front door, leaving her standing there, feeling foolish and more than a little surprised. She was relieved that she hadn't asked him to stay as she felt it was too early in their budding relationship, comforting though it would be to have him there. However, she had hoped that he might have made a move to at least kiss her goodnight and she had made her wishes pretty clear, she knew. Perhaps she had misread his signals?

'Ah well, Paws, it looks like it's just you and me then,' she told the cat as she settled back on the sofa and flicked through the TV channels before giving up and reaching for her laptop.

Going through the notes she had made about the various deaths again, she was sure that something untoward had happened with all of these patients that had been identified by her colleagues. Why did these patients suddenly deteriorate? None of the ones who had had a post-mortem had shown any evidence of a sudden heart attack or stroke, and yet they had all had cardiac arrests and then not been successfully resuscitated. While the not infrequent equipment failures must add to the numbers who died, it didn't fully explain it.

There were no two ways about it, she was going to have to go to the chief exec and lay her suspicions in front of him at some point if she was going to ensure new, better defibrillators were bought and distributed as quickly as possible throughout the hospital, before someone else died. But she also needed to be sure that he wouldn't block further investigation by NHS Counter-Fraud and the only way to do that, was to send the information she had uncovered to them first, as she had explained to Anwar. But if they contacted Hargreaves to verify the situation, was it fair on him that he didn't know what had been going on? After all, he hadn't even been at the hospital when all this must have started, some of the defibs had been bought years ago. The arguments in her head went back and forth. Should she tell Hargreaves first? Or the fraud team? In the end, she decided the only course of action was to let them both know at once, so she sent all her data to the fraud team and then, before she changed her mind, she sent an email to Hargreaves, asking for an urgent meeting and telling him that she was concerned that while top-of-the-range defibs were apparently being purchased, only cheap and unreliable ones were actually being supplied.

And she pressed send. That would put the cat amongst the pigeons if nothing else, she thought as she smiled at Paws, who was peacefully asleep by her side.

Killing him was hard, the hardest thing I have ever done. But he was weak, he would have destroyed me if he had gone to the police. It's time to finish it, make sure she is out of the way. She has got far too close for comfort. I saw her going to pathology and I can't risk her taking her evidence to the chief exec, not when he still believes in her despite all my hard work to undermine her. I can't go back to her home, not with all the security she's put in, but I have to do something. It has to end tomorrow. And tonight? Tonight I had to make sure there were no loose ends. I had no choice. She made sure I had no choice. I surprised myself with my tears. After all, what's one more death when you think of it? I never cried or shed a single tear for any of the others.

It's time to say goodbye Dr Wilson, and good riddance!

CHAPTER TWENTY-SEVEN

Alison was surprised to be met at the door to the senior admin corridor by Tony Grant.

'Mr Hargreaves asked me to take you straight to his office,' Tony explained as he opened the door and walked with her towards the chief exec's office.

'Can I at least put my things in my office?' Alison asked.

'No,' he replied before adding, 'I'm sorry, Dr Wilson.'

Alison couldn't imagine why she wasn't being allowed to go to her office. This urgent meeting had to be about her email about the fraud, hadn't it?

'What's this about, do you know?'

Tony didn't answer and Alison would have liked to ask more, but they had arrived at Hargreaves' office door, and Tony knocked.

'Come in,' Hargreaves called and Alison was disturbed

to note that Tony stayed standing by the door as if she were likely to run away. Inside, Selby was standing next to his boss, hands behind his back and looking serious.

'Good morning,' Alison said trying not to show her anxiety. 'Is this about the email I sent last night? About the fraud?'

'Sit down, Dr Wilson.' Hargreaves ignored her questions.

Alison sat down.

'It has come to my attention that you have altered the hospital figures in the central collection database.'

'I beg your pardon? I have done no such thing!' Alison was appalled. 'I don't interfere with that at all! I simply download what is on there so that I can see where we are.'

'And yet, the figures have been changed and IT say that it was done by you, late last night, or rather in the early hours of the morning. They are able to track who does what, you know.'

'Of course, I know that. Can I ask who alerted you to the changes I am supposed to have made?'

Hargreaves looked at Selby.

'And who told you?' she asked Selby.

'I am not at liberty to say,' he replied stiffly. Alison turned back to Hargreaves.

'Did you receive the email I sent last night about the fraud I have uncovered?'

'Yes, despite your attempt to recall the email, I saw it.'

'I didn't try and recall it. There have been a number of instances where my computer access has been used, I have reported it to IT—'

'And they have repeatedly told you that it is you who has done these things, Dr Wilson, no one else, and Jonathan here tells me it's not the first time you have tampered with the data, your first senior team report was also . . . *inaccurate*.' He looked as if he had a nasty taste in his mouth as he said this.

'But not this time!' She wished she could take that outburst back, because it was as good as admitting she had been guilty the first time, which she was but. . . 'I promise you, someone is logging in as me and—'

'And why would they do that?' Selby asked, unable to keep a smirk from his face.

'To get me out of the way, to stop me from investigating the fraud.'

'And as for that, I would strongly advise you against contacting the fraud agency until after I have had a chance to look into these wild accusations.'

As Alison had predicted to Anwar, Hargreaves wanted to keep it quiet.

'I have already reported it to them, Mr Hargreaves, and sent them the evidence, which I am happy to show you, if you would like.'

Both Hargreaves and Selby stared at her.

'How dare you, Dr Wilson!' Hargreaves was shaking with anger and Selby was looking like a rabbit caught in the headlights. 'How dare you go to outside agencies before coming to me.'

'I'm sorry, but I wanted to be sure you didn't try and stop me from doing the right thing.'

'The right thing?'

If Hargreaves had been angry before, he was absolutely livid now. Selby looked concerned and hurriedly fetched him a glass of water.

Hargreaves took a deep and calming breath and they were all relieved to see his colour return to almost normal as he got himself under control.

'This is just a pathetic attempt to put the blame on others and distract from your own crimes, Dr Wilson,' Hargreaves said with a shake of his head. 'Accept that you have been caught and suspended for gross misconduct.' Hargreaves stood. 'I am sorry, but that is the end of the matter as far as I am concerned. You will want to get legal representation before any further action is taken, but I will be recommending your immediate dismissal to the board. Now, Mr Grant will take you to your office to collect your personal possessions and see you off the premises.'

'But this isn't right! I didn't—'

But Hargreaves wasn't listening. He gestured towards Tony at the door and Alison knew there was little point continuing the conversation. She followed the head of security out of the office, shell-shocked by what had just happened.

She walked with Tony through reception to her own corridor, acutely aware of Mary watching her as she walked into her own office. She opened the door and put her tote bag down on the desk.

'I will need your laptop and security pass,' Tony told her gravely.

Alison took the laptop out of her bag and handed it to him, still unable to process what was happening. She sat down at her desk.

'What on earth is going on?' she asked him, 'I never altered the figures on the database, and it isn't my imagination that someone is deleting emails and meetings.'

Tony shrugged.

'Look, if IT says it was you—'

'No, IT say it was someone logged on as me, there's a difference.'

'But how could someone do that? I presume you changed your password?'

'Yes, pretty much daily once I realised what was going on.'

She saw Tony look at his watch and realised he needed her to get a move on. So she quickly went through the drawers, removing all her personal items and putting them in her bag. In the top drawer, she saw a data stick, the stick she had copied some of the hospital data onto, when she was worried about things going missing. The data stick was hospital property, as was the data, but she bundled it up with few items of make-up and the hairbrush she kept in the drawer and put it in her bag, relieved that Tony didn't notice.

'Right,' she said, 'that's everything.' She removed the lanyard with her ID card from around her neck and handed it to Tony. He took it and opened the door for her to go out. As she did so, she paused and touched the sign on the door saying: *Dr Alsion Wilson, Medical Director*. Perhaps the sign writers were right and she had never really belonged here.

CHAPTER TWENTY-EIGHT

If Paws was surprised to see her back from work so early, he hid it well and got busy winding himself around her legs in the hope that it might be feeding time again. She bent down and stroked him, trying to think what she should do. She was tempted to resort to a glass of wine and a good cry despite it being only ten in the morning. She could hardly remember the drive home she had been so distressed and she hoped she hadn't upset too many other drivers. But she knew neither wine nor tears would help, she had tried them in the past and they had only made matters worse. This time, she knew she had to do something. Action was the only thing that would make her feel better. She went upstairs and fetched her personal laptop and took it into the kitchen. She sat at the table, mug of coffee by her side, and set to work. She had to find out what was really going on at St Margaret's.

First, she transferred the data from the stick she had taken from her office onto her personal laptop, an action that was very much not allowed. IT regarded home computers and data sticks as a source of viruses, and they were certainly right about that. However, Alison knew she had good anti-virus software and, as she no longer had access to her work computer, she wasn't going to be able to infect them with any viruses, trojan horses or malware. From her previous experience, she knew that her NHS login would have been suspended to stop her from accessing the hospital system, so this would have to do. She was already in trouble so she might as well be hung for a sheep as a lamb, she thought. She wished she had been able to get hold of the data that Hargreaves said she had changed so she could compare things, but she knew she would never be able to now.

Her phone rang and she was tempted to ignore it but then she saw that it was Anwar.

'Hi Anwar,' she said. 'Have you heard the news?'

It seemed that he had and that he was very shocked.

'You have to believe me, Anwar, I didn't alter the data. I've been framed, someone wants to make sure I don't find out any more about what has been going on.'

'I am sure you didn't do anything wrong,' he reassured her and she was surprised at how relieved she was to have someone on her side, even if she wasn't entirely innocent. She cursed herself for changing the data for the first meeting.

'Why exactly did you leave London in such a hurry,

Alison?' he asked then, and she knew that hints must have been dropped that she had been forced out.

'I left because I couldn't stay, Anwar. I had done nothing wrong, I promise you. What have you been told?'

'They have said nothing definite, but at the senior team meeting, it was hinted that you left under a cloud and had perhaps not been honest about it when you were interviewed.'

'That's just not true!'

'Yes, I'm sure, but. . .' He paused and Alison could hear his bleeper go off in the background. She knew he was going to have to answer it.

'I am happy to tell you all about it, explain what happened,' she started. 'Both in London and this morning.' She tried not to sound like she was begging, but she needed him on her side.

'Perhaps we can meet for coffee later in the week, when I have a day off and can see you away from the hospital.'

'Of course, I'd like that.'

'And meanwhile, I'll see if I can find out any more about what has been going on here for you.'

'Look, Anwar, I'm obviously going to do all I can to clear my name, but watch your back, please. If they can do this to me. . .'

'Do not worry about me, Alison. I am retired, remember, I have no career to lose. And don't worry about the ward either, I have everything in hand, you just take care of yourself.'

She knew she could safely leave the ward and her patients in his hands, but looking into the unexplained deaths was different. While she hoped he did manage to find out more to help her, she was desperately worried about him, and about what might happen. She hoped he was careful.

Alison made herself a cup of coffee and went back to her laptop. She had copied the information she'd sent the fraud office onto a data stick, so now she sent it again, using her personal email address, just in case the email had been stopped by the hacker somehow. She had never used her personal email address on her NHS computer, so she hoped it was not compromised. She thought that she ought to find other ways of backing the information up as well, just in case, but didn't want to send it to Anwar as she wanted to keep him out of it as much as possible. In the end, she sent a copy to Ed, asking him to save it. She knew he would have questions about it and she didn't really want to talk to him but she couldn't think of anyone else who she could ask to do this for her. The long hours she had always worked meant that she had neglected friends and family to the extent that there was no one close, apart from Ed. He had always been the only friend she had needed. At least, she had thought that once, and now there was no one else she could ask.

Just as she pressed send, there was a ring at the door. She checked her phone, and could see it was Mike. Despite everything that had happened, she found herself smiling as she opened the door.

'I was just passing and saw your car,' he began apologetically, 'and I thought something must be wrong for you not to be at work.'

'That, Mike Jenkins, is the understatement of the year,' she said wryly, as she let him in.

It was a cold but sunny autumn day, so they sat in the garden with their cups of coffee as she told him about her suspension and all the events so far and he was suitably horrified.

'Someone has been taking money for equipment that doesn't exist? You have to do something about it,' he told her. 'You can't let whoever it is get away with it.'

'Don't worry, I already have,' and she explained about having sent the information to counter-fraud. 'Of course, I've added to the evidence against me by using my private address and using data that I have obviously taken from the hospital without permission, but I reckon that any charges relating to that would be minor compared to what I have shown has been going on at the hospital.'

He stood up and paced as he tried to take in all the facts.

'And this equipment is what is used when someone has a cardiac arrest?'

'That's right.'

'You know that my mum died when the machine used to try and resuscitate her failed.'

'I know, Mike. And I'm sorry.'

He shook his head, trying to think about what she was saying.

'It's unbelievable.'

'I agree it's hard to imagine anyone doing something like this.'

'And it must have been happening for some time, right? I mean, you don't just buy a job lot of defibrillators, you replace them as and when needed.'

'That's right,' she agreed. 'I think it must have started one, or maybe two, years ago. You don't change equipment all that often.'

'Years? It's just. . .' He shook his head again. 'My mother, and others, died because someone's been making money out of ordering high-cost equipment and replacing it with second-rate stuff that breaks down? It's just beyond belief.' He banged the table angrily and the coffee cups rattled.

'I'm sorry, Mike, but it will be hard to prove that any of the deaths are directly attributable to the equipment failures, they had all had cardiac arrests and might have died anyway . . .' She tried to calm Mike down, and wished in some ways that she hadn't told him the details of what she thought had been going on. He was too involved. She watched as he washed his face with his hands and thought about what she had told him.

'Who is doing this, do you know?' he demanded.

'No, I really don't know but I'm hoping the fraud investigators will find out. We have to leave it to them.'

'But someone pretty high up must be involved or

covering it up. Was it Atkinson? Was that why he was sacked?'

'I honestly don't know who it was, Mike, and this had nothing to do with Atkinson leaving.'

'So why did he go, then? He's been telling everyone he was pushed out to make way for you, but he must have done something.'

'Well, the hospital had poor ratings and he was held responsible.'

Mike looked her in the eye, clearly not believing what she had told him.

'There's more to it, isn't there?'

'No, well, I really can't tell you.'

'Can't or won't?'

'I can't, it's confidential.'

'No, you don't get to say things like that to me. My mother died and I want the truth!'

'I understand that, honestly I do, but it doesn't have anything to do with her death. . .' Even as she said this she wondered if it was true and Mike picked up on it.

'Tell me! Please. I have a right to know.'

'Look. . . ' She floundered, unable to lie to him. 'He was caught helping himself to some drugs.'

'What, like morphine?'

'Like that, yes.'

'He took drugs?'

She nodded.

'To sell?'

'I don't think so,' she admitted. 'I think. . . know he has a drug problem.'

'He has a what!' Mike couldn't seem to believe what he was hearing. 'That hospital allowed a drug addict to treat patients? This just gets worse and worse. How long has he been a junkie?'

'I don't know, look Mike, you have to calm down.' She touched his arm, but he didn't notice, he was too angry.

'I've a good mind to go around there and ask him if he is to blame for what happened. He stole from the hospital to fund his drug habit, that's what you think happened, isn't it?'

'No. Like I said, I don't know. Look, don't do anything stupid. I'm doing everything I can to find out what's been going on, but we have to do this through the official channels. Going to see him isn't going to help anyone.' But she was already talking to his back as he rushed out of the house, slamming the door behind him.

'Mike!' she shouted, and wrenched the door open again, but he was already out of sight, and all she could hear was his footsteps pounding their way along the pavement as he ran to confront Atkinson, she presumed. She grabbed her keys and went after him. She owed it to him to stop him from doing anything stupid.

CHAPTER TWENTY-NINE

Alison knew Richard Atkinson's address from his personnel file, but had never actually walked there. She headed in the direction she thought it was and in the end, it wasn't hard to find because Mike was banging on the door and shouting.

'Just come out and talk to me, why don't you?'

'Mike!' she called as she ran up the street, but he didn't hear her and, getting no response from the house, he rattled the door handle and leant on the bell.

There was still no answer, although, to be fair, Alison didn't think she would open the door when someone was shouting and banging on it in such an aggressive way.

'Mike!' she called to him again. She ran up and grabbed his arm just as he was about to bang on the door again. 'Come away! He's not going to answer even if he is there, which I doubt, and if he is, he's probably called the police.'

He shook off her restraining hand, but stopped for a minute, thinking about what she had said and knowing that she was right. He hesitated and then took a deep breath.

'I know, I know, I'm sorry. I just saw red momentarily. To think that, that man, might have killed my mother—'

'Or might not. I should never have told you about my suspicions, I'm sorry.'

'Don't you be sorry. He's targeted you as well! Look at what he's done to your home and car, let alone your career!'

She really didn't want to think about that, or she would end up banging on Dr Atkinson's door and swearing at him as well.

A police patrol car pulled up at that moment and two uniformed constables got out and approached them.

'That's all we need,' Mike muttered, and Alison tended to agree.

'What's going on?' the older, bearded one asked.

'It's all right, officer, we were just leaving,' Alison told him and pulled at Mike's arm to get him to come with her. He reluctantly turned away from the door.

'Just a minute,' the officer said and they stopped, right next to the two constables.

'We got a report of someone trying to break in and threatening the owner of this house,' the younger police officer said, quite aggressively. He seemed to be just itching for one of them to do something that would mean he could arrest them.

'I just wanted to talk to the man that lives here to give him a piece of my mind. I didn't try and break in,' Mike said firmly, a little too firmly for Alison's liking. She really didn't want him to kick off with the police, no matter how understandably upset he was.

'Look, officers, I am very sorry you have been put to this trouble.' She ignored a snort of disapproval from Mike and continued. 'DC Cresswell has been dealing with the harassment I've been getting, and she spoke to Dr Atkinson about it, yesterday, or maybe the day before.'

'Dr Atkinson?' the older, bearded constable asked.

'The man who lives here,' Alison explained. 'Who called you?'

'It was a neighbour who called us.'

'Oh, well, I'm sorry we disturbed them, it's Dr Atkinson who we wanted to speak to.'

'Why do you need to speak to him?'

'Because he's the one harassing her,' Mike said angrily

'Why would he do that?' the younger one interrupted.

'Because, well, it's a long story, but he thinks I took his job, at the hospital, but I didn't.' Alison really didn't want to go into all this with these two police officers, particularly on Dr Atkinson's doorstep.

'You work at the hospital?'

'Yes,' Alison tried to sound convincing. She didn't want to have to explain that she was currently suspended as that was hardly likely to help. 'Look, Dr Atkinson is clearly not in, and we've all calmed down now, so can we go back to my house? It's just down the road there. Glebe Cottage.' She pointed down the road. Her home wasn't quite in sight, but she had been surprised at how close she was. Richard Atkinson hadn't moved far from his old home when he sold the cottage and relocated here.

'And DC Cresswell has been dealing with it?' the older police officer asked.

'That's right.'

'Right, Bobby,' he told his young colleague, 'you accompany these two to their house and get all their details. I'll just check the building, make sure there's been no damage or anything.'

Alison would have preferred the older, more laid back one of the pair to walk back to her cottage with her, and from the look on Mike's face, he agreed, but they were not going to be given the choice.

They said nothing as they walked down the road and turned into Alison's driveway. The policeman stopped and looked at the garage where the remains of the message painted there were still faintly visible.

'Did he do that, then?'

'Yes, I think so, and slashed my tyres, poured paint stripper on my car and poisoned my cat. DC Cresswell went to see him, as I said, but he obviously denied it.'

Once inside the cottage, Alison offered the young man tea, and he declined. Paws came rushing into the kitchen having been asleep upstairs, took one look at the policeman and went and hid under the sofa.

'Your cat's okay now then?' the policeman asked.

'Yes, but still a bit wary of strangers,' she explained but the constable wasn't listening as something came through on his radio.

'Received, over,' he said as he turned and went back through the lounge and out of the front door, pulling it to behind him.

'Let's hope he's being told everything is fine and to leave it at that.' Alison went to the cupboard and took out a wine glass. 'Do you want one?'

Mike shook his head.

'If all was well, the other one would have come here,' he said. 'Something's up.'

Alison thought he was probably right, but she still hoped that the drama was over. She needed to contact her union rep and let them know what had happened. She really didn't need all this hassle right now.

'Sorry,' Mike said as if he could read her mind. 'I've just made things worse.'

'No, don't apologise, I can't tell you how good it is just to have someone who doesn't think I'm paranoid or unhinged.'

She poured herself a glass of wine and took a sip of wine, looking up as the policeman came rushing in.

'Okay, you two, you're to stay here, right? Don't go anywhere,' he said threateningly as he hurried out, slamming the front door behind him.

'That really doesn't sound like good news,' Mike said and sat down.

'No, it doesn't, does it.'

'Perhaps I will have that glass of wine, after all.'

It was a long afternoon as more and more police arrived, all asking questions, not just about that afternoon but where they might have been the night before. Neither had an alibi, as they had both spent the evening, and night alone, although Mike had popped into the pub for an hour. No one would tell them why they needed one either. Mike wanted to get back to his garage, he had work to do, and eventually they let him go. Once he had gone, along with all the police, Alison got on with contacting the Medical Defence Union and outlining the hospital case against her, as best she could. They promised to start the process of finding her representation and requesting information from the hospital.

Between phone calls to lawyers and unions, she heard from Mike. He said there were a lot of cars parked outside Dr Atkinson's house and people in white forensic suits, so it wasn't a complete surprise when he later called to tell her that Dr Atkinson had been found in his house, and that he was dead.

It wasn't much longer before DC Cresswell arrived and interviewed her again, in the presence of a uniformed constable. Alison was asked to give a formal statement of her movements over the past two days, which she did to the best of her ability.

'What happened to Dr Atkinson?' she asked when she had finished.

'We're still investigating,' Cresswell replied. 'Do you know if he had any family? Or friends who might have seen him recently?'

'I think he has an ex-wife, but Eliza would know. Eliza Jones, chief nurse at St Margaret's. I know she visited him sometimes.'

'Recently?' Cresswell asked as she jotted down Eliza's details.

'Two days ago, she gave me a lift home because my car was in the garage and she said she was going to visit him then. When do you think he died?'

'That's for the pathologist to say,' Cresswell told her curtly and Alison nodded her acceptance.

'And when you were there today,' she continued, 'are you sure neither you, nor Mr Jenkins looked through the letterbox?'

'No, we didn't, I'm quite sure. Mike was banging on the door and shouting, but it didn't occur to us to try and see into the house. We only wanted to talk to Dr Atkinson, ask him to stop harassing me,' Alison told her.

Quite what DC Cresswell thought about that, Alison couldn't tell.

'Would we have seen him lying there if we had?' she asked and saw from the expression on Cresswell's face that they would have. Alison sighed. 'Would we have been able to do anything if we had seen him?' Alison closed her eyes and tried to fight back tears, it had been a long and gruelling day, but DC Cresswell didn't know about her other problems and she really didn't want to go into them now.

'Don't beat yourself up about that,' she reassured Alison. 'He was already dead by the time you got there, and had been for some time.'

Alison smiled her gratitude for this small mercy and showed the police officers out.

Once everyone had left, Alison heaved a sigh of relief and thought about what she should do next. She tried to call Eliza to tell her about Dr Atkinson and warn her about the police, but the call went straight through to voicemail, and Alison wasn't sure what she should say in a message. Eliza and the doctor had been good friends, after all, so she just asked the nurse to call her as soon as she could.

Alison kicked off her shoes and sat down on the sofa. It had been quite a day, and all she wanted was for a few moments of peace and quiet, but the chime from her phone warned her that once again someone was approaching her home. With a groan, she sat up and went to the door, relieved to see it was just Mike.

'Have they been to see you about Atkinson?' he asked. 'They seem to think it was probably an overdose.'

'Yes. Well, it's logical, under the circumstances,' she said and sat down again.

He looked at her with concern. 'I was going to suggest going to the pub to eat, but you look too tired for that.'

'Exhausted,' she replied. 'And I'm not hungry, if I'm honest. Also it's been quite a day and I really don't want to face people just yet.' She knew that Atkinson, and by extension herself and most probably Mike, would be the main topics of conversation in the pub and shop and she really didn't want to listen to what was being said.

'Right,' he said and headed for the kitchen. 'Hungry or not, you need to eat.' He set about knocking together an omelette. She followed him and watched as he cooked.

'You're going to regret this,' he warned her as he grated some cheese to mix with the eggs. 'The chef at the pub is way better than me and as you've pointed out before, I don't really do green stuff.'

Alison smiled at this and, realising she had no choice if she wanted to eat healthily, she put together a salad. It felt very natural as they both sat at the table to eat dinner. Alison was surprised to discover that not only was the omelette delicious, but that she was ravenous as well. And she did feel much better for eating. She had, indeed, needed food.

Alison had only used the wood burner a handful of times since she had moved into the cottage because it hadn't really been cold enough, but autumn was in the air and the evening was chilly. So, once they had cleared away their impromptu dinner, Mike lit it. They sat on the sofa and Alison was surprised that Paws even deigned to join them. He had never really taken to Ed and was very definitely Alison's pet, but he seemed happy to accept

Mike's presence. They sat in companionable silence for a while before Mike spoke.

'You must regret ever coming to Wayleigh,' he said.

Alison gave it some thought before answering him.

'No, I don't really,' she told him, 'although I regret the circumstances of my having to come here, of course.'

'Why did you?' he asked. 'Why leave London, your home and your husband?'

So, she told him, all of it. About Ed's affair, Sara's accusation and the deal she made to resign.

'But why did you go if you hadn't threatened her? Why wasn't she the one who had to leave?'

'Because it was my word against hers and I was the one in the position of power, so I was the one deemed the most likely to be at fault.'

'But that's not fair!'

'No, I agree with you. It wasn't fair at all but I really didn't have any choice but to resign.'

Looking back now, she wondered if that was true, that she really hadn't had a choice. Battered by the humiliation of Ed's affair and the problems Sara had made for her at work, had she given in too easily? Accepted that the best option, the only option was for her to leave? Could she have fought it? But what chance was there for her to change anyone's mind if her own husband hadn't believed her?

'But you're not going to do that this time? You're not going to just resign and run away?'

Was that what she had done? Run away?

'No,' she reassured him with a confidence she didn't feel. She knew the advice from the lawyers would be the same as last time, accept the chance to resign, get out with a bit of dignity and find a job somewhere else, maybe even abroad, but this time she wasn't going to do that, this time she was determined to fight.

'Good,' he said simply, and she knew that he really believed her, unlike Ed. She sighed and snuggled into the crook of his arm. It was warm and cosy and it felt right. She looked up at Mike and smiled at him. He smiled back at her, and she thought that he had a lovely smile, a kind smile. She reached up and touched his cheek and he bent his head towards her and kissed her. He pulled his mouth away, and looked at her questioningly, but she didn't want him to stop and, putting her hand behind his head, gently pulled him forward and his lips back onto hers. It was a long time since she had kissed anyone other than Ed, and this was very different. Mike's need was more urgent, more passionate, less clinical in every way and he was breathing hard when they stopped kissing. She wasn't going to run away this time, and, she thought, as she took his hand and led him upstairs, she wasn't going to let him run away either.

CHAPTER THIRTY

The next morning, Alison woke to the noise of someone showering. She sat up, momentarily disorientated as she saw not her bedroom in London, but the cottage. Once she remembered where she was, and who was in the shower, she relaxed. Mike had stayed last night and she couldn't help but smile as she remembered how they had almost run up the stairs, already pulling at their clothes. The sex had been urgent and passionate, the first time. Slower and more satisfying the second. No wonder she had slept so well. She was surprised to see that there was a cup of tea already waiting for her on the bedside table. She sipped the hot drink and went over the events of the night before again. She was still smiling as Mike came in from the bathroom, naked except for the towel he was drying himself with. He came over and leant down to kiss her and she pulled the towel from his hand and dropped it on the floor.

It was a while later that Mike left, eating his toast on his way as he walked swiftly to the garage where he had a car booked in for an early service. Alison made herself more tea, and, having no work to go to herself for what seemed like the first time in many, many years, went back to bed. She lay there, with Paws curled up next to her, a happy cat who was loving the extra snooze time with her.

Despite her anxiety about what would happen at the hospital and what could happen, she was amazed to discover that she was less worried about it than she had been the day before. Even the worst-case scenario of being sacked didn't seem quite so bad, not the end of the world, anyway. She would bounce back, one way or another. No matter what else happened, someone believed her. Mike believed her. But that didn't mean she could just forget about her problems, she needed more than just Mike on her side if she was going to get her job back. That is, if she wanted to get her job back.

At least she had the time now to give it her full attention, to think about everything that had happened and to try and work out who was behind it. She mentally listed the facts that she knew.

Someone had managed to hack into her computer, she was certain of that. There was no other explanation for all the altered data, the changes to her report or the cancelled meetings. Someone seemed to be able to get into her computer files at will. Well, not quite, she corrected herself, there always seemed to be a lag after she changed her passwords, a period when they had to work out the new ones, at least at the beginning.

The time lag between changing her password and someone getting into the system as her seemed to have stopped after the time she had left her laptop in her on-call room.

Suddenly she sat up and Paws mewed his displeasure at the unexpected movement and dug his claws into her thigh.

'Ow! Oh, Sorry,' she said flinching and then gently stroked him back to sleep again as her mind raced.

She knew only too well how small and easily hidden cameras were these days, like the one they had used to catch Eliza trying to steal drugs for Dr Atkinson. What if there was one in her office? So that someone could see when she typed in her password? She had heard that scraping noise when she was in her office late at night, hadn't she? Could that have been someone trying to position the camera so that they could see her typing in the password? Someone watching her from. . . from where? The stationery cupboard next door? That would explain the sounds she heard, the doors that were just closing, everything. Then the scratching noises when she worked alone late at night had stopped and she had not heard them at all recently. Not since she had left her laptop in the on-call room. Something must have happened to it then which made it unnecessary for them to keep watching her, because now they had full access to her laptop. Could someone have done something to it while she was in A&E seeing patients? She knew there was malware that could track keystrokes and even give other users control of the laptop, as if they were her. If that was the case, then they would no longer need to physically see her type in her password.

Alison grabbed her phone and called Tony Grant. To her surprise, he picked up straight away but when she explained what she wanted him to do and why, he was sceptical.

'I'm not sure about this, if I'm honest,' he told her, 'I'm not an expert on that sort of thing, I don't know much about cyber-crime, checking for signs of a hidden camera is more my area. But I'll give it some thought.'

'Thank you, thank you so much, I really don't know who else I can ask, and it might just prove my innocence. So please, please, please check my office for signs that there was a camera and ask IT to take a look at my laptop.'

He only grunted in response and she couldn't blame him for that. She hadn't taken his advice when dealing with Eliza so he already thought she didn't do things by the book, and, in front of Selby and Hargreaves, she had admitted to changing the data once, so why would he believe her when she said the second time it was done by someone else? She wasn't even sure she would believe it herself under the circumstances, if she didn't know that it really wasn't her. All she could do was hope that, against the odds, he decided to do as she asked and looked in her office for evidence of a hidden camera and also managed to get IT to check for malware. He was her last hope to prove her innocence.

There was nothing else Alison could think to do but wait for news. She had so many questions it was frustrating. She wanted to know more about Dr Atkinson's death: was it really an overdose? Suicide? Was she in some way to blame because she had stopped his supply of drugs from the hospital? She desperately wanted to hear from Tony as to whether or not he had found evidence of a hidden camera in her office, or that IT found that there was some kind of software on her computer that shouldn't be there. She wanted to hear from NHS Counter-Fraud as to whether they were investigating her allegations, and she needed to know if someone had been allocated to her case at the MDU so that they could discuss her defence, not only for the gross misconduct charge but also for the bullying complaint from Dr Carrick.

She sat and then stood, made coffee she wouldn't drink, and paced the floor. There was nothing she could do but wait, and she had never been good at doing that.

So, she decided to clean the house from top to bottom, leaving dust-free windowsills and sparkling taps everywhere. She even cleaned out Paws' litter tray, only to watch him climb straight in, circle three times and make it dirty again. She checked her watch for the umpteenth time, but the day stretched out interminably in front of her, so grabbing some shopping bags, she decided she would go to the large supermarket a mile or so away to stock up. A little bit of her was asking, why buy groceries? Was she planning to stay in Wayleigh if she didn't have a job here? Shouldn't she go back to London as Ed had suggested she should? Not for work, there wasn't anywhere that would touch her with a bargepole under the current circumstances, but at least she had friends there and no one would be gossiping about her unlike here. Well, some of them would still be gossiping about her, but not her friends.

She tried to think about them, her friends, but actually when she started to go through the people who came to her house for dinner parties, or drinks, or who she went to see, they were mainly Ed's friends and she couldn't think of one person that she could drop in on and talk to about her current situation apart from Ed, and she really didn't want to go to him. There was no one in London, but here in Wayleigh she had Mike and Eliza. Especially Mike, she thought with a little smile of pleasure. So maybe that told her something, maybe that told her that she was better off staying put in the place where she had at least two friends. After all, she had a contract to stay in the cottage for a minimum of six months and she wouldn't be able to get out of that so she might as well stay here and front out the gossip. She could do that, she told herself. Gossip tended to have a short shelf-life, at least she hoped it did. It wouldn't be too long before someone else's troubles were the main topic of conversation and at least there wouldn't be any more attacks on her property, or Paws, now that Dr Atkinson was dead. Maybe she would even feel able to let her pet outside again. It would certainly be a relief not to have to live with his litter tray.

Before Alison even made it to the door to go to the shops, her phone rang. It was the MDU. She had a depressing video call with her representative. They discussed the case, with Alison doing her best not to sound too paranoid or unhinged, but her story of being hacked and set up was so bizarre that she was sure the lawyer thought she was either lying or severely unwell. They ended the call with the plan to speak again soon, once the lawyer had had a chance to get the case against her from the hospital.

The lawyer had said, probably correctly in Alison's opinion, that she thought the hospital would want to settle without any need to go to a tribunal or a formal disciplinary board, if Alison was agreeable. It wouldn't look good for the board if they had to publicly admit that they appointed a medical director who tried to fiddle the figures, particularly if her defence was that she was set up by someone trying to hide a larger fraud. The lawyer was not pleased to hear that Alison had reported the suspected crime to the authorities already as it would have given them a stronger bargaining tool if she was prepared to drop her evidence against the hospital in return for a settlement. Now it was out of their hands and for that Alison was grateful. She wouldn't have agreed to keep quiet, not with patients' lives potentially on the line.

To the lawyer's mind, the best outcome was for the hospital to accept Alison's resignation with no fault acknowledged on either side. Just like before. She might still be able to get another job – not as a medical director, everyone would know something had gone wrong if she didn't last six months in her previous job – but she might still be able to work as a stroke consultant, somewhere. If she wanted to.

Once the phone call was over, Alison felt thoroughly depressed and craved company more than a shopping trip. She decided to walk to Mike's garage. Perhaps she could make him a cup of coffee while he worked. Leaving Paws asleep on the sofa, she headed off. The route took her past Dr Atkinson's house. The police and crime scene investigators had all left, but there were the remains of some blue and white tape flapping in the breeze. Had she hounded the poor man to his death? Or was someone else responsible? Would she ever know? Alison hurried past, head down.

She hadn't been to Mike's garage before but had driven past it on her way to work, so she knew where it was. The garage building was an afterthought built onto the side of a house that itself looked in urgent need of some care and attention. There was a pile of tyres along one side of the concrete driveway leading to a ramshackle shed and the double garage where Mike worked. The doors were open and inside, one car was parked over the pit, and another was next to it with the bonnet up. There was a radio playing quietly in the background and a fair amount of revving coming from one of the cars. With houses close by on either side of the garage, Alison wondered what they thought about having a commercial garage next door. She would have to ask him if he got a lot of complaints or were people happy with the trade-off of having someone on hand to sort out their car problems.

She was brought back to the present by the clanging of an instrument being dropped. Mike appeared from behind the bonnet, wiping his hands on a rag that was probably dirtier than they were. For someone so fastidious about her own cleanliness and appearance, Alison was surprised to find that she didn't mind Mike's grease-stained hands and work clothes. After all, she knew he scrubbed up well.

'Hello,' she said and he looked surprised to see her.

'Is everything okay?' he asked, suddenly concerned.

'As well as can be expected,' she answered with a grimace. 'I just thought I'd come and see if you had time for a coffee break.'

'Of course,' he smiled.

He led her into the house and Alison was surprised to find it clean and almost obsessively tidy, although, she was pretty sure no one had decorated since the house had been built in the Seventies. There were orange and brown swirls on carpets, curtains and wallpaper and the kitchen cabinets were a yellow ochre colour that reminded her of the contents of baby's nappies. She was willing to bet there was an avocado bathroom suite somewhere in the house.

Mike was busy washing his hands but turned to see her looking at the décor.

'It was my parents' house,' he explained. 'They bought it new and never really changed anything. Well, Dad was too busy with the garage, and Mum worked in the shop and did the books and that, and then, long after they had given up hope, I came along.'

He went to the fridge and opened it.

'I'd offer you coffee, but I've no milk, I don't suppose you could take it black, just this once.'

'Don't worry, I've probably had enough caffeine for today, but don't let me stop you.'

He looked relieved and filled the kettle.

'So, you've always lived here?' she asked. Somehow that didn't fit with what she knew of him. He was at home here, yes, but he also had an independence about him that suggested he hadn't always lived with his parents.

'No, I joined the navy when I was eighteen, trained as a mechanic, travelled the world, and didn't come back until a few years ago when Dad died. Mum needed looking after and the garage was still here.'

'That must have been hard.' She meant it must have been hard to give everything up and come back, but he chose to deliberately misunderstand her.

'Dad was still working on cars up to the day he died, so it was easy to just slot in where he left off. And then Mum died.'

'And now?'

'And now, I don't know. There's enough work now, there's a lot of old cars around here but they or their owners will die eventually and I can't service all these new cars without specialist equipment, so eventually a lot of the work will dry up,' he seemed resigned to the fact.

'What will you do?'

He shrugged.

'I could sell up, or. . .' He looked up and grinned. 'Or I could turn the house into a museum of the swinging Seventies, a sort of time capsule.'

She laughed.

'Please tell me you've got an avocado bathroom suite,' she said.

'Worse,' he replied with smile. 'Chocolate brown.'

They laughed, and Alison realised that, despite everything that was going on in her life, she hadn't felt this relaxed and happy in a long, long time.

CHAPTER THIRTY-ONE

Alison was pleased to see when she got back home again that DC Cresswell was parked in her usual spot on the driveway, patiently waiting in her car for Alison to return.

'Hello,' Alison said as she unlocked the door and let the police officer into the cottage. 'How can I help you?'

'I wanted to give you an update on Dr Atkinson.'

'That's good of you to come in person.' Alison was surprised, she hadn't thought the police would be so thoughtful. 'Would you like a coffee? Or tea?'

As Alison busied herself preparing the tea, DC Cresswell sat at the kitchen table.

'Do you know how he died yet?' Alison asked. 'Or when?'

'Not exactly and no. We don't have the toxicology back yet, but it looks like an overdose sometime during the night before he was found.'

Alison stopped what she was doing and looked at the police officer.

'I did wonder about that.'

'You knew he was a user?'

'It's why he was made to resign. He'd been stealing controlled drugs from the hospital for some time apparently.' Alison knew the hospital would not like her revealing that to the police, but the time to worry about that was long gone.

'Well, it certainly explains a few things,' DC Cresswell said.

Alison placed two mugs of coffee on the table.

'I know I had nothing to do with him losing his job, his wife and his home. I mean, it all happened before I even came to Wayleigh, but it must have been hard for him to see me here, every day, taking over his life in so many ways.'

'I don't think you can blame yourself. We're not even sure it was a deliberate overdose, after all, it only looked like he used one ampoule of diamorphine.'

'And it was medical grade?'

'Yes, ten milligrams. It must have been the last one he had left, because there weren't any more anywhere that we could find.'

Alison frowned.

'Ten milligrams? That might be enough to kill him, if he injected it fast, but it's unlikely. I would have expected him to be more tolerant if he'd been taking it for a long time. Were there any signs that he injected intravenously usually?'

'Yes, his veins were well-used, according to the PM report.'

'And are you sure there was only the one open ampoule? He couldn't have thrown another one away or anything?'

'We checked everywhere. The only other thing there was the sterile water used to mix it. The ampoule was open beside a used syringe and needle and the tourniquet was loosened but still round his arm.'

'Was he still in his chair?'

'No, he'd fallen out of it onto the floor. That's how the PC was able to see him through the letterbox and then broke into the house.'

Alison thought about it. How had such a small dose proved to be lethal?

'Is the pathologist sure there was nothing else that might have caused his death? A heart attack or stroke, perhaps? Or other drugs he'd taken orally?' She knew as soon as she asked the question that the police wouldn't have missed anything so obvious. 'Look, I just can't quite believe one ampoule was enough on its own to kill him, but, if it was the only ampoule there, it must have been. . .'

'Or. . .?' DC Cresswell didn't look surprised. In fact, she seemed pleased that Alison had worked this out.

'Or someone must have taken the evidence away,' Alison finished for her. 'And you've come here, because you think it might have been me?'

The detective had the good grace to look a little abashed.

'There's nothing to suggest this is anything other than an accidental overdose,' she replied firmly. 'Apart from the small amount of drugs found there.'

'But once you get the toxicology results you will know more.'

'Yes.'

Alison thought about it for a moment. 'It wasn't me, I promise you that, even if I did think he was harassing me.'

'He denied it when I went round, you know.'

'Of course he did.'

'I know but he seemed genuinely surprised when I told him about your cat. Could anyone else have done that?' They both looked at Paws, contentedly asleep on the rug.

Alison thought for a moment and then shrugged. 'I have no idea anymore, but I still didn't give the man an overdose.'

'I can't honestly see him accepting drugs from you, or letting you draw them up for him, no matter how desperate he was.'

'Good point.' Alison shuddered, she wondered just how bad the things he had been saying were. 'What about fingerprints?'

'Dr Atkinson's on the tourniquet and syringe, but the ones on the ampoule were too smudged to be identified.'

There was little else the detective could tell Alison.

'We'll just have to wait for the toxicology report,' she said as she left and Alison agreed. It seemed as if her entire life was on hold in one way or another, waiting for other people to do their bit. Well, everything except for her relationship with Mike, if that was what it was. She thought about the way he made her feel, and thought that yes, it was early days, but it was definitely a relationship.

Meanwhile, she needed to contact Eliza, to let her know that the police would definitely want to talk to her now, if they hadn't done so already. Once again, the call went straight to voicemail and this time, Alison decided to leave a message.

'Hi Eliza, it's me, Alison, I understand that it must be awkward to speak to me while you're at work, but if you could give me a call when you get home, I really do need to speak to you, urgently.'

Having done her cleaning, and spoken to Mike and DC Cresswell, there was little more she could do but wait for a call back from Tony or Eliza. One of them would get back to her eventually surely?

In the end, it was Tony who called her. He hadn't found a camera, but there was a hole in the wall above the shelves in her office. The hole went through to the store cupboard next door and there were scratch marks around it that could well have meant that there had been a camera there, watching her every move and every keystroke. Once he realised she might have been right, he had asked

IT to take a close look at her laptop and they had promised to do so, when they had time.

Alison closed her eyes with relief, she wasn't going mad. Someone *had* been signing in as her and changing things.

'Tony, can I ask you to email me with all that information?'

He hesitated and explained that he wasn't keen to do that as he had been ordered not to have any contact with her. 'Look, I promise, if this goes to a hearing and you are using the fact that someone hacked your emails and changed things as a defence, then I will say that I think it's possible that there was a camera there,' he reassured her.

It was as much as she could persuade him to do, and she understood why. If he broke rules and sent her the information in writing, he could lose his job. If she were then to settle, or decide not to use the evidence, it would have been for nothing. At least this way she had the promise of a defence, even if she didn't have it in writing.

CHAPTER THIRTY-TWO

She was still expecting Eliza to call so she snatched up her phone as soon as it began to ring.

'Hello? Eli—'

'Alison?'

The last person she had expected to call her was Ed.

'I just wanted to know how you were holding up, it must be hard going through all this on your own,' he said.

'How on earth did you know about it?' she asked him, surprised.

'Anwar called me. He was concerned as he hadn't heard from you.'

Of course Anwar would do that. He was a good friend to them both, and she should have called him before now to let him know what was going on, and to find out how he was, too.

'What was all that data you sent me?'

'Don't worry about it, I just wanted to make sure it couldn't be changed, that I had a copy of the proof that there was fraud going on. Just keep it safe for me, please, and I'll let you know if I need it.'

'Anwar mentioned something about that. It seems. . . I don't know, a bit mad.'

'But we can't both be mad.'

'No. Look, Alison, I'll come down, if you need me, I can cancel my operating list, or come down as soon as I finish,' Ed told her. 'We can talk about the future, what you can do moving forward.'

His assumption that he had any say in her future irritated her, but she knew he meant well. Having persuaded him that she was okay and that his work was more important than her problems, she promised to be in touch soon, and let him know what was happening. Although she probably wouldn't. As soon as she had hung up on Ed, Alison called Anwar. She knew he would be busy, so left him a voicemail, asking him to give her a call and suggesting that they meet for coffee after work or whenever he was free.

He called back quickly, relieved to have heard from her and happy to meet later, provided it was somewhere not too far away. He said he had news for her, but he had no time to discuss it now as he was needed on the ward. She suggested a café on the sea front, and he agreed immediately before putting the phone down. It would be good to take advantage of being so close to the sea, she thought. She hadn't had much of a chance as work had been so all consuming, but now, now she had all the time in the world.

Before going to meet Anwar, she wanted to see Mike and tell him about DC Cresswell's suspicions about Richard Atkinson's death. Halfway there, she remembered that he didn't keep milk at his house and she detoured to the local shop so that she could buy some. Jenny was serving and when Alison came to the counter to pay for her milk, the shop manager ignored her and tried to get the basket from the woman behind her.

'Excuse me, I think I was next,' Alison said, but Jenny continued to take no notice of her and gestured to the woman behind to put her basket on the counter again.

'You're next,' she said to the confused elderly woman, who was next in the queue and really didn't know what to do. 'I'm not serving this woman.'

'Why on earth not?' Alison said. 'I don't know what I've done to upset you, but I just want to pay for this milk.'

'You really don't know what you've done?' Jenny turned on her. 'Don't give me that. Not content with taking that poor man's home and his job, you hounded him to his death. He was a good man, and you killed him!'

'I didn't take anything from him!' Alison almost shouted at Jenny. 'He threw it all away!'

Alison turned and ran out of the shop, leaving the milk on the counter and the elderly woman looking shocked. She ran all the way to the garage without stopping. Mike looked up in surprise as she ran to him and threw herself into his arms. He held her tightly, rubbing her back and making soothing noises until she stopped sobbing.

'What happened?' he asked once she had herself back under control.

'They think I killed him.'

'Who?'

'Richard Atkinson.'

'No, I meant, who thinks you killed him, the police?'

'No.' She fumbled in her bag for a tissue, and wiped her nose. 'Not the police, the people that live here.'

'Well, I live here and I don't think you killed him.'

'Jenny in the shop said—'

'Ah,' he said, his face growing dark. 'Jenny. She has no right to accuse you of anything.'

'No, I know that, but she did, in front of the whole shop.' Although, thinking back, Alison knew there had only been two or three people in there at the time. 'And it will be all around the village now.'

'I'll go and speak to her,' he said, grabbing a towel to wipe his hands.

'No!' she said sharply and grabbed his arm to stop him.

'She's a vicious old woman and she needs to know she can't go around saying things like that,' he told her.

'But it will only make things worse. I was just shaken, she was so convinced that I'd "hounded that poor man to death", as she put it. I'm just worried that no one will ever believe I didn't.'

'I'll tell them, every single one of them,' Mike said and as she looked up at him, she knew he would do exactly that, at the drop of a hat.

'Thank you.'

He handed her a clean tissue and she blew her nose.

'Are you sure you don't want me to go and duff her up?'

'Yes, I'm quite sure, thank you,' she replied. 'I just won't go in there to do my shopping.'

'So black coffee okay for you?' he said. 'As we don't seem to have any milk again.'

She looked at her watch.

'If it's a quick one, I'm meeting someone from the hospital who has been trying to find out what's going on.'

He frowned.

'What?' she asked. 'He's a friend so I'll be fine.'

'I'm sure you will,' he replied, 'but you might want to get changed first.' He looked pointedly at her shirt and she looked down to where there were a number of marks on her previously pristine white front.

'It's the downside of being in a clinch with a mechanic,' he said with a grin and thinking back to where his hands had been when he held her, she knew he was right. She would have to go back and change.

She was still a little flustered and worried about being late when she arrived at the café, and was relieved to see that Anwar had only just arrived and was standing at the counter, ordering.

'Alison, what can I get you?'

'Just a coffee please.' She turned to the lady behind the counter. 'A large cappuccino.'

There was a bit of a tussle about who would pay for the drinks but Alison insisted and Anwar gave way in the end.

They found a table in the far corner away from the lunchtime crowd of mothers and pushchairs.

'And how are you, Alison?' Anwar asked anxiously. 'It can't be easy with all this going on.'

'I'm fine, honestly.' She tried to reassure him, but she knew he wouldn't believe her.

'Thank you for telling Ed about it all, but I really am doing all right and I don't want Ed involved any more than is necessary.'

'I know you're worried whether or not he should know what is happening, but, you know, the more people who do, the less chance of it being swept under the carpet, plus he's concerned about you.'

She knew he was right.

'It's just. . . I don't know, awkward, given our circumstances,' she said.

'Of course.' He nodded.

'I need to concentrate on the evidence, make sure I have enough to make the case that I was framed.' She told him about Tony's opinion that someone had used a hidden camera to watch her and find out her passwords and that IT were going to look at her laptop for some kind of malware that might have been left on it.

'You see, I think that they had access to my email, calendar, files, everything. And they could make changes that were marked as being mine, even when they weren't.'

'It has to be someone with access to the senior admin corridor then,' Anwar said with a frown.

'Yes, but there are so many people who do, not just those with offices there, but cleaners, maintenance men, security, they all have master keys.' As she said it, she realised that security would have had access to the camera used to catch Dr Atkinson, too. Perhaps she had been wrong to think that Tony would help her. There was the possibility that he was involved and would then deny all knowledge of his conversation with her if she asked him to give evidence on her behalf. She felt momentarily panicked. She should have kept evidence of his call, recorded it perhaps. She shook her head and concentrated on Anwar. 'I sent an email to counter-fraud, telling them about my concerns with the equipment and they've acknowledged it. I don't know what their next move will be.'

'And they probably won't let you know what it is, either.'

'I know.'

'But I am pleased you have done that. I imagine they will ask the hospital to provide them with more information, show proof of purchase and such like.'

'Yes, but as we don't know exactly who was involved in the fraud, how do we know they won't just be fobbed off, told it's all evidence of my paranoia?'

'I doubt they would be put off that easily.'

Alison wished she shared Anwar's confidence.

'And anyway, it must have been the last medical director, don't you think?' Anwar assured her. 'After all, he had a drug habit to support.'

'But he was getting his drugs from the hospital and that didn't cost him anything.'

'Perhaps he needed other things,' Anwar said with a shrug. 'Or more than he could steal without it becoming too obvious.'

Alison hoped he was right. There was no doubt that Atkinson had needed money, his new home had been meagre compared to the cottage where he had lived before. Of course, he might have had to sell because of his divorce rather than because he was buying drugs. He had come down in the world, everyone could see that, and everyone knew that addicts would go to any lengths to get their next fix and she had got in the way.

'Do you know what is happening with your case?' he asked.

'My union rep and I have an initial meeting with Hargreaves the day after tomorrow,' she told him. 'I should know more then about how this is going to play out.'

'I expect they will offer you the chance to resign and go away.'

'Yes, I think so.'

'Will you take it?'

She sighed and thought for a moment or two before shaking her head.

'I don't know, Anwar. I honestly don't know.'

They drank their coffee in silence for a few moments and then Anwar surreptitiously glanced at his watch.

'What was this news you had for me?' Alison asked quickly, realising that he would have to go soon.

'Ah yes, I spoke to the pathologist that you spoke to before. Like all of us, he has been told not to have anything to do with you, but he wanted you to know about the hospital porter who died.'

'Dennis something.' She struggled to recall his name.

'Yes, that's right, his potassium was very high.'

'It often goes up after death.'

'Yes, but this was very high, too high and it should have been lower than normal because of his gastroenteritis.'

'Potassium chloride. He thinks Dennis had a lethal dose of potassium chloride and that's why his heart stopped.'

'Indeed. I think your suspicion that these people were killed for some reason could be possible, but it will be very hard to prove, and as to why? I have no idea.' He shrugged.

'Nor do I,' she admitted. 'All I have is that Mrs Rossi wanted to speak to me, so perhaps she had seen something, something wrong, something about Mr Andrews' death.'

'But then you have to ask why he was killed, what could he have seen? And the others, why them if they *were* all killed?'

'I wish I knew the answer to that, Anwar. I wish I knew.'

'And now, I must go because I have a clinic.' He stood up abruptly.

'Of course,' Alison agreed, distracted by what he had told her. 'Anwar!' she called when he was almost at the door. 'Promise me you'll be careful?' she asked. He smiled, waved and left.

Alison's mind was spinning. The idea that these people had died not just because of shoddy equipment, but because someone had actively wanted to silence them was truly shocking. She couldn't believe it. But what if it were true? She knew that there were lots of things that could be used to induce a cardiac arrest and potassium chloride was the obvious drug to use, but by no means the only one. The problem was going to be proving the level was high due to a malign act, rather than caused naturally or accidentally. It wasn't routinely used on the wards, but she was sure there would be some in pharmacy and she doubted that anyone would even notice if some had gone missing. It wasn't a controlled drug, after all. The more she thought about it, the more she realised that it was just too easy to kill someone in hospital, and hard to prove. Perhaps she should concentrate on why they were killed. That might be more straightforward.

She picked up her bag, as a thought occurred to her: of the five patients she had asked Malcolm to review, there were two pairs of deaths, in that they were mere days apart, and one that was on its own between them. That one was Mike's mother. Could she have been a coincidence, a natural death? Alison thought not. And what of the two pairs? A patient had died on cardiology and then Dennis had died. Several months later, Mr Andrews had died and that same day Mrs Rossi had said she wanted to speak to Alison about something but had died before she could do so. Had Dennis and Mrs Rossi seen something relating to the deaths that occurred just before them and therefore had to be silenced? And if so, what? And why were the cardiology patient and Mr Andrews killed in the first place? It was no use. She was going round and round in circles and getting absolutely nowhere.

CHAPTER THIRTY-THREE

It was the evening before the preliminary disciplinary meeting at the hospital and Alison was going over and over the evidence and the possible consequences if she failed to convince Hargreaves or her union representative of what had been going on at the hospital.

At nine the next morning, they were to meet with Hargreaves and Selby. Her union representative had warned her exactly what to expect. The offer to allow her to resign and go quietly, followed by the threat that if she insisted on a hearing she could be sacked or struck off, and if so, never work as a doctor again.

Of course, Hargreaves would know that because she had reported the hospital to NHS Counter-Fraud, his precious hospital was going to be investigated and the chances of him keeping his job were slim. He might decide that the only way forward was to be open, and to blame Atkinson for the financial fraud and her for the data fraud, so that he could try to come out of it as comparatively clean. Without the threat of reporting the fraud, she had no bargaining power, and if she was ousted, she knew that no one would pay for the deaths.

She went over what she knew, again. Her problem was that there wasn't enough proof that any of the patients were deliberately killed, let alone by whom. And all the evidence pointed towards her, and her predecessor, being the reason the hospital was in such a state. Her and Atkinson. She was beginning to wonder if, like her, he had been set up, or manipulated into turning a blind eye to what was going on. She had to convince Hargreaves that she was innocent and get him to agree to investigate.

Her only solace as her mind went round and round in circles was Mike. He came to the cottage, offering her hot drinks, glasses of wine, giving her a hug, listening to her when she needed to talk something through, and supporting her any and every way he knew how.

She hadn't been out in the local area, except to walk to and from Mike's garage in recent days, but she had been for long, healing walks along the coastal path. Since her run-in with Jenny at the shop, she had tried to avoid situations where she might meet with animosity. Mike had assured her that most of the village didn't blame her for Dr Atkinson's death, which they all still thought of as suicide or an accidental overdose, but she knew that some did, and that was enough. It seemed that the police had decided to accept that it was suicide as well and DC Cresswell never answered her phone when Alison rang her to find out what was going on. An inquest had been opened and adjourned while they waited for the police investigation to be completed. Alison had to accept that if the coroner decided that Atkinson's death was suicide, she would always be blamed by his friends and family.

'What kind of omelette would you like, I can do plain, or. . .' Mike trailed off to do a recce of her empty fridge. 'Er, cheese?' he finished, holding aloft a rather old piece of cheddar and eyeing it dubiously.

Alison looked over his shoulder.

'I know that cheese needs to be put out of its misery, but I have to admit, I'm not really tempted.'

'You have to eat,' he told her firmly, putting the cheese back and checking the freezer compartment and the cupboards for anything else he might be able to put in an omelette.

Giving up, he sat down at the table. 'Have you decided what you are going to do tomorrow?'

'It depends what Hargreaves has to say, and what he offers.'

'You have to fight it, Alison. You can't just give up, you are innocent.'

'No one is ever entirely innocent,' she told him. And even if they were, it didn't necessarily make any difference, she thought. 'But it would be so much easier to just resign and leave.' She rubbed the tense spot on her forehead trying to ease the headache that was building.

'And what then? What if you resign? What will you do then?'

'I don't know. Look for a job somewhere, I suppose. Maybe go away for a while, do some serious thinking.'

'Go away?' He seemed surprised.

'Well, yes. I have to think about my future. Where I could go. Where I might get a job.' She looked at his shocked face and understood that he hadn't realised any of this. 'I'm a doctor, Mike, that's what I do, what I want to do, but it's not going to be easy to get another post. There are bound to be questions about why I left St Margaret's, and you can guarantee I won't get any offers of work in this region. They will all know about the data. Hargreaves, or Selby, or someone, will talk.'

'But if you fight the case, then you'll be on suspension and you couldn't work elsewhere, anyway. You could stay here.'

'And do what? Potter about in the garden in the middle of winter? I would be bored to tears, Mike, with nothing to do, stuck in a house in the middle of a community that hates me.'

'No one hates you,' he tried to reason with her.

'Tell that to Jenny! I can't even go to the local shop or the pub.' She buried her head in her hands, desperately trying to hold it together but feeling the panic rising.

'She's not worth worrying about and all the gossip will die down in time.'

'I know but I don't think I can do it, Mike. I really don't think I can stay here.'

'I can't just up and leave and go with you,' he said. 'I've got the garage to—'

He stopped as he saw the surprise on her face. She hadn't been expecting him to go with her. His face fell.

'I couldn't ask you to move away, I know you can't do that,' she hastily told him.

'So that's it, is it?' he said angrily as he grabbed his jacket. 'Thank you and goodbye? Right, well I'll leave you to it, if you're going anyway.'

'Mike,' she called out but he was already leaving and she let him go, too tired to argue, too tired to stop him. She knew he wanted her to want to stay, to be with him, but how could she? She really would climb the walls if she didn't have work and it wouldn't be long before her boredom led her to destroy whatever they had anyway.

She heard the door slam as he left and suddenly wished she could run after him, fall into his arms, get him to stay. More than anything else, she didn't want to be alone. She wanted him to be there. She needed him, to help keep her calm, help her to get at least some sleep, didn't he know that? She knew it was her fault, she had pushed him away, so certain was she that she would mess up their relationship anyway. She was torn, but deep down, she knew it was better for him to go now, rather than later when it would hurt even more.

She went to the fridge and pulled out the open bottle of wine.

Perhaps a couple of glasses of wine would help, or not. She really needed to cut down on how much she drank, but was now the time?

As she was pouring herself a glass, the phone rang and she snatched it up, hoping it would be Mike, apologising for walking out on her in her hour of need.

'Hello, M—?' she said as the person on the end spoke simultaneously.

'Alison, it's me, Ed.'

'Oh, hi, Ed,' Alison tried not to sound disappointed.

'Just calling to find out how you are. Anwar told me about the hearing tomorrow.'

'It's just an informal meeting,' she corrected him.

'I know but it's your chance to get out of there, get back to London, then we can work out what to do next. I can help, Alison.'

'But it's not my fault, Ed.'

She could hear him sigh at the other end of the phone.

'Fighting this will take years, you know that. The hospital will string it out and meanwhile, you will be under a cloud, unable to work. How would you of all people cope with that?'

It was the argument she had used herself when she decided not to fight before. The thought of not being able to work.

'But I am innocent?' she said in a small, defeated voice.

'No one's entirely innocent, Alison, you know that, they'll be able to find you guilty of something, you can be sure.'

She was shocked to hear him say it, no matter how true it was. It echoed what she had said to Mike.

'I'll think about it,' she said and put the phone down, quickly.

CHAPTER THIRTY-FOUR

Alison had a feeling of déjà vu as she walked into the board room. It was just like before, when she was in London, although there were more people there now, a lot more people. She was holding onto her bag so tightly that her knuckles were white as she tried not to let anyone see how badly her hands were shaking.

'Good morning,' Hargreaves said but he wasn't smiling and there was no handshake today.

Alison and her legal representative, Lara Smith, sat down and faced the team lined up against them, waiting for Hargreaves to tell her what their decision was, what kind of offer they were going to make. Selby was sitting next to him, looking grim-faced. Hargreaves' hatchet-man, she thought. He'd be the one to tell her the bad news. Seated next to Hargreaves were a man and a woman

Alison didn't recognise, but she recognised their type and guessed that they must be lawyers for the trust.

Hargreaves cleared his throat.

'I think we have seen all the statements,' he started, tapping a file in front of him and looking up to check. He got a nod of agreement from Lara Smith. 'And there can be no doubt that you acted in bad faith when you altered the data to mislead us and make us think that you were getting better results than you in fact were, do you agree?'

There was a buzzing in Alison's head. She couldn't think clearly, and her heart was beating so hard she felt sure they could all hear it. She just kept going over and over the events that had led to this and how she wished she had someone sitting next to her who would support her, believe her, someone like Mike, rather than Lara who clearly thought she was guilty. Or didn't care if she was or she wasn't.

She had tried to call Mike that morning but he hadn't answered. He was probably still upset by her apparent rejection the night before and who could blame him? She had left him a message, a long rambling apology, so unlike her typically to-the-point messages, saying that he was the only reason she had to stay in Wayleigh and she would do that, if that's what he wanted. She became aware that they were all looking at her, waiting for an answer, but she wasn't sure what she should say. Of course she accepted that she had done it the first time, but not the second, didn't they understand? Realising that Alison was unsure what to say, her lawyer answered for her.

'We accept that.'

'And we have heard from Mr Grant that Dr Wilson also did not follow correct procedure when she failed to report finding the person responsible for the drug thefts. He says that he advised you to take it through official channels and that you decided not to.'

Alison wondered why Tony had volunteered that information. To stab her in the back? Make sure she was sacked? Or had he had no choice when directly questioned about her?

'We had no proof and Eliza was just trying to help Dr Atkinson,' Alison told him.

'And that didn't work out so well, did it?' Selby cut in and Alison had to concede he had a point.

'So, I think we. . .' Hargreaves turned to the two lawyers next to him, who nodded. 'We have enough of a case for gross misconduct,' Hargreaves continued, and he was right, she knew. Again, he looked at her, but when she didn't answer, he turned to Lara Smith who again nodded her acceptance of what Hargreaves was saying. 'However, it would not be good for either the hospital or yourself, Dr Wilson, if we were to take that course of action. It's going to look bad enough losing two medical directors in the space of six months and, of course we have also to consider what action we need to take against the chief nurse.'

'Please don't take it out on Eliza,' Alison pleaded.

'You also have to consider that counter-fraud will be looking into the purchasing records of equipment for the hospital,' Smith chipped in.

Selby shuffled the papers in front of him nervously as Hargreaves stared at Alison.

'I take it we have Dr Wilson to thank for that particular complication,' Hargreaves said finally.

'Patients have died as a direct result of that particular complication,' Alison replied icily.

Smith laid a hand on her arm to discourage her from further interjections.

'We will, of course, be cooperating fully with NHS Counter-Fraud, but I am quietly confident that while it is clear that someone has been defrauding the trust, it was in all probability Dr Atkinson, and that any investigation will find that there has been no impact on patients,' Hargreaves said firmly and his lawyers nodded their agreement.

'I, for one, will be happy to give evidence to the contrary.' Alison refused to be silenced. She wanted Hargreaves to know she would not support him brushing this under the carpet.

'Any agreement not to sack you for gross misconduct will include a non-disclosure agreement that will make sure you are unable to give evidence about anything that happened during your short time here.' He turned to his right where the man was hastily scribbling notes and the woman nodded again. 'So, there you have it, Dr Wilson.

Our legal team have the papers all ready for you to sign if you agree to resign.'

He held his hand out, and the woman looked at her junior, who hastily grabbed a sheaf of papers and handed it to her. She passed it on to Hargreaves. It was like pass the parcel, Alison thought.

'There is the NDA in there as well, which you must sign before you leave to ensure that you do not speak to anyone about this deal, or about any other information you may have as a result of your work here, and that would include disclosing information to the police or to NHS Counter-Fraud,' the woman said as Hargreaves handed the paperwork over to Smith and she started looking through them.

'I'd like a moment to go through these, and may need to take advice as I'm not sure of the legality of stopping Dr Wilson from cooperating with the investigation. I hadn't realised you were meaning to include that when I saw the documents last night,' she said.

'Of course,' the trust lawyer replied.

Alison was surprised to hear that her legal representative had already seen the papers and glared at her. If she had seen them and had known what the offer was, why hadn't she told Alison? When they had spoken the evening before, Smith had simply said she thought it likely the offer would be to resign and go quietly, there had been no mention of an NDA. If Alison had thought about it, she would have realised that there would be one, but not one stopping her from speaking to the authorities. If she had been warned about this, it would have given her time to consider the implications and perhaps insist on changes. Perhaps that was why no one had brought it up before. No one wanted her to turn down this deal.

'And I need a moment to confer with my legal advisor, is that okay?' Alison asked.

Hargreaves looked at his lawyer.

'I'm not signing anything I haven't had a chance to discuss with her,' Alison said firmly.

There was a moment of hesitation but finally there was a nod of agreement.

'Very well,' Hargreaves said and then turned to Selby. 'Jonathan, perhaps you could take Dr Wilson and Ms Smith somewhere quiet to confer.'

Selby leapt to his feet and ushered Lara Smith and Alison out into reception, where Alison was surprised to see Eliza sitting next to Mary at her desk and was glad that she had come to show her support. Despite the drug thefts, and the problems that had caused, it showed that Eliza still considered Alison a friend.

Tony Grant was sitting in the visitor's chairs and stood as they came out of the room. Alison had asked that he be made available in case she needed him to speak on her behalf.

'I'm sorry to disrupt your day like this,' Alison apologised to him with a smile.

'Am I needed?' Grant asked her pointedly. 'Only I've got IT on standby to give evidence as well, if you want them.'

Selby looked at Grant in surprise.

'No, I don't—' Smith started to say but Alison interrupted her, pleased that it looked like Grant had managed to get evidence that her laptop had had malware on it.

'We don't know yet, Tony,' she said. 'If you could just wait here a little while longer. I'm sorry.'

'He does have a job to do,' Selby said petulantly.

'I am aware of that,' she said crisply, 'I won't hold him up any longer than I need to. Now, I just need a word with my advisor.' She gestured at Smith.

'We'll need somewhere private,' the lawyer said, much to Alison's relief. She really didn't want anyone listening in and was relieved that Lara Smith seemed to have caught on that there might be something going on that she didn't know about.

Alison knew there was a small meeting room just off the corridor, so she suggested they go in there. Selby went to follow them in, but Smith very firmly shut the door in his face.

'What's the problem?' she asked as soon as they had the place to themselves.

'You've seen the papers already?' Alison asked her.

'Yes, they're pretty standard. They just say that you are resigning with immediate effect, that there will be no comeback on the hospital blah, blah, blah.'

'And the NDA covers everything, I won't be able to help the counter-fraud investigation or tell them about the deaths?'

'I would need to check that, but I'm pretty sure it will cover everything. Is that going to be a problem?'

'I honestly don't know,' Alison told her. 'I need to give it some thought.'

'Look, you've done your bit. You've reported your concerns, you have to leave it to them now. NHS Counter-Fraud have trained investigators who know what they're doing and if you don't agree to sign these documents, you may well lose the chance to resign quietly.'

'Yes, but if I go quietly, no one will be interested in the patients who died, they'll only be interested in who has been defrauding the hospital and the NHS.'

'You giving evidence won't bring them back, even if they were killed by the faulty equipment or some homicidal maniac and, speaking as a lawyer, I don't think you'll ever be able to prove it either way. You don't need me to tell you that being sacked will effectively end your career, and will also leave a huge question mark against any evidence you may give. You could end up not helping anyone, and ruining yourself.'

'Grant is here because he has the evidence that my laptop was hacked.' She crossed her fingers and hoped that was true. 'He can prove that I didn't do the things they say I did.'

Smith sighed. Clearly, this was proving to be a lot more complex than she had expected.

'You admitted to me that you did change the data on one occasion.'

'Yes but—'

'That's all they need. To be frank, everything else is moot.' She looked down at the papers in her hand. 'Look, let me check through these, and then we can talk. Why don't you go and get a breath of fresh air or something? I'll text you when I'm done.'

Fresh air was exactly what she wanted. She left the lawyer in the meeting room and went along to the door leading to the stairs. No one was in the corridor, but she could feel eyes watching her from the reception area. No doubt Mary would tell Selby that she was making a run for it.

Alison hurried up the stairs to the roof and once there, almost ran to the rail where she could look out, over the rooftops to the sea. She leant on the rail and took deep breaths, feeling herself relax. Why was sea air always such a tonic? She looked towards the horizon. It was a shame it was so cloudy and there was no sunlight glinting on the wave tops. She needed to think and, as always, her mind was much clearer up here on the roof.

It seemed such a simple choice: resign and let the fraud team do their work, and have a chance to start again elsewhere, or stay and fight and risk losing everything and helping no one. The sensible choice was to go, but shouldn't she at least try to give the relatives of those who had died some sort of closure? A real cause of death? Would she be able to do that, even if she stayed and fought?

Her phone rang and she saw that it was Mike calling. She dithered for a moment – should she answer? Her finger hovered over the green button when there was a bang of a door closing and she turned to see Eliza come out onto the roof.

'Hi, Eliza, did you get my messages?' Alison said as her friend walked towards her. 'I'm so sorry about Dr Atkin. . .' Something about the look on Eliza's face made her stop. There was no doubt she wasn't pleased to see Alison. In fact, she looked furious.

'You promised me you wouldn't tell them about the drugs!' she shouted. 'You promised!'

'I'm so sorry, Eliza, but Tony Grant had no choice but to tell them.'

'You're just using me to distract everyone from your own guilt. Destroying my career to try and save yours!'

'No, I promise—'

'Shut up! Shut up!'

Alison knew there was no point in trying to reason with people who were so far out of control, so she did as she was told, for the moment. Eliza came closer, until she was in touching distance of Alison.

'I'm so sorry about Dr Atkinson, Eliza,' Alison said quietly, trying again.

'Don't you dare say his name. It's your fault he's dead,' Eliza hissed as she came even closer. Alison had no chance to get out of the way of the slap that quickly followed those words, even if she had been expecting it. Her head jerked back and she dropped her phone.

'Ow! What did you do that for?' Alison was shocked

and held a hand to her stinging cheek. She stepped back, away from Eliza, but her back hit the rail at the edge of the rooftop terrace. She looked across the roof but her phone had skidded several feet away.

'He was my friend.' Eliza poked her painfully on the sternum as she spoke. 'My partner, and I had to kill him because of you and your meddling!' Eliza said coldly.

'What?' Alison was too shocked to take in what Eliza was saying.

'I could have helped him!' Eliza was almost wailing as she moved closer to Alison. 'I could have helped him get back on his feet, but he was so angry about your bloody cat, said I'd gone too far and it was time to give up, go to the police, tell them everything and I couldn't let him do that. Do you understand?' Eliza pushed Alison in the chest again as she asked this. Alison tried to sidle along the rail, but there was a corner and she couldn't get far. Eliza was right up against her, pushing her back. She was trapped.

'He was going to tell them about stealing the drugs?' Alison asked, trying desperately to keep Eliza talking, hoping that someone, Lara, Tony or even Mary, would come looking for her.

'The drugs were nothing, he would have just found another way of getting them. I told him that, not to use me anymore.'

'So what was he going to the police about?' Out of the corner of her eye, Alison thought that she could see someone by the doorway. She deliberately didn't look directly at them because she didn't want to alert Eliza.

'He was going to tell them about what we'd been doing, the deal we had going, everything,' Eliza said.

'What deal?' Alison asked. There was a slight movement at the door and she couldn't help but glance across to see who it was. She was disappointed to see it was Selby. Eliza turned.

'Jonathan!' Alison called out. 'H—'

'Leave us alone!' Eliza shouted at him quickly, drowning out Alison's plea. 'She'll be down in a minute.'

Alison pushed forward, but Selby had turned and was going.

'No, Jon—' Alison grunted as Eliza punched her in the face. Her head snapped back and there was a sharp pain across her face, followed by a warm trickle from her nose. Eliza was pushing her and by the time she was able to open her eyes, her back was right up against the railings again, and there was no sign of Selby. She hoped he had gone for help, but what if he didn't realise what was going on? What if he thought they were just having a heated conversation? What if he was involved, as she suspected? She couldn't rely on him, she had to buy more time and do this herself. She spat some blood from her mouth, pleased to see it spatter on Eliza. 'What deal?' she said thickly.

'I know someone in a supply firm. We'd order expensive equipment, and be invoiced for it, but cheap stuff would be supplied. Richard would sign it all off as correct and we pocketed the difference. Such a sweet little earner, plenty of money for everyone. Richard didn't want to do it, but I gave him no choice. I kept quiet about his drugs and he helped me. It paid off my mortgage.'

Alison couldn't believe she was hearing this.

'It was you? You and Richard Atkinson together? Do you have any idea how many people died because of your greed?'

'Most of them were dead already.' Eliza pushed Alison again, so she was leaning back over the railing with it digging hard into her back. 'I made sure of that.'

Alison was stunned. This wasn't the Eliza she had come to like and respect. How could she have got it so wrong?

'But why?'

'Because they saw things they shouldn't have and couldn't keep their noses out. Dennis even had the audacity to try and blackmail Richard about a patient who died!'

'The one on cardiology?' Alison was beginning to understand now, how it had all begun, how one thing had led to another.

'Richard was drugged up to the eyeballs and made a mistake, gave him an overdose. I covered it up and we thought we'd got away with it, but Dennis, of all people, had seen what happened and kept the evidence.'

'So he had to go.'

'That's right, just like you have to now.'

Eliza started pushing harder, and Alison shouted

'Help me!', desperately hoping someone was near enough to hear.

'Selby's gone, run away like he always does.'

'Was he in on it?'

'Selby, you must be joking,' Eliza said derisively. 'He hasn't got the stomach for it. He was just a useful tool, someone I could manipulate, feed information to, even if it wasn't true. He lapped it all up.' She laughed. 'He seemed to think I was only trying to help him and his precious career!'

Alison realised she had got it very wrong, but if he wasn't in on it, surely he would have got help by now.

'Why are you telling me this?' Alison tried to wriggle free, but Eliza had her pinned against the rail.

'Why not? You aren't going to be around to tell anyone. Poor Dr Wilson, so distraught she was going to lose her job, she jumped off the roof. Richard thought we could get you to go away without going too far. He just wanted me to frighten you off, not do you any harm. He was so angry when I poisoned your precious cat. He was always the weaker member of the team.' She laughed and pushed Alison again.

Alison realised that Eliza was stronger than her, and as she kept pushing, Alison was being bent further and further over the railing. Turning her head, she could see the cracked cement of the car park, several floors below. But there was nobody there, no one who could look up and see what was going on. She wrapped one arm around the railing, trying to get a grip, but she knew it wasn't good enough. She screamed as loud as she could.

'Help! Please, stop, Eliza! Help! Somebody, help me!'

Eliza moved her forearm so that it was across Alison's neck, making it almost impossible for her to breathe let alone shout.

'Shut it!' Eliza hissed and once she was satisfied that Alison could no longer call for help, carried on. 'I loved Richard, but because of you I had to kill him. He would never have gone to the police before you came here, you and your ruddy cat. You made me do it.' She looked at Alison. 'I think he knew, as I injected him with the second dose. He tried to pull his arm away, but he didn't have the strength. I held him, comforted him, until it was over. I didn't let him die alone.'

'What about the others? Why did you kill them?' Alison whispered, her voice almost non-existent with the pressure Eliza was putting on her larynx. She needed to distract Eliza, so that she didn't see Alison's hand creeping along the railing, desperately trying to find something, anything she could use as a weapon. She felt her arm slipping as she was pushed further and further over the edge. 'Why did you kill Mike's mother?'

'Interfering old bitch. She'd seen me with Richard. Heard me threaten him if he didn't do as I told him. So, she had to go.'

'And Andrews?'

'Well, he worked for the suppliers, a driver and knew there was some sort of fiddle going on. He'd seen me and his boss together and when he ended up here and recognised me, I couldn't take the risk of him saying something.'

Alison had found nothing to use as a weapon and she knew she couldn't hold onto the rail much longer. She could hear sirens in the distance, but this was a hospital and she knew it would be an ambulance not the cavalry.

Alison braced herself against the railing and gathered her strength. She had to try and stall the inevitable or try one more time to push Eliza away, before it was too late.

'And Mrs Rossi?'

'Oh, she saw me give Andrews a dose of potassium chloride, my weapon of choice. She'd come in to give him some homemade sweets or some such. I don't think she knew quite what she had seen but she tried to tell you about it, so she had to go. Once you've killed once it gets so much easier every time. It's amazing, none of them questioned me giving them an injection or flushing through their cannulas. I just told them the doctors had said they need it and they held out their arms. Like lambs to the slaughter. Of course, I made sure to tell Mrs Rossi you had asked me to do it. I knew you liked her, so it made killing her that much sweeter,' Eliza continued. 'I thought her dying might just push you over the edge.' Eliza laughed at her own wit. 'It's a shame I don't think you would sit still and let me give you an injection, and you have no handy cannula to make it easy, so jumping off the roof would seem a better way.' She went to grab Alison's leg to tip her over the railing, but Alison was prepared and used all her strength to turn and kick out, catching Eliza on the knee.

'Ugh!' Eliza grunted, but punched out at Alison, hitting her on the jaw. Alison's mouth snapped shut and she bit her tongue and fell to the ground, tasting fresh blood in her mouth. Eliza grabbed Alison's hair with one hand and tried to pull her back to the railing. Alison was stunned, but managed to grab Eliza's leg to stop being pulled closer to the railings. Eliza kicked her head, not hard enough to finish her off, but enough to make her see stars. It made Eliza swear too and Alison hoped she had done some damage when she kicked her on the knee.

Alison's vision was blurry, her thoughts scrambled and fuzzy, but as Eliza rubbed her sore knee, Alison saw her phone lying a few yards away by an air-conditioning vent. If she could just get to it, she could summon help. As Eliza lurched forward again, Alison rolled away, but didn't get far. Eliza grabbed her leg and although Alison tried to kick her, she was prepared this time and jumped out of the way, twisting Alison's leg as she did so.

Alison screamed in pain, but through her tears and pain, she thought she saw movement by the door onto the roof again. Had Selby come back? Had he got help? Then Eliza kicked her head again, and everything went black for a moment or two. She braced herself for another kick, but knew she couldn't move out of the way, couldn't defend herself if it came.

She heard some movement, footsteps, running.

'Stop!' someone shouted, she wasn't sure who. 'Get away from her!'

Alison turned over with a groan and saw Eliza back away. Grant was a few feet from her with Lara Smith, who was looking horrified at the scene in front of her. Alison could see Eliza weighing up her options before climbing up on the railings and putting one leg over the top. Alison's head was fuzzy and she couldn't work out what was happening. She shook her head to clear it. Eliza was still sitting on the railing, one leg either side, looking down at the car park below.

'Eliza!' she said and reached a hand out to stop her colleague, she couldn't forget that she had thought of her as a friend once. 'It doesn't have to end this way.'

'Doesn't it?' Eliza looked at her then back down at the asphalt again.

'Don't do it!' Tony said and took a step closer.

'Keep away!' Eliza shouted and lifted the other leg off the low wall.

Alison wasn't sure if lifting the leg unbalanced Eliza, or if she knew exactly what she was doing and then changed her mind at the last minute, but as she took her leg off the roof her hands slipped and the nurse tipped over the edge with a look of fear on her face. Tony rushed and tried to catch her hand. She screamed as she fell and desperately tried to grab hold of his outstretched hand, but missed and she slipped, still screaming, out of sight. There was a terrible thud as she hit the ground, and then silence.

Tony stood looking down, hand still stretched out as if to catch her. Alison knew that he would probably see her fall, and the moment of impact, in his dreams for the rest of his life.

People began coming out onto the roof.

'Don't move,' someone said as they checked her for injuries, and Alison was happy to comply. All she wanted to do was sleep and so she let the blackness descend again.

CHAPTER THIRTY-FIVE

There had been trips to X-ray and CT for a scan of her head and neck, but apart from a broken nose which had been set and what were likely to be some spectacular bruises to come, the doctor was pretty sure there was no permanent damage.

'But we'll keep you in overnight, just to be sure,' he told her. 'If we can find you a bed,' he added as an afterthought.

Knowing how hard it was to find beds for even those most in need, Alison was pretty sure she would be going home later. The sticking point was the fact that she lived alone and they wanted someone to check that her concussion didn't worsen. Having got her phone back, which seemed to work fine despite a cracked screen and a few scratches, Alison had tried to call Mike, several times, but his phone went straight to voicemail.

Anwar had miraculously appeared when she was wheeled into A&E and insisted on staying with her, even accompanying her to have her scans. He was horrified about what had happened, but had understood she didn't want to talk about it just yet, so had sat, silently supportive, by her side. Alison was working her way towards asking if he would come home with her and sleep on her sofa so she could go home, when DC Cresswell poked her head around the curtain.

'Are you okay to talk?' she asked.

'Yes, I'm fine,' Alison lied as she pushed herself up on the trolley, wincing at a newfound pain in her ribs and remembering a kick that had landed there.

'Careful!' Anwar admonished her and helped her to get comfortable.

'Good job she was wearing soft-soled shoes,' Alison explained with a smile that felt a little crooked thanks to her swollen lip.

'Yes.' The detective came into the cubicle, followed by a middle-aged man who looked more like an accountant than a policeman with his grey suit, pristine white shirt and migraine-inducing tie. 'This is Detective Sergeant Clarke,' she introduced him.

'If we could. . .?' He looked meaningfully at Anwar.

'I'll go and fetch some coffee,' Anwar said as he tactfully left, already pulling his phone out of his pocket.

'Now, if we could ask you a few questions?' DC Cresswell asked.

A few questions turned out to be a lot, and Alison tried to tell them everything that had happened. She found their questions kept her on track and helped her organise the events in her mind.

As she talked to them and thought back to how close she had come to being the one going over the railing and hitting the car park, she began to shake.

'I'm sorry,' she said. 'It's just been quite a day and I'm very, very tired.'

'Not at all, Dr Wilson,' the older detective said. 'We'll let you get some rest now, but we will need a formal statement from you later on.'

'Of course.'

'I'll be in touch,' DC Cresswell said as she left.

Anwar came back in as they went out, and Alison knew that he must have been waiting nearby.

'Hargreaves wants to see you,' he told her, 'but I told him to go away.'

'Thank you.'

'Rumour has it he wants to offer you your job back.'

'Really?' Alison was surprised.

'Well, now he knows for certain that you were set up.'

'How would he know that?'

'Grant told him about the hacking, plus, he heard some of what Eliza said,' Anwar told her.

'He might have come and helped me sooner, if he was there.' But she knew he was probably weighing up intervening against getting Eliza to explain everything and also waiting for the right moment. 'What about Selby?' she asked. 'He came up there before, did he tell them what was happening on the roof?'

'It seems that Eliza had been feeding him all sorts of details about you, and he thought you were angry about it and were just having it out with her. He swears he had no idea of what was really going on. He thought discretion was the better part of valour.'

'That sounds pretty typical of him. I knew he wasn't clever enough to have known all that he did without help.' How like Selby to slither away from a confrontation. 'Hargreaves can't brush this under the carpet now. Eliza confessed to it all, the fraud, the murders, even poor Dr Atkinson, and I'll happily testify to everything she said.'

'I don't think you'll need to, they have it all recorded.'

'How?' Alison was amazed.

'From someone's phone – you answered someone's call just before you started talking to Eliza. Your lawyer from the MDU apparently told Hargreaves he had to reinstate you after this, and anyway, no one would take the job if he tried to get someone new in, not after all this mess.'

This mess seemed to sum it up pretty well, Alison thought, but whose call had she answered? Who had thought quickly enough to record the call? It had to be Mike! That's why he wasn't answering his phone, the police had taken it as evidence. She sat up and swung her legs round. Anwar looked alarmed.

'You should rest.'

But she had to find a way of contacting him.

'I need to—'

'And there is someone here to see you,' Anwar added with a twinkle in his eye that Alison was pretty sure meant that he had called Ed and got him down here in a misguided attempt to get them back together.

'No. . .'

But Anwar had already left.

The curtain was pulled aside again, and she looked up, expecting to see Ed. She was prepared to use him to get out of the hospital and get him to drive her to Mike's house.

'Oh!' she said as instead of Ed, Mike walked in.

'Thank God!' he said as he rushed over and pulled her into his arms.

'Ouch!' she said, but quietly, because it hadn't hurt too much and he was kissing her anyway.

EPILOGUE

She was sitting in the lounge of her picture-postcard cottage, the warmth from the log burner making her feel drowsy. She had Paws on her lap, a glass of wine in her hand and Mike by her side. She felt cosy and settled.

'Do you regret staying?' he had asked her and she thought about it.

She was still not welcome in the village shop, but thanks to the diary that Eliza had left, parts of which had been read out at the inquest, everyone knew that Atkinson had been murdered by her and not died by suicide, she hoped that she would be forgiven by Jenny, one day, maybe soon or maybe not, and she could live with that. And more inquests were due to be opened in light of that diary. Alison could only hope it brought some peace and understanding to the relatives of those who had died, been killed by Eliza, just as it had helped Mike to finally know what had happened, even if he couldn't forgive or forget.

At the hospital, there were still squabbles on the stroke ward. Simon Bayliss was as feckless as ever and Dr Cheung stuck rigidly to his allocated hours, but she had Joyce and Anwar covering her back now. How long Anwar would stay was uncertain, but Dr Carrick had taken a post in Norfolk and dropped his claim of bullying against her. Anwar had promised to stay until she had found someone to replace him. Part of her hoped that it would take a long time.

She had her old job back at St Margaret's, they were busy recruiting a new head nurse and a new chief executive, Hargreaves having decided retirement was the best option. Everyone had been told that it was because he wanted to spend more time with his family, but they all knew that the real reason was his failure to notice a massive fraud going on under his nose – and no one was going to be appointing Selby to a top job anytime soon.

As for her, she was determined to stay and bring the hospital up in the ratings, and make sure the people of Wayleigh got the care they deserved. Of course, so many roles being empty meant that she was left with an absolutely mammoth task just to keep on top of the work, but somehow, not having anyone there to get in the way helped. She just got on with the job and she seemed to have the support of most of the staff.

Alison had refused to allow the deaths of patients from the faulty equipment and Eliza's killing spree to go unacknowledged and she was working with the coroner and the police to reopen inquests into all of them, including Mike's mother. DC Cresswell had told her they had found a massive stock of out-of-date potassium chloride ampoules at Eliza's home. The chief pharmacist was mortified that they hadn't been destroyed as correct procedure would have dictated, but it explained how she was able to induce cardiac arrests in any patients she found inconvenient. As Alison had thought before, it was all too easy to kill someone in hospital.

DC Cresswell had also told Alison that Eliza had enough money stashed in various bank accounts to keep herself in luxury for the rest of her life. It was clear from her diary that Eliza hadn't done any of this for the money, she did it for the power. The power over life and death. Alison shivered. Mike stroked her arm and she looked up. He was still looking at her, waiting for an answer and she snuggled up against him.

They were taking it slowly and she had warned him that there was no way that she was going to move into the Seventies museum where Mike had grown up and now lived. He had offered to do the place up, let her choose wallpaper and colour schemes but even then she probably wouldn't live there. She knew it and Mike knew it too. But that was okay with her and it seemed to be okay with him. He spent most nights at the cottage and having the house meant they both had space between work and home. There was no rush, and she could live with that.

Yes, sometimes she missed London, the feeling of being in the centre of everything, on the cutting edge, but Wayleigh had the sea and that made up for a lot. They often walked along the sea shore, or over the cliffs. Mike had suggested they should get a dog, but Alison wasn't sure that Paws would agree to that.

She looked up at Mike, still waiting for his answer and smiled.

'No,' she said, 'I don't regret staying at all.'

AUTHOR'S NOTE

Having worked in the NHS for many, many years, I have experienced the different pressures of A&E, midwifery, practice nursing and even managing clinical networks across large regions. I have worked part time, full time, and been able to mould my working life around bringing up children, writing for television and moving around the country when my husband changed jobs; the NHS always adapted around me and my needs as an employee. I would like to say I have loved every minute, but of course I haven't. There have been moments when I wanted more than anything to do something more normal, less stressful, less sad, and there have been other times when I have believed it to be the best place to work in the world.

Every day we seem to read about some new calamity, some new failure: patients left to die alone in corridors, ambulances that don't arrive, the vulnerable being mistreated in care facilities, but in all my time in the NHS I have never met anyone working there who didn't want to do good, to help people, who didn't care. Are doctors, nurses and carers really harming their patients deliberately? Most definitely not. In fact, the cases of deliberate harm are few and far between; what seems more common are mistakes, and as pressure increases from sheer numbers of patients or some new bureaucratic demand, the mistakes get more frequent and bigger.

This book is a work of fiction, and I am not in any way suggesting the events in it have happened and I hope that they would never do so. I know that around the world there have been a number of well-publicised events where health care workers have turned to murder – we can never forget Shipman, nor should we, but I cannot believe there are many like him, and I certainly hope there are not. I want to reassure readers that I have certainly never come across anyone that evil myself.

Whenever I have been seen as a patient, I can honestly say that everyone involved has treated me with respect and care and done their utmost to help me. Whether they were nurses, doctors, ambulance personnel or cleaners, they still all wanted to help to the best of their ability. They cared and they cared for me, sometimes under incredibly difficult circumstances. And I am very grateful. The food, however, can be pretty horrendous

– so if you are going to be a patient in the NHS anytime soon, I would recommend you take a packet of biscuits with you. And a good book!

ACKNOWLEDGEMENTS

A huge thank you to everyone at Avon for giving me the chance to work with them, and in particular Molly Walker-Sharp who has been so helpful and patient with my early drafts. A special thanks, too, to Dushi Horti who checked for medical errors along with grammatical errors (of which there were, and will always be, many). I promise them both that I will remember to be more positive and not to over use the word 'perhaps' in the future. Perhaps. Maybe.

Thank you to the cover designer, Toby James – it's a cracker! And thank you to all the lovely members of the team at Avon in editorial, marketing and publicity; across the board they have all made me feel welcome and are always so cheerful. It really is a happy team.

Thank you, too, to my husband Bob for knowing so many ways to kill people (a little worrying, if I'm honest), for always being patient when I talk through plot points and characters at length and for not minding that I disappear into my posh shed in the garden for hours at a time. I'm beginning to suspect he likes the peace and quiet while I'm gone.

And, of course, a thank you to everyone who buys and reads this book. I hope you enjoy it.